LEAVING BENNET BEHIND

volume 2

Cherished

SARAH JOHNSON

Cover Design by: Peculiar World Designs
Section Dividers by: vectorbeast

ISBN-10: 1503356248
ISBN-13: 978-1503356245

DEDICATION

To my husband of sixteen years, Paul. You are truly my own Mr Darcy. Without your love and support I would have never found the courage to complete this journey. *Thank you!*

TABLE OF CONTENTS

ACKNOWLEDGMENTS

While I would love to personally thank each person who has read the original version of this story online, I know such a task is not possible. Every comment written, and every nudge I received was what gave me the courage to eventually pursue publishing this story. So to all my readers – *Thank you!*

There are five ladies I would like to acknowledge by name, the first being Brenda. In her quest to draw new authors out of the woodwork she began a writing challenge on her forum. It was with her encouragement that I first put pen to paper – or rather, hit that first keystroke – thus beginning this journey. She has been behind me from the start and has reassured me every step of the way. I cannot effectively express how much I appreciate her friendship and guidance. *Thank you, Brenda!*

Two others who deserve my personal gratitude would be my original editing team – Linnea and Anita. Both of these ladies were willing to take on the enormous task of helping a new writer, and for their time and patience I am truly grateful. When they signed on none of us knew where this story would even lead, and yet they have stuck with me through it all, giving me wonderful feedback and ideas along the way. They have both become so integral to this story that I know it would not be the same without their help. So to both of them I must give a heartfelt – *Thank You!*

Also there are two who have taken on the task of helping me with athe editing for turning this story into a series. I enjoy hearing all their input, and look forward to finishing the three books to come with them. So to Rose and Zoe – *Thank You!*

CHAPTER

I

Friday, November 29, 1811
Longbourn, Hertfordshire

T he air was getting colder, but after the rush of the last few weeks, Jane enjoyed the stillness it brought on such a beautiful morning. Though she was not usually one to awaken so early, not like her sister Elizabeth, she did today and soon found herself eager to see the sun rise over the eastern horizon. She knew just the spot where the view was perfect. So, with a lightness to her step, she walked quickly through her mother's familiar garden paths, and to the stone bench that sat near the back wall.

When she sat, a chill ran through her body. *I should have brought a blanket—this stone is quite cold,* she thought. She wrapped her arms around her body, pulling the cape more snugly around her shoulders, and drew her legs up under her, hoping they would help warm the seat.

She closed her eyes and took a deep breath as the stillness engulfed her. She could hear the sound of birds chirping off in the distance.

Upon opening her eyes, her breath caught and she pulled her hand to her chest in awe of the gorgeous hues all around. Purples and pinks slowly gave way to a soft yellow rising from the distant hills, setting off the bright reds and oranges of the leaves as they were caught in the wind and pulled from their dwellings, to be scattered about and blanket the dying grass for another winter ahead.

Though autumn was a season for many to cherish and certainly contained its beauty, her favorite time of year was yet to come. She adored winter. Her heart soared at the thought of seeing snow covered hills, barren trees, and ice covered lakes. The heavy scents of the large evergreen trees and logs burning in the fireplaces all around made her feel warm all over and she continued to watch as the sky lightened to a dull greyish blue color that told of the season that would soon be upon them. A sudden wind sent shivers down her spine, but she lifted her cheeks to feel the nipping that always came with such weather. She could tell snow was coming—possibly in the next few days.

With a smile just gracing the corners of her lips, she pulled the letter from her pocket, opening it to once again read the words her sister wrote just the day before.

> November 28, 1811
> Darcy House, London
>
> My Dearest Janie,
>
> It is strange to say so, but I cannot imagine my life before my William. Oh Jane, the joy I get in waking every morning to see him beside me is so overwhelming I can hardly contain it within my soul. I find myself smiling nearly as much as you do, and we both know my disposition is not normally bent in such a direction.
>
> While the last two days have passed with the most amazing experiences, I would be remiss if I did not say how much I miss my dearest sister. How I wish you were here in Town as well, but I would never wish you to be away from Mr Bingley at such as time. Why, it is of a most critical season in your friendship. To know you are being courted by a man

so perfectly fitting to you is what gets me through the selfish moments when I wish you by my side. I know you would tell me if he had proposed, so I must find a way to endure until such news reaches me. I know not what is taking so long—he is obviously enamored with you. Who would not be? You are such a sweet and gentle person.

Jane chuckled, thinking to herself, *oh Elizabeth, I am not like you. I do not wish for a courtship that whisks me off my feet and passes by so quickly I cannot enjoy the moments in the middle. I shall never be like you in that regard. No, I am quite enjoying the pace at which my friendship with Mr Bingley is progressing.* She turned the page over and continued to read.

William has assured me that our plans are set and we will be back in Hertfordshire in just three short weeks. I shall be counting down the days, my dear sister, and shall hope for a turn of events in your life soon, for I dearly wish to talk with you of things only a married lady could understand—how I shall ever feel comfortable in my role as mistress of this house, for one. Oh Jane, what if we arrive at Pemberley and it is too much for me? What then? Will I forever be watching for the specters of the former Mrs Darcys over my shoulder? I know William says I am the perfect mistress, but what if he is wrong? What if this is too much for me?

I am not one to stay despondent for long, and so I feel I must change the tone of this note—I cannot have you pondering my words of melancholy when you should be looking deeply into the eyes of your beau and thinking only of what your heart feels for him.

She smiled broadly, then pulled the letter to her chest thinking on just what Elizabeth said she should be thinking—*Mr Bingley*. His lean figure and blonde hair were features she well appreciated, but most of all it was his blue eyes that drew her in. They looked into her soul in a way no other had ever done. Even her sister did not know some of the deep secrets Jane wished to tell to Mr Bingley when he looked at her a certain way.

She opened her eyes again, startled to see the man of her thoughts standing right before her. "OH! Mr Bingley! What are you doing here?" She looked all around, trying to catch her breath from such a fright and knowing her cheeks were flaming.

He gave a smile and bow, "Your father and uncle invited us to go shooting early this morning, but when I saw you here I could not help but come to greet you. You do not mind if I sit, do you?"

She scooted over just a bit, moving to a more proper position with her feet now on the ground, "No, I do not mind."

"Thank you," he said as he settled onto the stone bench beside her. "OH MY! This is a cold seat!"

"Yes, but the view is what has drawn me out on such a chilly morning."

He looked where she indicated. "It is a beautiful sky." The pink of the sky brought out the flush of her cheeks, but he dared not verbalize such a brazen statement.

"Are your guests not with you as well?"

"My brother would much rather not be up so early, but the viscount and the colonel are walking our mounts around to cool them off. We pushed them hard on the ride here. When we saw you sitting here, they afforded me the opportunity to sit with you until the others are ready."

Jane blushed and looked down at her clasped hands still holding tightly to her letter.

Bingley saw as well. "Have you already heard from Mrs Darcy? Were they not married but three days ago?"

4

"Yes, she was eager to send her first letter with her new name."

Bingley noticed the slight sadness in her eyes. "I hope you are not lonely without her here?"

She took a deep breath, "We have always held each others confidences, so in some ways I do miss her tremendously, but as she points out, it will be only three weeks and we will be together again."

Bingley could not help the excitement that rose in his chest at knowing his plan to propose to the lady sitting beside him would so soon be accomplished—just as soon as his friend returned with a *certain item* which he was to pick up in Town. Clearing his throat, he turned back to look where his companion still gazed. "My home is starting to settle already, but I greatly look forward to having the Darcys back in a few weeks."

His comment about house guests made her think of her sister Mary. "I pray my sister and Miss Darcy are doing well?"

Bingley chuckled, "Those two are such an odd pair, and yet they get along so well. Miss Mary is just what Miss Darcy needs right now in her recovery. That carriage accident and the crippling affects of it have taken away so much of that spark she always possessed, but with your family around, and especially Miss Mary, I have seen her slowly come back to the girl I always knew."

"I am glad to hear it, sir. My sisters and I are very happy to have her in our family now as well."

Bingley saw the two gentlemen and Mrs Gardiner walking their way, so he stood, "It seems our time has come to an end. Thank you for providing me such a lovely view upon my arrival to Longbourn today," he gave a simple bow, tipping his hat, then walked off to join the gentlemen.

Jane was uncertain if he meant the sky or her. Her cheeks flamed a deep scarlet at such a thought.

Mrs Gardiner joined her niece on the stone bench, sitting as close as she could and running her arm through Jane's as they watched the gentlemen walk towards the stables. "It is a cold morning. What has brought you out here?"

"I just wished to embrace the stillness of the sunrise."

"Yes, the last few weeks have been quite overwhelming with the entertainments, dinners, guests, a ball—then there was the wedding on top of it all. Now you can find the time you need to learn all you can of Mr Bingley. Enjoy this time, my dear. I know Elizabeth chose a faster approach to her marriage, and that worked well for her, but you have always been in need of a little more time with something before you are truly comfortable."

"I am content aunt. I am in no rush to leave home just yet."

Maddie reached for her niece's fingers, squeezing them in a knowing manner. A cold wind swept across them, sending chills down her back. "Oh, my! Come, we will return inside and warm up by the fire. It would not do to have a red nose when *your Mr Bingley* calls later today."

"Oh aunt, he is not *my Mr Bingley*."

"Not yet, but I assure you my dear, he will be… one day."

Saturday, November 30, 1811

Lady Emily Lucas was on a mission and nothing would stop her. Not even her husband's need to use the carriage or the bitter cold and thick fog that settled in the Hertfordshire air overnight. *I am certain it will snow soon*, she thought as she plodded down the road. Her nose became colder and her feet moved faster until she was nearly tripping over her own skirts. Her fingers were so frozen she did not flinch when they came in contact with the chilly brass knocker. Her teeth began to chatter as the housekeeper, Mrs Hill, answered the door.

"Lady Lucas! Come in, come in! We must get you by a fire." Mrs Hill helped her out of the damp spencer and ushered her into the empty sitting room. "You warm yourself by the fire while I go find Mrs Bennet."

She knocked on Mr Bennet's study door and was bid enter. "Ma'am, Lady Lucas has walked from Lucas Lodge and is awaiting you in the sitting room."

"She walked? In this weather? Oh my, she must be half frozen. Thank you Hill; we will need some tea and cakes in the sitting room."

Mrs Bennet went to join her friend and find out what was so important as to bring her out walking today.

"Lady Lucas, what has brought you to my doorstep without your carriage for protection from this bitter cold?"

Turning to face her friend, with her teeth still chattering, she answered, "I have some information I must pass on to you."

Mrs Bennet easily positioned two chairs in front of the fire and replied, "Sit and get warm, then we can talk." Mrs Hill came in the door with a tray of tea and cakes and Mrs Bennet prepared their beverages and handed a cup of the hot liquid with a spoonful of honey (and a splash of some of Mr Bennet's liquor) to her friend.

Lady Lucas picked up the cup, cradling it in both her hands, and slowly sipped the tea. She closed her eyes as the warmth spread from the inside out and the shivers that shook her shoulders finally calmed. When she was sufficiently thawed, she placed her teacup back on the table and turned towards her hostess.

"Thank you, I did not realize just how cold it was outside until I was nearly here, then I could not turn around."

"This must be important news for you to walk here in this weather. What is it? Has someone been injured?"

"I had a visitor today;" Lady Lucas said warily, watching for the reaction her hostess gave, "—your sister."

Mrs Bennet sighed. "I am certain she was upset over not being included in the wedding."

"Yes she was; especially when she heard from Mrs Long that my family joined yours for the exclusive and private ceremony."

"I left the decision up to Elizabeth and Mr Darcy. My sister and her husband were invited to the breakfast afterwards, but I never saw them. Miranda has never fostered a relationship with any of my daughters and Elizabeth is wary of her, often speaking of not trusting her in the least."

"Elizabeth is a very perceptive person. There is something about your sister that makes me uneasy also, though I cannot determine what it is," Lady Lucas said. "That is what I came to speak with you about. I do not know why, but she was *especially* unusual in this visit. She mentioned that sometimes *tragic events* follow happy ones, and for some reason the look in her eye when she emphasized those particular words has haunted me since."

"I know exactly what you mean. I have often heard her say something that makes me nervous. As far as I know though nothing has ever come from her overt insinuations. My brother and I have often wondered if she is mad."

"She also said your brother has been in the neighborhood for the last month and has yet to visit her."

"That is true; the last time he and his wife took the time to visit, she told them they were not welcome in her home. So this time they have avoided her."

"I cannot imagine treating one's family as she does," Lady Lucas said in a shocked manner.

"She is ten years older than me, and we were never close. My brother, being seven years my junior, hardly knew Miranda. Her own mother's death hung over the family for years and she was raised apart from us because of her refusal to accept our mother as her father's new wife. I heard stories of her rage at his marriage, but my father kept us from her for many years. She did not marry until after Mr Bennet and I were wed, and my brother has told me our father settled the law firm on her to convince Mr Philips of her worth."

"Does your brother regret that he was unable to take over your father's business?"

"No, even at the young age of three and ten he knew he did not wish to be a country solicitor. Instead, my father sent him to schools where he learned all he needed to be the prosperous business man he is today. Did you know his warehouse is one of the most successful in Town?"

"No, I was unaware of his great success. Sir William rarely takes me to Town when he goes."

"He has been thinking of selling to his business partner and buying some land just as Sir William has done, but I do not know if he would do as well as a land owner."

"I am grateful for Mr Bennet taking Jonathan under his care and teaching him all he has. I have a feeling when the lodge is under his management it will prosper in ways my husband has not been able to accomplish."

"Your son was such a blessing to our family through all of the hard times. My husband has looked at him almost as a son for so long, and in a small way I am sad he and Lizzy did not marry." Mrs Bennet immediately realized what she said, "Oh, not that I bemoan Mr Darcy—he is just perfect for my Lizzy, though I did so wish for many years for Jonathan to one day be our son-in-law."

Lady Lucas smiled and reached over to pat her dear friend's hand, "Well, you do have *four* other daughters."

"Yes I do! I will not lose hope that one of them may catch his eye in the future."

"In truth, I should say three others, as Mr Bingley will surely speak of his affections for Jane very soon."

The two continued to talk of their expectations of the future until it was time for Lady Lucas to return home. This time she gratefully accepted the carriage ride Mrs Bennet offered, glad to not have to walk out again in such cold weather.

CHAPTER II

Netherfield Park, Hertfordshire

Colonel Richard Fitzwilliam entered the library to peruse Netherfield's shelves and found his brother at the desk writing a letter.

Alex put his pen down and looked at his brother as he wiped the ink from his fingers, "What has brought you to the library?"

"This winter wind that settled in overnight has made it too cold for a decent ride, so it seems I am trapped inside." Fitz picked up a few books on the table, looking through the titles. When nothing interested him, he walked over to the bookcases, running his hands along the spines. "Does Bingley not have anything of use on these shelves?"

Pointing to the other side of the room, the viscount quipped, "The romance novels are over there."

"Ha ha," he said with a groan.

Alex smiled, "I am writing to Anne; is there anything you wish me to convey to her?"

"I need to write her myself." Pulling a chair over to the desk, he asked for some paper and a quill, saying he could slip his own letter into his brother's. The two sat side by side, quietly writing for the next half hour, and when they were done Alex folded both letters together and sealed the thick package.

"Would you like a drink?" Fitz asked as Alex melted wax for the seal.

"Yes, thank you." He dropped the letter onto the silver tray to be sent out in the next day's post and wearily sat down in the chair near the fire.

"You look tired," Fitz remarked.

Closing his eyes and rubbing his temples, Alex answered, "I have a headache."

"Too bad Miss Bingley is no longer around to nurse you back to health."

Alex glared at his brother, "Yes, I have been spared her effusions—for now. I dread when we are both in company together again though. Bingley cannot keep her secreted away in Scarborough with his aunt forever."

"It is lucky for you, Georgiana, remaining here while Darcy is in Town with his bride. It has given you the perfect reason to stay on here yourself." He looked to ensure the door was securely closed, then turned back to tease his brother some more. "Would you like me to go get Miss Mary? She might be just what you need to feel better."

"Not funny, Fitz," Alex replied, bringing the glass to his lips for a drink. "I regret ever telling you how I feel."

"I do not regret that decision at all. It is not often I have the opportunity to tease you so."

"She is avoiding me anyway, so I doubt she would worry too much over my pain." Standing, he said, "Please keep an eye on Georgiana in case she needs help—I am going to lie down until it is time to dress for dinner."

"Of course; she prefers me anyway."

Fitz followed Alex out of the library and stood at the door to the music room, watching his brother as he walked away. *Just how much he is willing to endure from Mary Bennet is unclear. Perhaps I can help put my brother in a good light with her,* he thought, then turned to enter the room.

He stood by the door until the short piece the two ladies were playing together was completed, then he clapped, and walked over to the instrument, "What a beautiful rendition, ladies."

"You really think so Fitz?" Georgiana was nearly bouncing with excitement. "We had to change a few parts that I cannot play well enough yet."

He leaned down and kissed her forehead, "Absolutely, Sweetling." Then he turned to her companion, "Miss Mary, I must thank you for all the ways you have helped my cousin. You truly are a blessing to my family."

"It is Georgiana who practices, sir. I contribute little—it is her natural ability that shines through."

"Well, I cannot say I have any musical abilities. No, I think my brother is a better catch as far as that goes." He noticed her pale and turn away to go through the stack of music sitting on the pianoforte. *Maybe she just isn't ready yet,* he thought. He turned back to address his cousin, "When you are ready to return to your room, call for me. Alex has gone to lie down."

Mary stopped shuffling the papers, listening intently to what was said about the viscount, though she tried to convince herself she did not care to know anything of him.

"Oh? Is he ill?" Georgiana asked.

"Do not worry, it is only a headache."

Why should I care if he is not well, Mary told herself, trying to focus once again on the music sheets before her as she put them back in the proper order.

Fitz excused himself from the two, smiling when he closed the door and heard them begin to play again. Georgiana's accident had caused such a loss of strength in her hands that it had been a long recovery to get where she was now. It nearly brought tears to his eyes when he thought of all she had gone through over the last seven months. Clearing his throat and shaking his head, he looked around, ensuring the servants did not see his unintentional emotional display, then he heard the crack of balls coming from the billiards room and turned to follow the noise.

As he entered, Bingley was talking, "I am certain Caroline will write to Louisa when she arrives at Aunt Hamilton's, but I will write to you also when I hear from her. Hopefully she will learn her lesson and stop throwing herself into the paths of men who will never give her a second glance."

"You mean like my cousin and my brother?" Fitz said.

"Yes, exactly; come on in, Fitz," Bingley said.

"Thank you." He closed the door behind him.

"Where is your brother?" Hurst asked.

"He has a headache and has gone to lie down."

Bingley said as he walked to the bell pull, "I will have Mrs Benson take him some of her special tea. I am sure it will do wonders for his head and he will be feeling better before the day is through."

"I think he would appreciate that."

When the housekeeper came into the room, Bingley explained the situation to her. As she was about to leave, Fitz asked her, "What is in your special tea, Mrs Benson?"

"Oh, that is a family secret, Colonel," she replied.

Smiling, he urged her to reveal the secret, but she would not say. "What if I am sitting in my barracks in London with the most horrible headache, and I do not have you to question? You simply must tell me or I shall blame you for my agony," he prodded.

With a lift of her eyebrow at the antics of the amiable Colonel, she turned to walk through the door, "Why, Brandy, of course."

Fitz let out a roar of laughter, and they were all soon doubled over with tears in their eyes. The three men sat in the chairs trying to gain control again. It was a few minutes, but eventually Bingley offered some drinks to his companions, and the three calmed enough to carry on with their game.

Fitz, remembering what he heard when he came in the room, asked, "Before Alex came here, we received a letter from you, and in it you mentioned a situation; did it have anything to do with your sister?"

"Alex has not talked with you of all that has taken place?" Bingley inquired.

"No, he has been a little *distracted* in the week since I arrived," Fitz answered.

Bingley leaned down to take his shot, "Oh, right; with the wedding and guests and Georgiana I am sure he has not had much time for that."

Taking a drink, Fitz thought, *he has been quite distracted, but not for the reasons you surmise, my friend. The lovely Miss Mary Bennet is what is keeping his mind busy these days.*

"We found Caroline attempting to be *caught alone* with Darcy and when we confronted her about it she insisted he asked for a *private discussion*. We, of course," Hurst explained, indicating he and Bingley, "knew he was gone that day and did not see or talk with her before he left."

Bingley picked up the story from there, "Then after Alex came to Netherfield, she was caught jostling his door handle one night."

"I am sure he is glad he learned long ago to lock his door."

"Yes, fortune has shined upon him in *that* regard, has it not?" Bingley said. "The worst was when she made some comments where Miss Bennet could hear proclaiming me to be a rake."

"A rake! You are anything but that," Fitz was in awe of what his friend's sister would do to get what she wanted.

"Yes, that was my reaction as well," Bingley said.

"I would guess you were able to clear up the misunderstanding with Miss Bennet?"

Bingley smiled, "Yes, I was. For now I am courting her, but soon I am going to ask for her hand."

Fitz settled onto the sofa, "Though she smiles and seems easily pleased, her countenance does not tell much. Do you think she is delighted with your attentions?"

Bingley' eyes closed and a big smile graced his lips as he said, "She is an angel, a perfect beauty both inside and out."

Fitz sat forward in his seat, intently looking at the man who had been his friend now for thirteen years. "Yes I gathered so from meeting her, but that does not answer my question. Does she care for you?"

Hurst smiled and answered, "I can honestly say I have seen her face light up when he comes into a room. She smiles often, but when it is at Bingley, it is different. I believe her heart has been touched."

Bingley's cheeks flushed at hearing what Hurst had to say on the subject. Being the youngest of their group growing up, the others tended to linger over him in protective mode often, but in this he needed no protection— he trusted Jane Bennet with his heart and knew she would handle it gently and return the love he was ready to give to her.

"So when will you propose?"

Bingley was jarred from his musings. "I am waiting for Darcy's return. He promised he would find the perfect Christmas gift for me to give to her and bring it with him when they return on the twentieth. I intend to propose sometime during the holiday celebrations. I do not have any set plans yet, but I want to make it special for her. She deserves no less than my best effort."

Hurst chuckled, "I am glad I will be leaving in three days. If I had to put up with this for the next month I cannot say I would not want to hurt someone."

"Yes, I too am glad I will be leaving as well."

"Just wait, Fitz; when your time comes I will torment you just as harshly as you are tormenting me now."

"Ahhh, but the difference is, when I have lost my heart, I do not intend to tell anyone. I will just sweep her off to the church without anyone knowing, and will return with a wife on my arm."

Holding up his drink in mock salute to Fitz's plan, Hurst added, "Weddings are overrated, I say."

"Yes, but you showed up, did you not?" Bingley laughed.

"Indeed I did," taking a sip of his drink and thinking of his wife, "*indeed I did.*"

———————◆◆◆———————

Sunday, December 1, 1811

Fitz sat at the desk in the library organizing the notes of the investigation that would take him back to Town tomorrow. He had spared as much time as he dared and knew he must return. He must find the reprobate who was responsible for the deaths of two of his soldiers. This was the only thing stopping him from selling his commission and putting the rough life of an investigative officer behind him for good. The door opened and Mary entered. Startled, he stood, shuffling the papers, "Good day to you, Miss Mary."

"Oh, I am sorry for disturbing you, sir," she answered as she turned to leave the room.

"You are not disturbing me," Fitz said. "Can I help you with something?"

"After the service this morning, Georgiana is resting. So I thought I would find a book to read."

"And this being the library, naturally you have come here in your search of the perfect tome." He watched as a small smile alighted on her face.

"If you do not mind, I will just find a book and then leave you in peace," Mary said, turning to the bookshelves.

"Do not feel you must leave on my behalf, I will not be here much longer myself. What sort of reading material do you fancy today?"

"I am not certain, sir," she answered as he came up beside her, perusing the shelves.

"I hear tell the novels are kept on that shelf over there," Fitz said with a smirk as he pointed to the bookcase on the other side of the room.

Smiling at his response, she said, "I do not read novels often."

Stepping back, he crossed his arms over his broad chest and looked at her. After studying her for a few seconds, he said, "I have found you to be a very sensible person. I would surmise your interests lean towards histories, maybe religious texts, and possibly the Bard himself—not all of his works mind you. I do not see you liking the tragic deaths of *Romeo and Juliet* or *Anthony and Cleopatra*. The darkness of *Macbeth* might draw your attentions sometimes, but I see you more as a comedies type of person."

"Your assumptions are astoundingly correct, sir."

"It is my job to be so, Miss Mary. So, which will it be today—Fordyce, or possibly the greatest story William Shakespeare ever penned, if I do say so myself," he said as he pulled two books off the shelves and held them up for her appraisal.

Mary smiled, "If those are my only choices, I would have to choose *The Merchant of Venice*. While religious texts do sometimes draw my attention, I never read *Fordyce*."

With a gallant bow, he held the book out to her, "Your book, my lady."

Mary smiled and curtsied as she accepted it, then sat on the couch to read. *I know why Georgiana laughs at this cousin so often*, she thought as she took a seat. *He puts a person at ease very easily. If I had a brother, I imagine he would be very much like Colonel Fitzwilliam.*

Seeing the perfect opportunity to ask about his cousin, Fitz sat in a seat near her and asked, "Miss Mary, may I talk with you about a serious matter for a moment?"

The look on his face concerned her. Putting the book aside, she answered in the affirmative and waited for him to begin.

"I am not certain what you know of Georgiana's injuries."

"I know only that she was in a carriage accident and sustained injuries that continue to cause her discomfort, including not being able to walk," Mary answered.

Nodding, Fitz said, "Have you been told of her recovery prior to coming here?"

"Your brother informed us that she was not even removing from her rooms before coming to Netherfield Park."

He nodded again, "I know you have been around her more than anyone else, and so I must ask you—how is she? I know physically she is doing as best as can be expected at this time. To own the truth, I was surprised she was so willing to attend church services this morning. It has been a long time since she was able to do so. But how is she *really* doing?"

Taking a minute to think while she studied the worried look on the man's face, she finally answered, "Beyond the physical, I think she is having difficulty with the aspect of this being for the rest of her life. She refuses to use her bath chair because she says it is as if the finality of the situation afflicts her when she sits in it. She has not talked often of anything she is feeling, but sometimes I can see the sadness on her face. I think once she realizes life can continue, just not in the same manner as before, she will be able to put these things behind her and go forward embracing all that will have to be done differently from now on."

"Do you think she is close to that acceptance?"

Mary shook her head, "Just judging from what my father went through, no I do not. She is young and has so very much to undertake. I think it may be another few months at the least, possibly even longer, before she will be ready for the next step. I am certain, however, that my sister Elizabeth will be able to draw her out and help her on this road to recovery."

Nodding his head in agreement, Fitz stood, "Thank you for your honesty, Miss Mary. It gives me comfort to know she has found such a dear friend in you. It is not easy to leave her, but when you are by her side, it becomes a little easier."

"Are you leaving again soon, sir?"

"Yes, I am needed in Town and must leave on the morrow."

"I am sure we will all miss you, sir," she said.

"Thank you." He gave a small bow of his head, "I will leave you to read in peace now."

Mary picked up the book again and sat back to read as Fitz returned to the desk and gathered the papers now laid out in proper order, placing them in his satchel. He capped the ink, positioned the quill in its holder, and excused himself from the library, leaving Mary to ponder their conversation, the book she held no longer holding much of her attention.

Sarah Johnson

CHAPTER

III

Monday, December 2, 1811
Rosings Park, Kent

L ady Catherine was lost in her own thoughts as her daughter rubbed
her head, the pounding finally subsiding with the gentle pressure to
her temples. She was brought to anger once again by the limitations her
husband set in his will, but that anger always came with a headache. In fact,
they were coming more frequently than ever these days.

"What will Mr Collins preach on next week, Mother?" Anne asked.

Lady Catherine inwardly groaned—*Mr Collins*. The man was sent by the
Archbishop as a replacement to the parson her husband had chosen
years ago. Just when she thought she would finally be out from under
her husband's controlling reach and be able to influence his brother,
Commodore de Bourgh, who was in charge of the estate until Anne
married, she received a letter from the Archbishop. It stated that Sir Lewis
de Bourg had left *specific requirements for the spiritual needs of all his loved ones*
with his brother, and that Mr Collins would fit those requirements. Lady

Sarah Johnson

Catherine had no say in who filled the newly vacant position. *Why does my husband continue to haunt me even from the grave? What did I do in life to deserve this treatment, even still, so many years after his death? The man has been gone for over twenty years, and yet I still cannot rid myself of the control he holds over my life.*

"Are you well Mother?" Anne asked when she noticed her mother's features paling more than usual.

She reached up to touch her daughter's hand, "I am well, my child. I just do not wish to endure any more of Mr Collins."

"He was here again this morning for his usual meeting?"

"Yes."

"If you are not feeling well, why not just send him away?"

"He would not go," she said wearily as the rubbing of her temples was finally starting to calm the pain in her head.

Sir Lewis' directives were followed by Mr Collins as if they were the sacred words written in the stone tablets. Every week she must endure not only his inept attempts at morality, but also him bestowing his never-ending endearments towards *his patroness* on a daily basis. For it seemed her husband had also laid out specific daily tasks for the parson to perform, and William Collins would not ignore the final wishes of the *obviously* most loving husband and father, even if those actions were not favorable to those upon whom they were bestowed. Every morning, whether rain or sun, he would arrive at Rosings, list in hand, and he would not leave until the tasks of the day were completed.

Today that list included his talking for exactly two hours on the subject of his family. Last week he talked of his much-loved mother, and this week it was of his distant cousins, the Bennet family of Longbourn in Hertfordshire, and about the family rift that had torn the previous generation apart. With the recent death of his father, Collins was now next in line to inherit the estate because of an entail on the land and the family's lack of a male child. Several years ago, his father tried to talk Mr Bennet into an invitation to visit Longbourn, but one was never garnered. Being a parson, Collins was now determined to heal this chasm that was formed by his father, and he had written to his cousin in order to start them towards rebuilding the family harmony. Collins was certain any day now he would receive a response which would surely be an invitation to visit the family for at least a week, possibly two, if he could be spared from his duties for such a generous amount of time.

Lady Catherine had to endure the two hours without complaint and without interruption, for if she tried to change the direction of his speech, he would only extend the time he spent in her presence. She had learned many months ago just to let the man talk. Unfortunately, she also learned that she must pay attention to him at least a little; otherwise he would start it all over again, prolonging her agony even further. She determined that if this Henry Bennet did write to her parson inviting him to visit, she would try to talk him into staying for more than just a week or two. It would be truly heavenly if she could talk him into a full month of leisure! Maybe if she convinced him it was now his duty to be married, and that it was also his duty to his family to offer for one of his cousins as an olive branch of peace, he would stay away while settling on and becoming familiar with his intended.

Anne continued to run her small fingers through her mother's hair in a soothing manner, and replace the cold cloth on her forehead every few minutes. These headaches were coming on more frequently, and Anne had no idea what the cause could be. She feared the local doctor was not very well acquainted with whatever malady that plagued her mother and something of a much more serious nature could be the underlying cause. *Maybe Uncle Hugh would know of a trustworthy doctor,* she thought. It was with a great determination she decided she must find reason enough to write to her relations soon, and hopefully in such a way as to keep the letter's contents from her mother's eyes. She had spies everywhere, so it was not often such an opportunity presented itself for the sheltered and only child of this controlling woman. It was disturbing to see someone she dearly loved become someone she hardly recognized. Her mother had never been verbose about her affections, but she was now acting as a completely different person altogether.

When her mother's breathing evened out and sleep finally came, Anne quietly left the bedroom for her own suite of rooms. As she walked out the door, a maid holding a small silver tray of letters was coming down the hallway.

"An express has come, Miss de Bourgh, and another letter in the regular post," the girl said as she came closer.

Anne lifted the two letters from the tray and immediately recognized the Darcy seal upon one of them. Having heard from her uncle already about Darcy's wonderful news, and knowing it was this that was likely contained within the letter, she decided it would be best to let her mother rest for now. It would not do to disturb her after such an episode, and if she was correct, the news would surely set her off on a tirade the likes of which had never been seen before. She was not known for her calmness under pressure, but rather for her explosive manners, especially when she had the least control over the situation, as was the case here. "Thank you; I will deliver these to my mother once she is refreshed. It would not do to disturb her right now."

"Yes, ma'am," the maid answered, then returned to her duties.

Anne watched the maid retreat. When she was alone in the hallway, her eyes turned back to the two missives. She lifted the weightier letter, addressed to her, with a smile. It was from her cousin Alex, and from the feel of it, there might be another letter contained within. She retired to her rooms to open it in privacy.

There was, indeed, a second letter within, and it was from Fitz. Anne quickly skimmed the letter from Alex and put it aside. Her fingers trembled as she opened the thicker one from Fitz.

> November 30, 1811
> Netherfield Park, Hertfordshire
>
> My Dearest Anne,
>
> How I long to call you such in person, but it is not to be—yet. Do not lose heart, my love, for my task

will one day be completed and we will be able to marry.

I was fortunate enough to find Alex writing to you, so I have been able to add my own letter to his, hopefully without raising the suspicions of your mother. I suppose I should spare one sentence asking about the old coot, so how is she? Does she allow you to go into the garden on your own yet? I am sorry you must endure such a controlling mother for my sake.

I often wonder—is it selfish of me to continue on this investigation when nothing new comes of it at our every turn? Will I have to one day decide to let this murdering fiend go? I fear this long wait will pull us apart before we have the opportunity to even be together. A person can only endure so much in patience before it is too much to bear, and I would not have my own actions and choices burden you so, my love. I know what you would say to me, and I can just now here your soft voice telling me you wish me to pursue this last investigation. That the families deserve to know their soldiers did not die in vain, and that one day they too will sleep more soundly in knowing the person who has haunted their families all these years no longer holds such power over them.

I will agree with this continued path, for now, with my promise to put every bit of my energy into catching this killer and finally closing this investigation that keeps us apart. Perhaps the new year will bring information we have yet to find. I must continue to hope for such a turn of events.

It is with great purpose I have set aside such ominous words to announce much happier ones, for us and our cousin—Darcy is now a married man! For many years it was your mother's belief that you were meant to marry Darcy that has kept us from pursuing our own happiness, but now that he is settled with a wife, perhaps our own time will finally come. I must say, it has loomed over my head for a long time now. Even after Darcy stood up to Aunt Catherine after the accident I did not fully believe you would not be forced to marry him. My heart beats more solidly knowing you truly will one day be mine, no matter what your mother says. Has she heard the news yet? I hope it has come from either Darcy or my father, and not from your mother's perusal of the paper. I can just imagine her reaction, and while it may play out comically in my mind, I would never wish you to endure such treatment as I know will come with such news. If it is too much, promise me you will write to my father or brother so we can get you away from her. Please, promise me!

I cannot dwell too long on such melancholy, so I must move on to better thoughts. This last week I have been privy to one of the greatest love matches I have ever seen, and it has reminded me over and over again of what I feel for you. One day I will sweep you off your feet and be able to hold you and kiss you as you deserve...

Anne felt tears sting her cheeks as she read the pages from Fitz. He promised her over a year ago that only this last investigation stood in their way of his being able to sell his commission. As the commanding officer of two soldiers who were killed, he felt it his duty to find the man who murdered them before he set aside his uniform for good. This turned out to be the most challenging assignment of his career, and the two were left pining for each other as the months wore on, but she understood and encouraged him on his quest. Their day would come soon enough, and until then she would have patience enough to endure.

Anne read the letter through three times before she laid her head down to rest until it was time to dress for dinner. She clutched the letter in her hand as the weariness of the day became too much for her, and she soon drifted off to a sleep filled with wonderful dreams of her love coming for her.

Her maid, Lucy, woke her in time to dress. She pulled her hair up into the tight bun Lady Catherine insisted Anne wear, wrapping the thick shawl around her shoulders to hopefully ward off the chill of the dining room. Its grandeur was astounding, and although the mantles were quite costly, the fireplaces they framed were not very well built and did not adequately heat the large room. Anne descended the stairs for the two-hour long, full five-course meal her mother required every evening.

Upon entering and seeing Lady Catherine already in her chair, Anne apologized for her tardiness and sat down at the opposite end of the long table. Why they must sit so far from each other was something she always wondered, but never dared ask. "I hope you rested well, Mother?"

With her nose in the air, Lady Catherine unfolded her serviette, nodded at the servants to begin their duties, and answered her daughter, "Yes, it was quite adequate, thank you."

Anne cleared her throat and pulled the letter for her mother from her pocket, "An express came this afternoon just as you began your rest. It is from my cousin Darcy."

Lady Catherine nodded to the servant who went to Anne's side with an empty silver tray, upon which she set the letter. Then the servant walked to the far side of the table where the mistress sat and again held out the tray with practiced ease, bowing and backing into the corner again when Lady Catherine took the missive. However, she did not choose to open it. Anne looked down at her soup bowl, and quietly stirred the hot liquid. She had hoped to know what was contained within, but it seemed her mother did not intend to open it until later when she was alone. Anne would have to determine what was in it another way.

"I was told you received another letter as well."

Anne tried not to let her cheeks flush, giving away her feelings to her mother. "Yes, from Alex."

"Be sure to answer him directly. It would not do to offend a *viscount*, even if it is just your cousin."

"Yes, Mother," she answered, then looked back to her soup bowl. She was shocked at not being told she must produce the letter for her mother's perusal, as was the usual way. *Perhaps it is a blessing bestowed from above,* she thought.

After the meal, and after Anne was required to read aloud for an hour, she was bid leave to retire.

When Lady Catherine was finally alone, she opened the letter from her nephew. As she read the few lines contained on the page she became incensed. She had never been so angry in all her life. *Why did my sister and that man she married have to put the notion of love into my nephew's mind? Now what am I to do? He has married this woman, this Elizabeth Bennet, and it will ruin all of my carefully laid out plans.*

Elizabeth Bennet...Bennet, where have I heard that name before? Ahhh, yes, Collins' family was named Bennet. What was the name of the place he said he would one day inherit? Was it Longbourn, in Hertfordshire? If she remembered correctly, it sounded like this could be the same Bennets he expounded upon for two hours today. For once, the sycophantic parson and his long-winded soliloquies might have come in handy. *I will have to question him tomorrow and see if there truly is a connection. If there is, I am certain I will be able to persuade him to do my bidding and ruin this family. They must pay for thinking they are worthy of such a connection. Then my Anne can marry Darcy, as it is meant to be.*

In the spring, she was so very close to having her wish come true. If only George Wickham did as he was told, but no, instead he caused Georgiana's nearly fatal accident, putting such stress on her nephew that when she approached him about his marrying Anne, he expressed himself in a most inappropriate way, cutting her off from his family and insisting she leave his home immediately, never to be welcomed again. *If I ever get my hands on that boy again, I will make him regret crossing me!*

CHAPTER IV

Wednesday, December 4, 1811

Jane shuddered at the icy wind that whipped around her skirts.

"Are you cold?" Bingley asked her, drawing her arm just a little closer to the side of his body.

"A little," she said, "but I do not wish to go back inside."

"Maybe if we walk a little faster you will warm up a bit," Bingley suggested. At her acknowledgment, he quickened the speed of their footsteps.

"Have you heard from Miss Bingley yet?" Jane asked, trying not to let her teeth chatter.

"No, though I do not expect to hear from her until at least next week. She left six days ago, and the winter may have made her journey longer than the four days it usually takes to travel, so she may not arrive in Scarborough until today."

"That is quite the distance," Jane said, unable to fully grasp just how far Scarborough was from Hertfordshire. "The furthest I have ever journeyed is to London."

"Your family does not travel much, then?" he asked.

"Elizabeth has gone to the north with my Aunt and Uncle Gardiner once when she was younger, but otherwise, our travels have only taken us to London."

"Do you go there often?" Bingley asked.

"Elizabeth and I have been there with my Aunt and Uncle Gardiner for the Season three times."

"I am surprised I have not met you then," he said.

"I did not think we had many common acquaintances, sir."

"It was my understanding Darcy has known the Gardiners for many years. I know he has taken me to their warehouse before and has mentioned he knew the family well," Bingley said.

"Really? I was unaware of the connection. My Aunt and Uncle have never mentioned the acquaintance," Jane replied.

Changing the subject back to travel, Bingley asked, "If you could choose one place to visit, where would it be?"

Without even a pause, Jane answered with a small bounce to her step, "Italy."

"Italy! I did not think you would be interested in traveling so far," Bingley said, shocked.

"I have wanted to travel to Italy ever since I was young and learned of the

Roman Empire in our studies."

"If you had to choose a closer destination, where would it be?" Bingley asked.

Cocking her head to the side as she thought, she bit her lower lip. "I think I would like to see the sea. I cannot say where precisely, but I have never seen what I have read in many books of the waves as they slide onto the shore, rolling back out into the abyss of sea that merges with the horizon far off in the distance. It sounds very peaceful and serene, does it not?"

Bingley smiled. "I spent my younger days on the cliffs and rocks of Scarborough's shores. It is far from peaceful when you have such harsh terrain." Looking off in the distance, he continued, "I remember the first time I went to Brighton. I was fifteen and Darcy and I traveled there with some friends from school while we were on holiday." Bingley looked down at the lady on his arm and smiled, "I often walked along the shores picking up shells or sat in the sand watching the surf as it came in. There was one place along the shore where the rocks jutted out into the water, and it reminded me a little of Scarborough. Darcy often found me sitting on the rocks, wet from the rough waves as they splashed up onto me. I would sit there for hours not realizing how much time had passed."

"That sounds beautiful," Jane said quietly. She smiled, "You make me want to visit Brighton, sir."

"My sister and her husband just left two days ago for Brighton."

"Yes, Mrs Hurst and I talked of her travel plans. She was very excited for her winter holiday," Jane replied.

"They should arrive there today; it is not too far of a drive, only eighty miles or so," he said.

Jane's eyes widened, "I cannot imagine a life where eighty miles is *not too far.*"

Chuckling, he thought to himself, *I hope to one day give you that kind of a life.* When he felt her shudder again, he said, "I think it is time we join your family inside. I would not have you fall ill because of my taking you for some fresh air, and I am certain we will have snow before the day is done."

Mr Bennet watched the couple from his window as they made their way through the garden. Their arms were entwined and both smiled and leaned towards each other in the way only those in love are want to do. *I have a feeling I will soon have another visit from Mr Bingley, and this time he will be requesting the hand of my eldest daughter*, he thought to himself.

Saturday, December 7, 1811

The stench of urine and sweat hit his face as he entered the run-down establishment. He swallowed the bile rising in his throat and walked on through the door, hoping his stomach would not empty at any moment. His mother said for years she did not understand how, with his weak constitution, he had lasted so long in the King's service. He could think of many worse situations he had been in over the years. Shaking the memories from his mind, he ambled up to the bar to order a mug of their finest brew; he would have preferred something stronger, but knew he would need his wits about him tonight.

When the drink was slammed down in front of him, he grabbed the handle and turned around to lean his back against the counter, looking over the top of his mug around the dark, smoky tavern. Seeing a card game at the table in the corner, he tipped his head that direction and asked the man behind the counter, "Open table?" When he received a nod, he asked, "What's the buy in?"

"A quid each, winner takes all. Game don't stop til ever'uns out. I seen 'um go fer days withot ev'n sleepin."

34

"Big stakes!"

"Keeps it to the ser'ous."

Nodding his head, he answered, "Yes, I am sure it does." Taking another drink, he asked, "You know the man in charge?"

"In the corner, dark hair—they call 'im *G.W.*"

Drinking what remained in his mug, he threw down a coin and said, "another for me and a round for the table."

Mugs were prepared and a girl, barely old enough to fill the dress she wore, sauntered over to the table, flirting with the men and passing out the drinks. The man in the corner of the room with dark hair looked over at the bar. He lifted the drink in thanks and indicated that the benevolent stranger join them. Picking up his own mug, the stranger walked over.

"Mighty generous of you," the man at the table said. Taking a swig of the mug, he said, "Care to join in?"

"I might be interested; what'll it cost me?"

"A quid to sit down, from there it's up to the hand and wager called." Eyeing him, he asked, "Too steep for you?"

Throwing down some coins on the table, the stranger said, "I think I can handle it if you have a new deck to pull out." He sat down and a new deck was given to him to inspect.

"So what do we call you?"

"Carter," the man said with a firm voice. "You?"

"G.W.," he said eyeing the stranger. "Well, Carter, you ready?" With a nod, the game began.

Seven hours later, he left with an empty pocket but a head full of knowledge for the man to whom he answered. As the sun came up he made his way across town, making sure he was not followed. He arrived at his intended destination, knocked on the door, and was led into the office inside.

"Carter to see you, Colonel Fitzwilliam, sir."

The colonel stood, "Thank you. Call Captain Chamberlayne and put a guard on the door; do not let anyone except him in until I say otherwise." When the corporal left the room, the colonel turned to his comrade, "Have a seat, Lieutenant Denny. I received your note; so tell me how the meeting went."

When Captain Chamberlayne arrived, he made a sketch of the characteristics described by Lieutenant Denny of the person known as G.W., focusing on any scars or physical markings that would help identify him. There was not much to go on with his face, as the lighting where the game took place was not adequate enough for a detailed description. He was of average height and build with nothing that stood out as distinctive. There was one scar that Lieutenant Denny could remember very clearly; it was a scar on the man's right forearm that he saw when one of the card players accused G.W. of cheating. He rolled up his shirtsleeves to prove his innocence. It was a jagged scar of about six inches in length along the top of his forearm. It looked like it had not been stitched up well and had healed with a lot of scar tissue. When Lieutenant Denny was certain the drawing was as accurate as possible, Captain Chamberlayne was dismissed.

Colonel Fitzwilliam and Lieutenant Denny decided their next plan of action. The new intelligence seemed to be accurate in pointing them to this man, but now they needed to pull another undercover man from his current assignment to watch this G.W. With Lieutenant Denny having already met G.W., it was important to find someone they could not tie back to them. Saunderson was just who they needed for this assignment. Lieutenant Denny would hunt him down, and then the three would meet together again in a week, at a secret location and all dressed to blend into their environment, something they had to do often in their line of work.

Robert Denny finally left for his barracks room to crawl between the sheets of his bed and sleep whatever was left of the rest of the day away. He would leave in the morning, once again posing as *Carter* to find Saunderson; that alone might take him a few days, but the man was now essential to this investigation.

Monday, December 9, 1811

The pounding would not stop; why could they not just leave him alone? In a sleepy haze, he heard the proprietor calling through the door, "YOU PAY ME TODAY, OR I'LL THROW YOU OUT MYSELF! I WANT MY MONEY NOW!!"

Cursing and pulling on his trousers, he stumbled to the table and dug through the purse, heavy from his winnings, yelling back, "I'M COMING!" When he finally found what was needed, he opened the door to the irate man.

"Here's your money, old man; now leave me be!"

"This ain't the poorhouse, and I don't trust ya to give me what you owe, so you'll pay for tonight too or leave!"

"Fine, just stop beating the door down," he grumbled and went to get some more coins to appease the man. Handing them over, he slammed the door closed and crawled back in bed to sleep a few more hours. The drunken state in which he had spent the majority of the last two days was beginning to wear off, leaving him with a pounding head and a short temper—two things he often eased with more spirits. Unfortunately he was out and was too tired to go get more now.

It could not have been five minutes before someone else was banging on his door. He got out of bed again and swung open the door, saying gruffly, "WHAT do you want NOW?"

The servant girl jumped with the harsh tone of his voice and timidly held out a note, "B…b…beggin' yer pardon, sir, but this come fer you."

Taking the letter and closing the door, he turned it over and recognized the seal. Groaning, he mumbled to himself, "And here I thought my day could get no worse."

The note was brief, as always, and only gave a time and place to meet. Looking at the clock, he cursed again. If he were to make it on time, he would have to leave immediately. He had a good mind to not go, but knowing what he did of this person, that might not be the smartest move. He grabbed his clothes and quickly dressed.

A half-hour later, he walked into the place indicated in the message. Looking around, he did not see who he was there to meet, so he chose a corner table and sat so he could see the door. He called for a drink and two glasses, hoping it would dull the continual throbbing in his head. When the servant came with the glasses and bottle, he ordered, "Leave the bottle," threw a coin onto the tray and poured himself a drink and drank it down quickly.

When *she* came through the door, she caught the attention of several patrons. Seeing him in the corner, she smiled as she passed the tables, running her hands over the shoulders of a few of her favorite men. One reached out to pinch her, but she scooted away, shaking her finger at him in a teasing manner as she sauntered over to the table. "It has been ever so long. I am so glad…"

"What do you want?" he interrupted.

"I have a job to be done, and I would like your help."

"Sit," he said gruffly as he poured two drinks and slid one over to her. "What is this job?"

With a glint in her eye, she replied, "It is simple—we need to bring ruination to a certain family."

"And which family would that be?"

"The *Bennets* of Longbourn in Hertfordshire."

"I have never heard of them, so they cannot be so well off. What made you accept this job?"

"They are now connected to *Fitzwilliam Darcy*," she said, raising her eyebrow and watching his reaction.

He took a slow drink, "Ahhh, I see; you took this because of revenge."

With an evil smile, she replied, "I cannot let what he did to us go unchallenged. I have lost some of my best contacts because of that last disaster of a job, and now that I can pay him back and receive a nice tidy sum to boot, I will not turn it down."

"Who is paying for this one?"

"I am sure you already know."

Cursing, he said, "So I do not have any say in whether I am helping you or not?"

Taking a drink, she leaned back and said with confidence, "No, you do not."

"I have a price."

"Of that I have no doubt. I will try to get what you want, but cannot be certain whether it will work in your favor. What is your price?"

"Unfortunately I lost some very important *items* while hiding out a few years ago. If you can acquire these for me, then I will charge you only half my usual fee."

"Hmmm… I think I might just be able to work that into the negotiations. It is quite the encouragement for me, is it not?"

"Yes, the extra would pad your pockets nicely." He pulled a scrap of paper and pencil stub from his pocket and started writing down said items.

"I will meet with my *associate* in two days and will be in contact with you again soon." As she stood, she drew her finger across his hand and said, "I have missed you Geo—…"

"DO NOT call me by that name," he ground out, fury clearly evident on his features. "I have done well to avoid the authorities in London so far, and I will not have you ruin it for me now." He stood and handed her the paper, "I have already paid for my bed for the night, so your services are not needed." He turned and quickly left.

She took one last drink and read the list of items he gave her. Placing the paper in her reticule, she rose to leave. As she passed the table of men again, one caught her hand and pulled her onto his lap. "I see you are leaving alone. Does that mean you are free for the night?"

Smiling, she said, "I am."

"What a coincidence, so am I," he said.

Pulling out her card she whispered, "I have moved since I last saw you." She stood and quickly left.

He looked down at the card in his hand—*Mrs Younge's Boarding House.* Noting the address, he pocketed the card and called to the server for one more round of drinks for the table.

CHAPTER

V

December 8-19, 1811

The next two weeks were spent enjoying the activities the month of December always brings. Winter weather set in, and on days when the wind was calm, it was nice to be outside and feel the cool crisp air as it brightened cheeks and made noses red. Their first snowfall was only a light dusting, but they knew the heavier covering was soon to come.

Fitz heard from Anne, and the love of which she wrote strengthened his determination to end this last investigation as quickly as he possibly could.

Miss Bingley arrived in Scarborough, and while she was not exactly having a pleasant time, she was glad to have the traveling over with for a while. Aunt Hamilton introduced her with much aplomb at all the holiday parties, and Caroline soon grew weary of the season's gatherings and revelry. She wrote to Louisa, hoping to talk her into letting her join them, but had yet to receive a response from her sister.

The Hursts enjoyed being in Brighton and spent most afternoons strolling the boardwalk and listening to the musicians as they played the songs of the season. Louisa found some special gifts for all her friends and family, and one particular item her husband had wanted for a few years.

The residents of Netherfield Park and Longbourn were often in company with each other and the two homes were decorated for Christmas with much care. Boughs of greenery and berries were strung along the banisters and doorposts, and Georgiana enjoyed decorating wreaths with Mary, Kitty, and Lydia. Mary managed to avoid Alex as much as she possibly could, but it became harder once Fitz returned to London, as the viscount was now Georgiana's only means of getting around. Alex noticed her reticence and did not push her to interact with him. He did not want to offend her again, and she had clearly stated she wished to abide by formalities for now. From a distance, he observed her and took note of things that might help him in eventually winning her affections.

The Darcys were seen at the museum and in Hyde Park when the weather permitted, and once those who attended the wedding arrived back in Town, the Ton was all abuzz with the details. The Earl and Countess of Rosebery invited the Darcys to the theater, and before the couple could make it through the lobby they were stopped over a dozen times by people wishing to meet the new Mrs Darcy. They shared many lovely evenings at home, just the two of them curled up in front of the fire, reading and talking.

Mr Bennet knew he could put it off no longer, so he sat down with his brother-in-law to discuss the details of his financial holdings to see if he had enough to possibly end the entail on his lands. He knew he would have to contact the Collins side of the family soon. With their plans drawn out, it was decided the gentlemen would first discuss the details with Darcy. He might have some foresight they had overlooked.

Not everyone had such a pleasant time. Mrs Philips was heard more than once complaining of the Bennets and how she was treated so ill by her own relations. She was determined to come up with a way to make her sister pay, and the man she saw watching Longbourn from the wood might just be her best hope. Hoping to learn why he was watching the Bennets, she followed him and tracked him down to a small establishment in a town five miles away. Questioning the owner, she found out the man had given the name of *George Wilson*, and he was in the area surveying the wood. The innkeeper thought maybe a new road was to be put in, but he could get no specific information from the man himself.

Mrs Philips kept an eye on the stranger until one day he disappeared. He left no tab at the pub, and bribing the maid who cleaned his room revealed nothing. He seemed intelligent enough, having impressed upon the locals his higher education, though his clothes were not that of a gentleman. She sketched a rough drawing of the man, lamenting the fact that she could not draw as well as her niece Kitty. He seemed to be a man of average height and features, but something about his eyes told her he was not there surveying the land for a new road.

Friday, December 20, 1811

"They have come!" Lydia excitedly called from the window seat. "Two carriages have just turned off the road."

Mr Bennet smiled at his youngest daughter's enthusiasm. As he looked around the room he saw the sweet smile on his eldest daughter's face and knew that she was just as excited, even if she would never show it as boldly as Lydia.

Outside, Darcy helped Elizabeth and Mary down from their carriage and went around to the other side to lift Georgiana out. He confidently picked her up and told her how much he missed her these last few weeks.

Bingley eagerly exited his own equipage and put his arm out to Elizabeth, "Mrs Darcy, may I escort you inside?"

With a smile, she answered, "Yes, thank you, Mr Bingley."

He leaned a little closer to her and quietly said, "I have a request to make of you. Since you will want to see your family often during your visit, I thought I would invite them all to stay at Netherfield. However, with both of my sisters away, I am in need of a hostess. Would you be willing to fill that role for a few weeks?"

"I will need to speak with my husband, but…"

Interrupting her, Bingley said, "Oh I have already spoken with Darcy about this. He felt you would rise to the challenge admirably."

Elizabeth looked over at her husband and caught the sparkle in his eye. *Yes, I am certain* you *were the one to suggest this to Mr Bingley*. Looking back to her escort she said, "Then I would be happy to do so, sir."

"Capital, it is settled then. I will extend the invitation to your father today, and if he is amenable to the plan, I will write a note to Mrs Benson to start preparing rooms for your family to join us tomorrow."

Alex did not wish to force Mary into any uncomfortable situations as he had in the past, but he knew his duty. Putting out his arm, he asked, "May I escort you, Miss Mary?"

With a nod, she gently wound her arm around his. Tingling started in her fingertips and rose up her hand the moment her glove touched his sleeve and she closed her eyes as her stomach knotted.

Noticing the look on her face and how pale she became, Alex grew concerned. Leaning down a little he asked, "Are you well, Miss Mary?"

When she opened her eyes and saw the distress on his face she stumbled to assuage his fear, "I am sorry to worry you, my lord. I am —well, I just felt dizzy for a few seconds, but I am better now."

Alex tightened his grip on her arm and said, "We must get you in from the cold."

She started to pull away and distance herself from this man to whom her body reacted so strangely, but he would not release her arm. So she let him escort her inside. When he did finally let her go so the maid could help her with her spencer, she felt a shudder as a cold chill swept over her. She again felt his hot touch as he gently guided her by the elbow to the sitting room.

Mr Hill announced the visitors, greetings and hugs were exchanged, and Georgiana was settled into the seat that had come to be thought of as *hers* over the last few months.

Alex guided Mary to the chair closest to the fire and sat nearby in case she began to feel ill again.

"I did not think you would be here so early," Jane said to Elizabeth as she hugged her neck.

"When William and I arrived at Netherfield Park, the carriages were ready to leave, so we did not tarry. I believe Mr Bingley was eager to see you."

The two sisters smiled at each other and knew they needed to talk privately later.

"Mr Bennet, Mrs Bennet, Mr Gardiner, Mrs Gardiner, it is a pleasure to see you all today," Bingley said with a bow to each.

"You are always welcome in our home, Mr Bingley," Mrs Bennet eagerly replied.

"Thank you, ma'am," he said. "Mr Bennet, if possible, may I have a moment of your time privately?"

"Yes sir, right this way." Mr Bennet led them to his study. When the door was closed, he asked, "What can I do for you today, Mr Bingley?"

"I know you would wish to spend as much time as you can with Mrs

Sarah Johnson

Darcy before they must leave for town again, and I know how crowded Longbourn can become when we are all here visiting," Bingley said.

"Yes, it does become quite the crush, does it not?"

"Also, sir, with the winter weather upon us, I am certain we would all feel safer knowing others are not having to travel such a distance in a carriage so often as the festivities will require."

"You make an excellent point," he said.

Bingley smiled, "That is why I wish to invite all of your family to stay at Netherfield Park during this holiday season. I have spoken with Mr and Mrs Darcy and they are amenable to this plan. Mrs Darcy has agreed to take on the responsibilities of hostess in lieu of my sisters being away."

"Thank you sir. We would be honoured to accept your invitation."

Bingley smiled, "If you do not mind, I will write my housekeeper a note to have her begin preparing rooms, and your family can join us on the morrow. Will that give you adequate time to prepare?"

Bennet chuckled, "Yes, that is plenty of time." He pulled out a piece of paper from the desk drawer and watched as Bingley hastily wrote a note. "I will have this delivered immediately."

The two found Mr Hill to pass it on and then entered the sitting room once again. Clearing his throat to garner everyone's attention, Mr Bennet said, "Mr Bingley has invited our entire family to join him and his guests at Netherfield Park for the next few weeks of festivities."

Enthusiastic exclamations were heard throughout the room, and specific plans were soon being discussed among the different groups. The rest of the day passed quickly, and when the Netherfield Park party left, the residents of both houses were eagerly looking forward to the following day.

CHAPTER
VI

Saturday, December 21, 1811

Bingley entered the dining room whistling a merry tune, and was pleased to see his best friend alone. He took his place at the table, quietly saying, "When you have a moment, I must speak with you privately."

Knowing what Bingley likely wanted to discuss, Darcy answered, "I believe my wife has asked Mrs Benson for a few hours of her time this morning after we break our fast."

Lifting his fork, Bingley said, "Capital! Do you feel like taking a ride?"

A small smile appearing on Darcy's lips, "You know I do after being in Town for so many weeks."

"Yes, you never could resist the draw of a speeding horse beneath you," Bingley chuckled.

"Is this a conversation we must have alone, or may I invite my cousin to join us?" Darcy enquired of his friend.

"Oh, by all means, he may join us as well. I imagine you have some things you wish to discuss with him about your sister and her care since you left the county."

"Yes, precisely—you read my mind," Darcy replied.

Alex entered the dining room with Elizabeth on one arm and Mary on the other, having met with the two sisters as they descended the stairs together. Greetings were exchanged and Darcy pulled out the seat beside his for his wife. Alex pulled out the chair in which Mary usually chose to sit, and then, wishing not to distress her, he chose the chair further down the table and across from Darcy for himself.

"Mrs Darcy," Bingley said, "I was just asking your husband if he would be free to join me on a ride this morning. He indicated you would be busy with Mrs Benson, so he is, indeed, at my disposal."

"Yes, your housekeeper and I have quite a bit to discuss with so many joining us over the next few weeks. I have asked my sister Mary to join me in our meeting, and then she and Georgiana are to help with a few other holiday preparations this morning," Elizabeth answered.

"Well then, if you do not think I will be needed, I will steal these two gentlemen from you," Bingley indicated Darcy and Alex with his head.

Elizabeth chuckled at his enthusiasm, "I believe my husband has missed the country fields these last few weeks. He said he usually rides in Hyde Park every morning, but lately he has been lazy."

"If I had a beautiful bride such as you at my side, I doubt I would wish to leave her either," Alex replied with a smile. The corners of Darcy's mouth

48

came up and Elizabeth saw the love in her husband's eyes as he looked at her.

Within half an hour, the three men were seated on their horses and ready for an invigorating jaunt across the cold winter landscape.

"I hope it stays cold enough to freeze the lake," Bingley said to the others as they mounted. "I have heard Miss Bennet is fond of ice skating and would greatly enjoy the exercise myself. It has been years since I have enjoyed the Christmas season as much as I am enjoying this one."

"I am certain the lake will freeze soon enough," Alex said as he tried to rein in his jittery horse, "although I usually spend my winters much farther north than Hertfordshire, so I may not be the one to ask."

"Whitie is eager for a good run," Darcy said as his horse circled about the others. "Are you two ready?"

At their acknowledgment, the three took off across the bare fields that surrounded the picturesque estate.

Mary stood by the window watching the three men outside on their horses. Ever since Miss Bingley told her of the viscount's rakish character she had avoided him—or tried to anyway. However, she was beginning to question whether Miss Bingley spoke the truth or not. He had been solicitous of her needs over the last few months of their acquaintance, but he was careful not to force her into situations she would find too uncomfortable. He also made no advances towards other ladies in the neighborhood. She knew of nothing that would truly make her think such low of his character other than Miss Bingley's words of warning.

Mary flexed her hand and looked at her fingers as she remembered the tingling feeling that ran up her skin each time she held his proffered arm. When she looked back out the window, she saw him speed off on his horse and could not help the small flutter in her chest. As the gentlemen disappeared, she turned away from the window to go check on Georgiana before she was to meet with her sister and the housekeeper.

After a vigorous winter ride, the three men were too cold to remain outside and talk, so Bingley invited them to join him for some tea after they were cleaned up.

Alex entered the billiard room last to find Darcy and Bingley both laughing. "What did I miss?"

Bingley answered jovially, "Do you remember me saying I asked Darcy to pick up something special for me to give to Miss Bennet when I ask for her hand?" At the nod, he continued, "Well, it seems your cousin is finding out just how hard it is to keep secrets from his wife."

Darcy then took over telling the story. "The first time I tried to go shopping alone, Elizabeth insisted she join me. So, I altered our plans, and we went a few other places before we found our way into a jewelry shop. I decided to see if I could covertly question her about what her sister likes. Unfortunately, my subtle questioning only led to more confusion, as I was soon reminded my wife has *four* sisters, each with vastly different sentiments with regard to jewelry. She was more than eager to point out pieces throughout the shop that any one of her family members might like for this reason or that, but I could not distinguish what features Miss Bennet would enjoy from the small details my wife focused on in the pieces."

Alex chuckled at his cousin and accepted the tea cup from Bingley. "Yes, I can see how that could put you in quite the predicament."

"The second time I tried to go shopping without Elizabeth, some urgent business came from my steward at Pemberley and I spent several hours dispensing with that instead." He stopped to take a drink of his tea, then continued. "By my third attempt, I did actually make it out of Darcy House alone, and after only a half an hour in the jeweler's shop I found some earrings I believed would complement Miss Bennet's simple elegance. I had them wrapped and delivered to my home, as I had a few other places to go first before I was to return myself. By the time I stopped by the book sellers to look at something he recently received, and by my uncle's house to speak with him about the note from my steward, the package had been delivered. Unfortunately, my very efficient staff thought I purchased the jewelry for my wife and placed it on her dressing table. I arrived home in time to quickly dress for dinner and did not realize my mistake in not confiding in Mrs Tucker of my outing until I saw my wife wearing the earrings. She so proudly showed them off to me, thanking me for such a generous and special surprise, that I could not tell her they were not meant for her."

Bingley was now laughing so hard he nearly spilled his tea, so he set the cup and saucer down on the table beside him.

Darcy was glad to see the situation could be appreciated for the catastrophe it became, even though at the time it was quite frustrating. "I was to this part of the story when you came into the room, Alex."

Holding up his drink in mock salute, Alex chuckled. "Do continue then."

"So, once again, I attempted to go shopping without Elizabeth, and of course, once again she unknowingly thwarted my plans. Instead, we spent the entire day at the museum and the chocolate shops. My wife had her own plans for shops we needed to visit, and a jeweler was not on her list."

"This is turning into quite the tale. Do not tell me you failed in every attempt?" Alex asked.

"No, I did finally find something. The day before we were to leave Town, I was able to go back to the jewelers and found what I think may be a gift even more perfect than the earrings I originally chose. However, it would have to be delivered the following afternoon. Knowing I could not delay our trip without giving my wife good reason, I had to find another way. I explained the situation to Mrs Tucker and she assured me the package would be delivered to Netherfield Park by my most trusted footman upon its arrival at Darcy House."

"Has it now come?" Bingley eagerly asked.

"Yes, it was with my valet, Foster, when I returned from our ride." Darcy pulled the box out of his pocket and presented it to his friend, "It is with great pride in accomplishing such a feat that I must now hand this over to you."

With shaking hands, Bingley accepted the tiny leather box, cradling it in his palm. He slowly opened it and looked at the ring inside. The stunning light blue stone shone against the gold band. He took the ring out of the box and looked it over with a discerning eye before quietly saying, "It is perfect!" After fingering the cut of the stone one last time, he placed it back in the folds of velvet and closed the leather casing, then he turned to his best friend. "Thank you, Darcy. I know it has caused much anxiety, and for that I am truly sorry, but I appreciate your help. This is simply perfect."

Darcy patted Bingley on the back. "Think nothing of it Bingley; it is the least I can do for the man who I hope will soon be called my brother."

Bingley smiled broadly, "I have felt we were as close as brothers for many years now, so it is a very fitting tribute to our friendship to finally be considered so in the eyes of everyone else as well."

The three gentlemen played a few rounds of billiards before Mrs Benson knocked on the door saying she and Mrs Darcy were finished with their tasks, though Mrs Darcy began to feel light-headed so the decorations would have to be completed later as she wished to rest for a little while. Darcy thanked her for letting him know and excused himself from the others to check on his wife.

As he walked into their chambers, he saw Elizabeth sitting on the edge of the bed, her hand on her chest and her face pale. He rushed to her side, lifting her hand in his. "Elizabeth! What has happened?"

She clutched his hand tightly and he helped her lie down. When she had sufficiently caught her breath and the color began to return to her cheeks, she answered, "I do not know what happened to me. I began to feel ill and told Mrs Benson I would like to rest, and by the time I entered our chambers I was dizzy and could hardly stand."

He placed the back of his hand upon her forehead, "You do not feel hot. Does your throat hurt?"

"No, I feel well enough now, though I am a little tired," she answered wearily.

Darcy removed his shoes and climbed onto the bed, resting his back against the headboard. "Come here," he urged to his wife. When Elizabeth was settled on the pillow next to him he covered her with a small blanket and began to run his fingers through her hair. He had calmed his sister in just this same manner since she was a young girl, and since getting married he learned it worked well for his wife also. She was soon asleep. He could not bring himself to leave her side, so he cuddled up closer to her and watched her features as the peaceful of sleep shown on her face, his own features indicating just how worried he was for her health.

Maddie knocked, but did not receive an answer, so she looked into her niece's room. Seeing Kitty curled up in the window seat and looking out over the wintery lands beyond the frosty glass, she walked over and placed a hand on her shoulder. "Are you ready to go?"

The gentle touch drew her from her revelry, and Kitty turned to look up at her aunt. "What was that?"

"I asked if you were ready to go, but you seem lost in your thoughts," Maddie said.

Kitty sat up straighter and placed her stocking-clad feet onto the cold floor, a shiver running up her back as she answered her aunt, "I was just thinking of all that has changed for our family in the last few months."

Maddie smiled and sat down beside her niece, "Yes, so many changes have come, and I have a feeling this next year will bring even more. You are all growing up, and I suspect that by next Christmas we will be adding a few more new members to the family."

With a dreamy look to her eye, Kitty said, "With Lizzy now married, it is very possible I will be an aunt by next Christmas." She blushed and looked down, her hands worrying the fabric of her wrap.

Maddie reached for her niece's hands and stayed them with a gentle squeeze, "I understand the sentiment. It is a position I find myself loving very much, and I do very much hope you will one day have the great pleasure as well. As much as you love children, I know your nieces and nephews will be adored."

Kitty smiled, "As we have been by having you as a wonderful model to follow. Thank you, Aunt Maddie."

The two hugged. When Maddie stood to leave, she replied, "The carriages are being loaded as we speak, so do not tarry long."

Kitty tugged on her half boots and securely tied the laces. Then she stood and retrieved her spencer from the bed and pulled it on as she followed after her aunt, joining her family for the short ride to Netherfield Park, where they were sure to enjoy the next few weeks with many festivities.

The carriage jolted to a stop and the footman opened the door. Mr Bennet was stepping down when his foot slipped on the icy step, but he found Darcy's strong arm immediately there to help and was grateful for his son-in-law's assistance. He gave a nod of appreciation and turned to assist his wife and daughters, insuring they too did not slip on the step.

As they followed the others into the house, Mr Bennet said to Darcy, "Thank you; that could have been a disaster for me if I had fallen."

Darcy looked down at the ground, "I would not see any harm come to you if I can in any way prevent it from happening."

Knowing this was as close to an open admission of love as he was to ever receive from his stoic son-in-law, Mr Bennet patted his shoulder, "Thank you." The two then continued inside, Darcy taking his wife's arm to ensure she did not have another spell as she had earlier in the day.

CHAPTER

VII

Sunday, December 22, 1811

J ane was enjoying seeing her family all together once again. Though her sister had been married only a few short weeks, it felt like an eternity since they all sat in the church as they did now in their usual bench. Of course, this morning there were so many they took up two benches. Mr Bingley sat to her right, and he scooted a little closer each time the Bible or prayer book was needed. She thought she could not blush any more than she had, until her father glared over at the gentleman and gave him a look strong enough to make him slide away just a bit again.

In front of her sat her aunt and uncle and their three young children, along with Mary, Miss Darcy and Lord Primrose.

Sophia and Rebecca shared a Bible, both trying to follow along the reading as best as they could, eight year old Sophie having a little easier of a time than her sister, younger by two years and not reading yet. David, their four year old brother, was not as enthused about the story being told as the others, and he began to bounce on the hard bench, swinging his legs out to kick the bench in front of them. Jane chuckled when her uncle gave the same look to his son that her father had given to Mr Bingley. Her cousin's legs stilled, but only for a minute. When he began to swing them once again, the viscount, sitting next to him, reached over and stilled them with a gentle touch. He then lowered his own Bible, pointing to the portion being read and focusing her young cousin's attention just enough to get through the service without any more major distractions.

Jane was not the only one to notice. Mary did as well and found her mind wandering as the voice of the reverend faded behind her own thoughts. The viscount truly baffled her. Even if what Miss Bingley had said was wrong, and she was beginning to believe it could be, she still could not excuse away the harsh words he spoke and that she heard with her own ear about the state of her dress when he came across her that day on the road. She could not excuse away those insulting words as they rolled through her mind once again.

Mary noticed everyone beginning to stand, so she closed her Bible and rose to join the other congregants in a hymn to commemorate the birth of the Savior—the reason for this festive season of the year—though her mind was still plagued with confusion over the viscount.

Mary smiled when she saw Mr Bingley look towards Mr Bennet, then when her father gave a short nod, he stepped just a little closer to Jane, offering to share his hymnal with her. Though she did not need the book, she accepted the offer. The two were so sweet and kind, and a perfect match. She was certain they would soon be engaged and probably married before spring.

The final notes of the last song were sung and the congregants began to gather in small groups to discuss the latest gossip. The Darcys, of course, were approached by several as well wishes for their recent marriage were given. When the crowd finally began to clear, Darcy lifted his sister in his arms to take her to the carriage.

"I was just about to get her myself," Alex said.

Darcy smiled as he looked at Georgiana, "I have looked forward to seeing my sister in church once again for so long that it is a joy to provide her this small service."

"Then perhaps I shall escort your wife instead," Alex joked.

"By all means, please do." Darcy chuckled when Alex stepped over to Elizabeth and offered his arm, smiling back at his cousins when she accepted.

"It is good to see him smile again," Georgiana replied.

"Oh? Has he not been his normal self lately?"

"I would say not! It is shocking just how distracted and pensive he has become. I know not what is on his mind, but perhaps you being back will draw it out of him."

Darcy followed after the others, assuring his sister, "I will do my best, Sweetling."

As he descended the stairs with his sister in his arms, he saw a flash of black and noticed a horse running full speed towards those gathered. He turned his head and saw who was directly in the path of the wild beast— *ELIZABETH!* The name froze in his throat and time slowed as the next few seconds played out in front of him in dreadful horror. He saw the flaring nostrils of the horse and the crazed look in its dark eyes. Bingley and Jonathan Lucas tried to catch the reigns as the animal raged and kicked, coming closer and closer to his wife. Just as he thought how horribly this could turn out, Alex lifted Elizabeth out of the way and the two men were able to the animal away from the onlookers.

Tension filled the air and Darcy hurried to his wife's side, giving Georgiana to Alex and helping his wife to a nearby bench. "Are you well?" he asked, wrapping his arm around her shoulders and looking into her pale face.

She was dazed, but not injured. However, the sudden intensity of the moment did cause her to become quite fatigued and her head began to ache, so she assured her husband of her own health and promised she would lie down when they returned to Netherfield Park. That seemed to appease him.

Bingley and Lucas came running back, assuring everyone that the animal was now under control. They did not know where he came from, or even who he belonged to, but the local blacksmith saw the commotion and stepped in to help calm him. He offered to take him to his stable until the owner could be located.

Had the incident played out any differently, Elizabeth could have been severely injured or even killed, and no one could understand the gravity of that any more than those who surrounded her now, especially her own father and Georgiana.

Assured of Elizabeth's safety, they all returned to Netherfield Park. The rest of the day was spent in rest and quiet contemplation. Though the air was tense from the events of that morning, the incident was not discussed. Words were not needed, only assurances of love from her family and husband, which they gave in bountiful amounts. So much so that when her head finally lay on the pillow that night, Elizabeth breathed a deep breath of relief and finally began to relax again.

Tuesday, December 24, 1811

The day Bingley planned finally arrived. Christmas Eve promised to be eventful. He looked out his window in his chambers to the snow-covered ground below, happy to finally see enough of the white powder to be assured the lake might be frozen. This day just might turn out better than he planned, especially if he could propose to Jane while they were ice skating. It was, after all, one of her favorite wintertime activities. With a swish of the curtains, he stepped away from the window and quickly readied himself, making his way to the dining room in hopes that Jane would be there alone. Unfortunately, this morning she was accompanied by her sister Mary. Greeting the two, he sat down at the end of the table and amicably chatted with them while the others slowly filtered into the room.

Knowing Bingley intended to propose today, Alex tried to offer an easy way for him to speak privately with Miss Bennet. He said to his cousin, "One thing I miss about the north is all the snow. While it is not as much as we are used to having by now, I dare say Georgiana and I would love to go for a ride around the neighborhood in the sleigh." Turning to the others seated around the table he asked, "Would anyone else care to join us? We have two sleighs at our disposal, and I would guess we can fit twelve people easily—possibly more if we want to squeeze the children in as well."

Bingley immediately chimed in, "Yes, that does sound grand." He looked over to Elizabeth, "Perhaps Mrs Benson can provide some warm drinks and a fitting fare?"

Elizabeth smiled, "I will go and speak with her directly after breaking our fast." She was becoming quite comfortable in her new role as mistress of a large household and was beginning to think perhaps she had underestimated her own abilities.

"Do you think the pond out front is frozen? Maybe we can go skating also?" Bingley asked.

"No, it will not be solid enough yet," Mr Bennet said. "However, there is a smaller pond near Lucas Lodge that may be solid enough by now. If you would provide a footman, I can write to Sir William and ask if they mind us using it today?"

"Oh, yes, use whomever you need. My servants are at your disposal, sir."

Elizabeth looked at her father, "Maybe Mr and Miss Lucas would like to join us today also?" At the mention of Jonathan Lucas, Kitty's cheeks burned. Luckily no one noticed her quietly pushing the food around her plate.

"I will be sure to extend an invitation to the Lucas family to join us. We have not had enough time with our good friends in a while, and a day of fun is just what we need."

The note was written and dispatched and within the hour Jonathan Lucas was announced in the drawing room.

Bingley stood to receive his guest. "Mr Lucas, it is good of you to come. We only expected a note in return."

"My father was not certain if the pond was frozen solid or not, so he sent me to check. I volunteered to come and deliver the invitation for your household and guests to join us at Lucas Lodge for dinner, if you will not be too fatigued from skating all day."

A squeal of glee came from Lydia who dearly loved to ice skate almost as much as Jane.

Looking at Mrs Darcy, he continued, "My mother has assured me our dinner will be simple but delicious. Our cook has somehow talked Longbourn's cook into relinquishing her favorite soup recipe. I know how much we all used to look forward to a hot bowl and crusty bread after a long afternoon on the ice when we were younger."

Elizabeth smiled at her husband, who then nodded to their host.

"We graciously accept the invitation," Bingley jovially replied, "and look forward to this afternoon's activities, along with this evening's shared meal with your family."

Bowing to the room, Jonathan turned to leave, catching Kitty's visage out of the corner of his eye. He smiled when he saw her rosy cheeks. *Is she blushing because of my presence?* Clearing his throat, he replied, "Until later, then," and left.

The residents and guests of Netherfield Park returned to their rooms to dress for the excursion, each also packing a change of clothes for their dinner at Lucas Lodge. The trunks were loaded into a wagon and sent ahead of the party by way of Longbourn to gather enough skates for everyone.

Bingley paced the foyer, waiting on the others and growing more nervous with every passing minute.

Mr Bennet came down the stairs, and, seeing the anxiety all over the poor man's face in front of him, asked, "May I get you a drink, Mr Bingley?"

Shaken from his reverie, Bingley answered, "What? Oh, no, thank you. I am well."

Mr Bennet looked up the stairs, making sure they did not have an audience. "Is there a particular reason for your pacing, or are you trying to see how well made your rugs are?"

The impertinent question made him think of Mrs Darcy. "I see where your second daughter gets her wit, sir."

"Yes, she takes after me in many ways; fortunately she did not get my facial hair also." He scratched at the long sideburns covering his cheeks. "While we have a minute to ourselves, I was wondering if I might speak with you privately."

"Yes, absolutely; right this way." Bingley led the man to his study, closed the door, and took up his pacing in front of the fire.

"Mr Bingley, I can see you are rather distracted today. Does this have anything to do with my family being here?" Mr Bennet had his suspicions that it was actually his firstborn causing such a reaction in their host, but he did not want to come right out and say so.

"Oh, no, sir. Your family is welcome at my home any time." Feeling his courage rise, he continued, "In fact, I soon hope to call your family my own." Sitting, Bingley continued before he could stop himself, "Sir, I know it is typical to ask for the lady's hand first, but since you are here—I intended to ask for Miss Bennet's hand today, and I now ask of you if I have your approval?"

Mr Bennet's impertinent reply stopped in his throat when he saw the sincerity in the man's eyes before him. He could not goad him—not right now at least. "Mr Bingley, if I did not see the looks my daughter gives you, and if I were not assured of your mutual affection, I would have no problem telling you *no*. However, I cannot fault you for loving such a creature as my Jane." He saw the ease on the young man's face as he finished, "It is with great pleasure I can assure you of my approval to your plan, and I know your suit will be well received."

A smile the likes of which he had never seen crossed the young man's face. As they quit the room Mr Bennet noted that Bingley was nearly bouncing with excitement. Chuckling silently, he followed the younger man back to the foyer where everyone else was preparing for their ride.

All were soon seated in the sleighs with rugs over their laps, Darcy and Alex at the reins. Elizabeth was seated next to Darcy, one arm wrapped around his and the other holding her four year old cousin David on her lap. Mr Bennet suspected grandchildren would soon be joining the family over this next year, especially with another daughter to soon be married. *Of course, first the young man has to get up the nerve to ask her.* He looked at the two and had to hold in the chuckle that wanted to escape. *Was I ever so nervous around Susannah? It seems such a long time ago, and yet I love her more now than I ever thought was possible.* He wound his arm around his wife's shoulders and settled in for the ride around the neighborhood that would eventually lead them to Lucas Lodge's pond.

CHAPTER

VIII

When they finally arrived at their destination, Sir William had a surprise for the younger ones. He had pulled out the sleds his own children used many years ago. "Welcome!" he cried jovially, his arms wide open. "We are glad to share this day with you." He excitedly helped everyone out of the sleighs and positioned the children onto the sleds, then he, Jonathan, and Alex pulled them around the ice.

The others skated around them, all laughing and having a jolly time. Darcy, having grown up ice skating at Pemberley every winter, was known for his speed, but he met his match as his wife skillfully whipped past him. He won their race only because of his long legs.

Not being very athletic, Mary chose instead to sit on a nearby bench and watch the others. She had just received a letter from Miss Bingley which contained details of the tragic events surrounding a former friend of hers. Events that, according to the letter, even the *Haute Ton* did not know all the details of. It seems this friend formed an attachment with *a certain peer of the realm*, and they were well on their way to soon walking down the aisle. That is, until the lady was put upon by said *gentleman*. When her father found out what happened and confronted the gentleman, he refused to do his duty. Her friend then had to be sent away to the north to live with another family member, and Miss Bingley only heard from her twice more before she came to a very sudden end in childbirth. The words at the end of the letter rolled around in Mary's head now knowing that this gentleman to whom Miss Bingley referred was obviously Lord Primrose.

> And so, Miss Mary, it is with this specific situation in mind that I once again caution you of the attentions of *certain gentlemen*. It would break my heart if another close friend of my family were to have to deal with a *similar situation*.

A familiar tingling interrupted her quiet revelry and Mary knew *he* was behind her before he opened his mouth.

"You are not skating, Miss Mary?" Alex asked.

"As you see, my lord," she answered curtly, Caroline Bingley's warnings at the forefront of her mind.

Quickly regarding the others, Alex noticed no one looking their direction and decided to use the relative privacy to his advantage. He sat beside her and asked, "Miss Mary, have I offended you in some way?"

Mary was taken aback by his forward question. Not wanting to reveal just how hurt she truly was when she overheard him telling Darcy his opinion of their first meeting, nor wanting to discuss the contents of the letter from Miss Bingley or her previous conversations about the viscount, Mary chose to remain silent.

"I take it by your silence that I have. If my assumption is correct, then please tell me, as I wish to properly apologize to you." Alex waited for several minutes, the silence still eerily held between them. "*I am truly sorry, Miss Mary.* As I see you are not willing to tell me what I have done, that is the best I can offer. I can only hope you believe me and that one day you receive what I am more than willing to give to you."

"And just what exactly *do* you want from me, my lord?" she asked, her eyes flashing in anger.

He knew he must tread carefully, so he replied, "Friendship."

Mary returned her gaze to those still skating. "I am not certain that is even possible. Perhaps you should return to your games with others—I want no part of them."

Thinking she meant his playing with the children, Alex stood and walked away. They were already cold enough to return indoors, so instead of returning to the others he sat with his back against a tree while he watched the activity on the ice. His mood was somber and he did not want to ruin this day for the others, but he could not shake the gloom he felt from his conversation with Mary Bennet.

Alex knew the moment Bingley awaited would present itself sometime today, and he knew his friend's hand would be well received. Even though he was happy for Bingley, he could not help but feel a pang in his chest at his own cold reception from the woman who held his heart.

Alex watched as the couple skated around in the middle of the pond, Bingley's tall, lanky legs allowed him to skate circles around Miss Bennet. The two were playfully smiling as Bingley soon skidded around to face her and dropped to one knee. Alex was transfixed as Bingley lifted his lady's hand and deftly pulled the leather box from his pocket.

His voice was shaky, but quiet, as he opened the box and went down to one knee, "Miss Bennet, I have wished for months to ask this of you, and though others have questioned why I waited, you never did. However, it is now time."

Jane blushed, her eyes transfixed on her love's eyes.

He took a deep breath, then asked with confidence, "Miss Bennet... Jane... will you marry me?"

Even knowing the words that would escape his lips did not prepare her for the rush of emotion that overcame her. She closed her eyes as a warmth rose within her. Finally she let out a simple, "Yes."

Bingley rose immediately and lifted her up in his arms, spinning around on the frozen lake as a squeal escapes her lips. By now he was certain every eye was on them, so he skidded to a stop and took her hands in his, stepping back to a more appropriate distance, and drawing her hands to his lips.

The kiss he placed on the back of each glove made Jane shiver. She could not imagine being any happier than she was in this exact moment.

Bingley looked over to the shore where Mr Bennet stood, a question on his features which was answered by the father when he gave a small, almost imperceptible nod. His eyes went back to his intended's and he lowered to place a simple kiss on her cheek. He knew more would have to wait; for now this would have to do.

Jane lifted her hand to cup her cheek, the blissful feeling on the inside shining out for all those around to see.

Bingley lifted her hand again, stretching out their arms between them as he began to skate, encouraging her to join him once more.

Alex had to chuckle at his friend—only Charles Bingley would have the nerve to propose to a lady right in front of her family.

The rest of the evening passed quickly, with the Lucas' extending an invitation to join them for a small gathering to be held for Twelfth Night. The invitation was accepted, and soon the Netherfield Park residents and guests took their leave. Tomorrow they would go to Christmas services and then exchange some small gifts. The servants would have the day off, so the group intended to play games and spend time doing whatever caught their fancy. They were all happy for the extended family they now had and only

Alex was left wanting something more, though he was grateful for what he now had.

───────◈◉◈───────

Wednesday, January 1, 1812

"Mr Darcy, sir," Hill announced.

"Would you like some tea gentlemen? Or I can have some coffee brought if that is more to your liking?"

"Tea is fine with me, sir," Darcy said. Mr Gardiner agreed, and Mr Bennet called for a tray.

"I am sorry for insisting we have this meeting here at Longbourn, but my wife is not privy to these dealings, and I do not wish to burden her with them just yet."

"Understood, sir," Darcy said.

Mr Bennet shuffled through the papers and the gentlemen talked of nothing of import until Hill returned with the tea tray. Then once they were assured of their privacy, Mr Bennet said, "I was desirous of your time today to see if you would look over some papers and give me your opinion, Darcy."

"I would be glad to, sir."

"Jonathan Lucas was detained and could not join us today, but he is aware of the details contained within these papers." Receiving a nod from Darcy, Bennet continued, "I do not know how much you know of Longbourn and the entail; has Elizabeth spoken with you of it?"

"The subject has come up a few times, but not being very knowledgeable of the intimate details, she had little to say other than that it is a typical property tail away from the female line."

"Well then, I shall fill you in on the particulars." Henry settled into his seat. "My grandfather, James Bennet, did not approve of my father and knew him to be irresponsible. But he was the heir, so he did the only thing he could do and placed an entail on Longbourn. He hoped his son would grow to be more responsible with age, but that never happened. It turns out the entailment was a good thing for this land. My father nearly devastated the estate and if it had not been in place, I am certain he would have sold off pieces to fund his debaucheries. As I grew up and saw what my own father did to these lands, I was glad for my grandfather's wise decision. My wife and I were generously blessed with daughters, so it is now a situation to which I must seek an outside solution."

Gardiner interjected, "My sister cannot know of the particulars though, as it would be quite distressing to her."

Darcy nodded, "Elizabeth has told me of her mother's anxiety over the loss of your son and heir. Knowing what it is to lose someone, I must offer my condolences."

Bennet's eyes began to tear, but he quickly looked away, "Thank you. The years do not ease the pain."

"No, they do not," Darcy said quietly, thinking of the loss of his own parents so many years ago.

Bennet cleared his throat and shuffled the papers in front of him, then continued, "I have been working to try to find a way out of the entailment, but as you probably know, they are nearly impossible to break."

"Yes, I do have some knowledge of the particulars of entailed lands. I have not heard of too many secure ways in which to end them," Darcy answered.

"As there is no male issue, Longbourn was to pass to a distant cousin of mine, Thaddeus Collins, with whom I have had no contact since my marriage. He chose to insult my wife and thus led to a break in the family. I learned about six months ago that my cousin has died and therefore his son, William Collins, is the new heir. He is a man of the cloth."

Darcy thought, *Collins... Collins... now why does that name sound so familiar?* Suddenly he remembered, "My cousin wrote to me of my aunt's parson dying and the position, I believe, was filled by a man of the same name as your cousin."

Bennet chuckled, "I did not know where to find him, so I have had an investigator looking these many months. I received word just last week that he is, indeed, the rector at Hunsford, which, I believe, is where your aunt fills the living."

Darcy shook his head in amusement, "I feel for your cousin."

"On the contrary, if he is anything like his father, it is your aunt for whom I must have pity. I can only hope the family connection will help in my endeavor."

Bennet went on to discuss the details of the plan to offer enough compensation for the estate that he hoped his cousin would see the value in giving up the rights. After saving and investing for years, he was now financially prepared to offer a fair price, but was not certain if the offer would even be considered.

It was decided Darcy needed to look over the land to determine if it was a fair price, so they made plans to ride around Longbourn's fields and visit some of the tenants the following afternoon.

Two days later the three, also joined by Jonathan Lucas, sat in Mr Bennet's study once again. Darcy suggested making a few changes to the offer, and after all four were happy with the particular wording, a letter was drafted inviting Reverend Collins to visit Longbourn as his schedule permitted to discuss the particulars. Darcy hoped Mr Bennet's cousin was an agreeable sort of man and would see what could be gained from this endeavor to end the entail and keep Longbourn and its land in the Bennet family. Surely, the man was sensible enough to consider the money being offered instead of having to wait for untold years for Mr Bennet to die before he could inherit? It would be worth it to purchase his own land and start his family as part of the landed gentry ranks as a young man. Unfortunately, William Collins was not such a sensible man

When he received the invitation and the packet of papers from Mr Bennet's solicitor, he went immediately to his patroness to determine what he should do.

Lady Catherine immediately saw the benefit of having her own spy within the family when she learned of the connection nearly a month ago, but she had not been able to convince him to do her bidding yet. She tried once more, but it was in vain. It was always in vain. The man was good for nothing and would only get in her way. She remembered her meeting just a few days ago with someone who offered a solution. At the time she was unwilling to go to such extremes, but she now saw that it would be necessary if her plan was to be a success.

When he finally left, she quickly wrote a note and dispatched it to her contacts. She would have her spy, one way or another.

CHAPTER IX

Saturday, January 4, 1812

He was dreading this meeting. G.W. had been back in town for over a week now and had dodged Mrs Younge so far, but there was no avoiding her today. She sent a note telling him where to meet, and he knew she would be livid.

He knocked on the door to her establishment and was told by the servant in which room she awaited him. Stepping into the dimly lit space, he did not expect the punch to the jaw he immediately received.

"Next time you defy me, it will be much worse," she said in a sickly sweet voice as he rubbed his jaw. "Thank you John; that will be all." The burly man who delivered the punch left them alone. Securing the door with a key and pointing to a chair, she brooked no opposition in her tone, "Sit."

"I can explain..."

"*I WANT NO EXPLANATIONS!*" she exploded, "I hired you because of your connection to my client, and I expect you to do as you are told! If you cannot do that, I can *and will* find someone else willing to do my bidding."

G.W. had never seen her so furious, but he had heard of her wrath from a few people. He knew now would not be the time to sweet-talk her, so instead he said, "What do you want from me?"

Sitting on the sofa with an air of confidence, she answered, "My client is willing to forgive this blunder, *if* you do not disregard what you are hired to do again. Otherwise, I cannot guarantee your safety."

Nodding his head in understanding, he asked what the new plan would be.

"She must be killed," Mrs Younge said with a note of finality to her voice.

"I can do that, but unless you want us all to hang for this it needs to look like an accident. It will take time to make it believable."

Smiling, she replied, "Luckily, I had a feeling you would say that. I have assured my client that the happy couple will not see their first anniversary, and though she is not favorable to such an extended timeline, she is willing to be lenient and has a possible way for us to become closer with the family."

"That must have taken some persuading," he said.

"I can be very *persuasive* when I need to be," she answered.

"Yes, I can see that of you," G.W. replied.

"Now, what is her plan?" The two talked for over an hour of all the possibilities.

"I may be able to do as asked, but it might take some months before I am able to bring about the situations we have laid out. This will not be an easy job—my performance must be flawless, and that does not come as easily as some might think."

She nodded her head in agreement, "Keep me informed, and do your job, that is all I require."

G.W. left with his mind in a whirl over all they discussed. He would now have to speak with the client on his own, a job he never particularly enjoyed, but it could not be helped. So he set out for Kent, annoyed at his having to take a horse the whole way as it set him to sneezing every time he rode.

"Lydia, you will never believe what has come in the post. You will be so happy for me," Maria was giddily bouncing with excitement as she led her friend through the crowd gathered in the drawing room of Lucas Lodge for her parent's Twelfth Night party. "Oh, but I must not get too excited." She stopped and demurely continued, "My father is watching me, and I must prove to him I am able to act appropriately."

"What is it? You must tell me!" Lydia was starting to get just as excited as her friend.

"With my sixteenth birthday coming in a few weeks, my father thought it was time I be given more responsibility."

"Oh no! What will he have you doing now? Surely he will not have you join the cook in the kitchen as Charlotte is sometimes required to do?"

She giggled, "I thought the same thing when he told me, but he said I must wait for the confirmation before he would tell me anything more."

"And you have now received this confirmation?" Lydia asked, spellbound by the tension Maria was creating with her story.

"Yes I have. In yesterday's post I received an invitation to visit my Uncle Murphy, my mother's brother, and his family in Brighton for six weeks!"

"Six weeks in Brighton—oh, how wonderful that will be!"

"Yes, but that is not all. My aunt and uncle have given their *specific* permission to invite a dear friend to go with me." Maria watched as Lydia's eyes got bigger. "My father says he will speak to your father today and extend the invitation to you!"

The two girls clasped hands and jumped with excitement. Lydia immediately started her incessant chattering, "Brighton! What a wonderful place to be able to visit. Think of all the shops we will patronize, and the beach—we can pick up shells along the shore! I have wanted to do so since I read about it in a book. We must walk along The Steyne and listen to the musicians. I have heard they play such wonderful music as they march down the promenade. Oh, and the tearooms! And sea bathing! Though, I guess, it would be too cold for that in January. I have heard you can hire out to take a day trip in a boat. Do you think your uncle would allow us such an excursion? I have always wanted to take a boat trip."

"Lydia, Lydia, we must remain calm about this. We must prove to my father, and to yours, that we are old enough for such a journey," she said as she nodded the direction of the two fathers looking their direction.

Calming and taking a deep breath, Lydia said, "Yes, we must." She smiled broadly and jumped slightly once again, "Oh, this is too much. I hope my father allows me to go with you."

"I do too," Maria said. "We will have such fun. My cousins are around my age, and I am certain they will know of other local places to visit during our stay."

Mr Bennet and Sir William Lucas walked up, interrupting the two. "I see Miss Maria has told you of her invitation, Lydia,"

"Yes, Papa, she has." Lydia could not help the smile on her face.

"Well, it seems your mother and I have some things to discuss then."

"Yes, Papa," Lydia's face fell a little.

"Do not look downhearted, my dear; I have a feeling your mother will be a proponent of your going. She visited Brighton when she was younger, and she has talked of its diversions as being the most entertaining trip of her life." Mr Bennet hugged his youngest daughter, "You are growing up too fast, my child. Why, it seems just yesterday you were toddling around holding onto your mother's skirts, and now here you are invited to go on a trip without us."

Lydia hugged her father back, "If you do allow me to go, I shall miss you tremendously, Papa."

"Now, now, let us not get caught up in emotions when I have yet to give you a final answer."

Mr Bennet and Sir William walked away, listening to their giggling girls once again start talking of the attractions of Brighton and all they wished to do while there.

"Did my father tell you of Lydia's invitation to join Maria Lucas in Brighton?" Elizabeth asked William as she sat down beside him on the bed.

He stopped untying his cravat and replied, "I heard of it from your mother."

Noticing the displeased look on his face, she asked, "You do not think she should go?"

"You think she *should?*" he asked back harshly.

"Yes I do. Lydia has grown up quite a lot in the last year, and I do not see a problem with her being invited to join her best friend's family for a few weeks. It is not as if she is out and would be going to social events, they will just be visiting the Murphy family and taking in the fresh sea air."

"I do not like it," he stated firmly. "I will be talking with your father about not letting her go."

The scowl on William's face shocked Elizabeth. "I do not think it is our place to say anything unless we are asked."

"Whether it is my place or not, I will *not* stand by and let this happen *again,*" he growled as he stood and quickly went into the dressing room.

What was that about, Elizabeth wondered? She finished with her preparations and was plaiting her hair when he came stomping back into the room. She watched for a minute and soon determined that something else was bothering him. "What is wrong, William?"

"Nothing," he said shortly.

Elizabeth was almost willing to let it go, but there was something about his demeanor that urged her to continue. "I know you are not being honest with me."

"What am I being dishonest about?" he asked in a huff.

"William, I want to understand why you are so adamant about Lydia not going, but you must give me a good reason, otherwise I shall continue to believe it to be an exciting opportunity for my sister."

"She just should not go———*that is all!*" He threw his dressing gown on the chair and climbed into bed, turning his back on his wife.

Elizabeth excused herself to the dressing room, and when she returned she saw his shoulders shaking. She climbed up onto the bed and placed her hand on his back. In a soothing voice she said, "Georgiana's accident was not your fault. You could not have known what would happen in allowing her to go on that trip without you just as we cannot know what will happen to Lydia on this trip to Brighton. But do you not see that it is not a reason to deny her request? Does she not deserve to be trusted just because of a mad man who haunted your family?"

He turned over to look into her eyes. "You are absolutely correct. She does deserve to go, and she has proven to be trustworthy enough to know if something is amiss. I just do not…"

"Shhhh, I know," she said, running her hand through his dark curls. "I know."

Smiling slightly, she said, "I know many people think my little saying is a bit trite, but I have had to learn through the hardest of times that *you must look on the past only as its remembrances bring you pleasure.*"

"You told me that the day Bingley and I walked with you to feed the Goulding's horses," Darcy said.

"Yes I did. At the time, I was not aware of why you were so sad, but I know how arduous my own father's accident was on me. I have had to learn to not dwell on the tragedy, but instead look to the triumphs. Before the accident, my parents were not as close as they now are. My mother was lost in grief that plagued her for ten years since my little brother Luke died, and my father was distant with all of us. Mary was searching for her own identity, and Kitty and Lydia were only looking for acceptance from one parent or the other. If the accident had not taken place, I fear my family would not be as close as we are today."

"You did not say anything of Jane," he said with a half smile.

"*Dear, sweet Jane*—I fear she would have accepted the first person to show her any kind of attention, simply because she never wishes to hurt others. Can you imagine if she had given her heart to some unworthy cur?"

"You cannot convince me she would be so easily swayed by a golden tongue. She is quite perceptive, though she may not express all she knows to everyone around her."

She poked him in the chest with her finger and joked, "You, sir, have come to know my dearest sister very well, but I just do not know…"

"Well I should hope I know her well enough after all these months. As for who *has* won her heart, I think my friend worthy of the great honour."

"Yes, they will be such a pleasant couple, never disagreeing on anything; unlike us."

He smiled, barely noticeable in the low light from the candle, "I quite like having a passionate marriage."

She smiled. "I do as well. I will miss her when we leave again tomorrow."

"I know, but you will see her in London in just a few weeks when she and Charlotte come to visit."

Elizabeth snuggled down beside her husband, allowing him to draw his arm around her shoulder as she laid her cheek on his chest. "Yes, we will have a wonderful time purchasing my sister's trousseau."

"Although Georgiana will miss your sister Mary, I know she is ready to go back to our home in London, and my cousin will be appreciative of letting his arms rest from lifting Georgiana so much. Perhaps it is time we add to our employ someone who can carry her until she is more comfortable with using her wheeled bath chair?"

"She has been through so much, but I know she will come around sometime."

Wanting to change the direction of their discussion to a less emotionally drawing direction, he smiled and asked, "Did you see Bingley this evening? He was so happy he was bouncing around the room."

She smiled as well, "Do you think they will be as happy as we are?"

"Never!"

She looked up at him in shock, "Why not?"

"Because no one could ever be as happy as we are."

"You, sir, are a tease."

"And you, madam, are encouraging." William's lips descended upon his wife's and the two were soon lost in a lovers' embrace.

Sarah Johnson

CHAPTER X

Friday, January 10, 1812

"What does your brother have to say?" David Hurst asked his wife as she read the most recent letter from Bingley.

A smile formed on her lips as she excitedly announced, "He has finally proposed!"

Hurst chuckled, "I knew he would eventually."

"If I am reading this correctly, he proposed while they were ice skating, with her whole family looking on."

"That sounds like your brother."

"Charles says all his house guests have now gone—the Bennets back to Longbourn, and the Gardiners, Darcys, and Lord Primrose have all returned to London. Miss Bennet will be visiting her sister, Mrs Darcy, next week to buy her trousseau, and Miss Lucas will be traveling with her also." Louisa looked up from the pages, "I have a feeling my brother will find a reason be in Town next week."

"Yes, I am certain he will find some sort of business he must see to while his *most cherished angel* is there," Hurst said, chuckling when his wife looked at him disapprovingly. "I am only saying what he has said many times before."

Looking back down at the letter, Louisa continued, "The wedding has been set for the middle of February and he asks if we will attend. He wishes to host a house party for the week leading up to the date, and asks me to be his hostess for that time, if it is convenient for us to travel."

"I do not see why we cannot. I have no pressing business which would interfere with such a schedule," Hurst answered. "I will write to your brother with our travel plans once we have them set."

Louisa shifted the papers and continued to read through the letter. When she came to something else of interest, she said, "Hmm, Miss Lydia Bennet and Miss Maria Lucas will be visiting Brighton and Charles asks if we would check in on them when we can. He has sent the address of the Murphy family with whom they will be staying. If I am not mistaken, I believe it is but a few blocks from here."

Showing the nearly illegible letter to her husband, he squinted his eyes, trying to read what was scratched on the paper between the blobs of ink, then agreed, "Yes, I believe you are correct. We pass by there on our walks to the promenade. It will not be out of the way to call on the girls while they are here. Maybe they would enjoy a few excursions to the shops or the tea room?"

Louisa smiled, "Yes, I imagine they would."

Hurst continued to read his letter from his father as Louisa went back to her own missive once again.

When she finished, Louisa asked, "What does your father have to say?"

"Not much, he just has some business he wants to discuss with me and wished to know when we will next be at Serenity Place. He said it is not urgent, but it is a matter he wishes completed before next harvest." Looking over the letter in his hand, he added, "My mother made him chronicle the entire contents of the Boxing Day baskets they gave to the tenants this year. She has been working extra hard in her endeavors to provide clothing for the little ones."

Louisa quietly added, "I think it is how she accepts, as best she can, the knowledge she will never be a grandmother."

"Yes, my brothers' death when we were young has loomed over my own life for a long time. Though she would not say anything to me, I know it is a harsh reality for my mother."

A knock at the door interrupted their conversation. The maid entered, a tray laden with tea and their dinner in her hands. As she set the table, she carefully watched the couple. Talk throughout the house was that they had been married for ten years, yet they had no children. It was obvious theirs was a marriage of affection, so the reason for their lack of progeny must be another reason. It was possible they lost a child, but she began to think they could not have any children of their own. Polly was touched by their caring nature and would miss them when they left Brighton. It was not often she saw such a caring couple lease this house.

Fitz received a disturbing note from his father about his brother and quickly left to find out what was amiss. When he was announced, he could see the worry on his father's face. "What has happened?"

"I do not know," Hugh said to his younger son. "He will not talk with me or your mother. I have never seen your brother like this before. Even last year when… well you know what happened, so I shall not speak of a scheme again. He was never like this though, even throughout that whole situation."

"Is he drinking?"

"No," Hugh answered quickly. "I had all liquor removed from those rooms and locked away, though I doubt he would touch the stuff. He would have to come in here to my study to find something stronger than the wine we serve with dinner, and as I said, he is avoiding me."

Fitz sat down, his heart heavy for his brother.

Hugh's concern shown in his voice; he had to clear his throat several times before he could speak, "I cannot imagine what has affected him so very much."

Looking up at his father, Fitz said, "I have an idea."

"Care to enlighten me?"

Shaking his head, he replied, "Not yet; let me speak with him first. I have a feeling this has something to do with a situation he has only spoken with me about." Fitz stood and turned to the sideboard to retrieve two drinks. Holding them up in salute he said, "Wish me luck," and strode from the room.

The melodramatic tones echoing through the halls told Fitz where his brother was. As he opened the door to the music room, he saw Alex's disheveled form hunched over the pianoforte, his long fingers banging out the soulful melody. "I have never heard that piece played with such melancholy before."

"Not now, Fitz," Alex warned as his fingers continued their dance across the keys.

Ignoring the warning, Fitz closed the door and walked over to the pianoforte. "Here," he said as he set one of the drinks down on the dark wood. Alex disregarded him and continued playing. Fitz soon chose a nearby seat and watched his older brother.

Alex had shed his coat and cravat, and his shirtsleeves were rolled up, revealing his lower arms. Fitz watched as the sinewy muscles contracted with the intensity of the music he played. As the notes were hammered out with much force, he could see Alex's neck tighten and his face grow dark. The faster the tempo, the darker his looks became until finally, in a flourish of emotion, Alex jumped up, knocking over his stool, and exploded, "WHAT do you WANT Fitz? WHY are you here bothering me?"

Not wanting the situation to become physical, Fitz leaned back in the chair and crossed his legs in a relaxing posture. He sipped his drink, and calmly asked, "What happened?"

Arms flying out, Alex yelled out, "What Happened? WHAT HAPPENED?" Starting to pace, he continued, "NOTHING happened, that's what!" His long legs took him from one end of the room to the other quickly and he pivoted around on his heel as he continued his pacing.

After watching his brother for a few more minutes, Fitz finally stood and stepped into his way, nearly making Alex trip. "Is she worth all of this?"

"What? What do you *mean* is she worth all of this?" Alex spat out.

"Well," Fitz said diplomatically, "is she? Is she worth your time and effort? Is she worth your heart and your love?"

"Of course she is," Alex said with fire in his eyes.

"Then you must find a way to get through to her."

"But HOW? She will not even hold a civil conversation with me. I do not know what I have done to offend her, but it is obvious I have done something. Yet she will not even tell me what it is. What am I to do?" Alex sat down dejectedly.

"You must woo her," Fitz said simply.

Alex snorted, "Easy for *you* to say—*you* are not the one with whom she refuses to talk. She walks away from me every time I approach her."

"So do it from afar. Let other things woo her for you. Send her a flower, play her a song, find ways to offer your services in any way in which she is in need, whether that be a hand as she steps down from a carriage or an arm on a walk. Above all else, you must prove to her you are a gentleman, not only in status but in comportment."

"I am not good at this sort of thing. I have avoided giving attention to any woman for many years, and now I find myself at a disadvantage and severely lacking knowledge that would come in handy."

"Alex, look at me," Fitz said sternly. When his older brother's eyes looked up, he continued, "I have seen in her and her family a quality that is lacking in most of the Ton. I understand why you are drawn to her. She is not a classical beauty as Miss Bennet, and she does not have the fiery spirit of Mrs Darcy, but she possesses something on her own that, when displayed, makes her a lovely woman in her own right."

"Yes she does," Alex said quietly.

"Do you want me to tell you what I think is happening here?" At Alex's nod, Fitz went on, "I think she is scared and does not understand what is taking place. She is young and has not been exposed to very many young men in her limited society there in Meryton. She has only been out a year, and as far as I know she has never had a season in Town, has she?"

"No, she has not," Alex answered, leaning his arms down onto his legs and looking at the floor.

"Give her time, big brother. She does not know who you are, only that you are a very rich and very prominent cousin to her new brother-in-law. Show her the man you truly are, and over time I am certain she will warm to your presence."

Looking up, Alex said, "But I have tried doing just that, and she still wants nothing to do with me. I do not see what else I *can* do."

"Give her time. You will not see her again until Bingley's wedding, and I think that may work to your advantage. In that time she will be able to remember all of her interactions with you, and hopefully your reception will be more civil. If not, then wait until she arrives at Darcy's for the Season. She cannot avoid you forever." He thought for a minute before he asked, "Have you ever done something to frighten her?"

Thinking back to his first encounter with her, Alex closed his eyes and, trying to swallow the lump that formed in his throat. "I had not thought of that before." Cursing under his breath, he continued, "Upon our first introduction she may have been frightened."

Confused, Fitz asked, "I thought you met her at a dinner party? What could you possibly do to alarm the poor girl at such a function?"

Rubbing his hands together anxiously and looking down at the floor, Alex said, "We met previously that day." Standing to once again pace, this time much more slowly, he continued, "When I rode out of Meryton on my way to Netherfield Park, I saw Miss Mary sitting on a log on the side of the road, waving her hands and calling for help. She had lost her footing and fell down a hill, muddying her dress and losing her spectacles in the process. She could not see to get back home, and I offered to help her." He continued to pace as Fitz quietly listened to the story unfold. "She is unnerved around horses, but the only way to return her safely back home in a timely manner was to have her ride. She said she was more comfortable riding if I were to ride with her, so I put her in front of me on my horse. I could tell she was completely terrified, and at one point when the horse turned, she was so scared she buried her face into my chest." His voice caught and his cheeks grew pink as he remembered the feeling of her in his arms. Shaking his head back to the present, he continued. "She was then embarrassed at her own reaction. I tried to reassure her all would be well, but knowing what I do now of Miss Mary, I can see how a meeting with a stranger in such a manner could completely set her on edge. As you said, she has not been exposed to many young men, and that day she was already uneasy because of not being able to see properly. I can imagine having to put your trust entirely into a stranger, and a man at that, is a very hard position for a young lady such as her to be placed." His voice grew quieter as he said, "I once told her she is the bravest young woman I know. I cannot imagine being in such a situation and still keeping my head about me as she did that day."

Fitz watched as his brother talked, seeing the compassion and love for this woman as it shone from his face. "You will have quite the time of it convincing her you are worth her time, but somehow I think it will all work out. Just take your time and do not frighten her again. She may be treating you this way because she is embarrassed, as you say, from her own actions that day. Then your presence was thrust upon her almost daily for the last two and a half months. It will be a month and a half until Bingley's wedding, and maybe by then she will have dealt with her own heart on the matter."

"Yes, maybe." Alex finally walked back to the pianoforte and picked up the stool that lay on the ground from his fit of ire earlier. Sitting back down, he fingered the cold keys, absentmindedly picking out a song he wrote when he was ten.

Fitz stood and stretched, "Well, if that is all, I think I may go have a bath before dinner. Mother would wring my neck if I showed up in her dining room smelling and looking as I do right now." Walking over, he patted Alex's shoulder, "Give her time; I am certain she will come around. And for God's sake, go get cleaned up and have your valet shave your face—*Father* may wring *your* neck if you continue to upset Mother as you have been doing since you arrived back home."

Alex chuckled and stood, hugging his brother. "Thank you."

"It's the least I could do," Fitz said as he picked up Alex's jacket. "Now go," he said, tossing it to him.

Fitz followed Alex out of the room and watched him climb the stairs. Turning down the hall that led to his father's study, Fitz knocked on the door and was bid to enter. As he sat down, his father asked, "So what is this all about?"

"Unfortunately, I am not at liberty to say. What I *can* say though, is I think he will be well in time." Fitz took a long drink from the glass his father handed him.

"He alarmed your mother—she thought for sure he had gone mad," Hugh said, tapping the quill he played with in his fingers.

"Yes, he was quite a sight, was he not? He is now upstairs letting John clean him up."

"Good," Hugh replied, "I would not like to see the looks he was sure to receive if he showed up at your mother's dinner table looking as he did." Hugh thought for a minute and then asked, "Does this have anything to do with a young lady?"

Lifting his eyebrow, Fitz asked, "What makes you ask that?"

"I do not know—it just seems the only logical conclusion. Your brother does not live from one drama to the next as some in his our society do, and I know he has avoided women in general. With his thirtieth birthday coming up in a few months, I am sure he is itching to find the right one and settle down, especially after Darcy's recent marriage and Bingley's tying the knot next month."

Fitz stood, "Well, as I said, I do not have his permission to discuss this with you, but I will say, it *might* be as you say," he quirked his eyebrow. Turning to leave, he quipped, "Now it's my turn to clean up. I cannot have my older brother outshine me at our own mother's table."

Hugh laughed, "No, that would never do." Looking down at his desk, he was reminded of the letter that came earlier today, "Oh, Fitz—Anne has written to you. It came in my own letter. Here," he said as he tossed the missive to his son.

Catching it, Fitz smiled and placed it in his pocket. "Thank you. See you at dinner."

He made his way up to his room and called his valet in to help him remove his boots. Hearing the tub being filled, he asked, "Did my brother tell you I was on my way up?"

"No sir, your mother told us over an hour ago that you and your brother would both be in need of baths," the man answered.

Shaking his head, he said under his breath, "*When Father sent the note…* if we only had enough soldiers with *her* intuition, Boney would not stand a chance." Making his way to the bath, he dismissed the valet saying he did not need any further assistance. Settling down into the warm water, he thought of all Alex revealed. *I wish my own situation were as easily solved as yours, Alex,* he thought to himself. Remembering the letter his father gave him, he quickly washed and was soon clad in a dressing gown, rummaging through the pockets of his jacket to find the letter. He pulled it out and sat down beside the fire to read.

> December 26, 1811
> Rosings Park
>
> My dearest Richard,
>
> Boxing Day being what it is, my mother has decided to personally oversee the handing out of baskets to ensure the tenants are not cheating her or taking too much of her generosity. This, of course, leaves me all alone and able to write to you. Hopefully she will be remain distracted long enough for me to take this to the post myself, otherwise I fear it may be a week at least before I can get this letter into your hands.
>
> Thank you for the birthday gift. I have never before seen a shawl with such sheen—it sparkles in the light of the fire. I imagine your arms are wrapped around me when I pull it over my shoulders, which

only makes me miss you even more. Is there any hope of your investigation ending soon?

Mother's headaches are coming on more strongly than before, especially with Reverend Collins coming daily for a meeting with her. She has now convinced the poor, foolish man of a mission of compassion to some far away county on the other side of our dear England. I know not how this came about, but I am happy he is gone. Perhaps her headaches will ease now.

It is so frightening to see how horribly she is affected. There are times they hit her with such force that she cannot even stand. What could be causing so fierce a reaction from a strong woman such as my mother? I am frightened they may be a sign of something much worse, but she refuses to call for anyone except her own doctor. I will write to Uncle Hugh. Perhaps he will be able to talk her into being examined by a London doctor.

Mrs Jenkinson will be back soon, so I must end this letter before she sees it. I miss you and hope the day we can finally be together comes very soon.

With all my love,
Your Anne

Fitz read through the letter again, stopping to ponder what his aunt could possibly be up to. It did seem an odd situation, especially the way Anne described it. Without much time left, he dressed and went down to join his family for dinner.

Sarah Johnson

CHAPTER XI

Tuesday, January 14, 1812

Jonathan Lucas knocked on his older sister's open door, "Are you ready?"

"Yes, my trunks are all packed."

"Right over there," he said to the footman following him. After the man left with the trunk, Jonathan looked at his sister. "Do you have a minute?"

"Yes? What do you need?"

"I just want to be assured you are well."

She turned around to look in the mirror as she tied her bonnet, "I am. Why are you concerned?"

"Ever since I returned home a few months ago, you just seem a little more withdrawn than is your want. I know you have assured me several times of your well-being, but there is something you are not saying. Please confide in me, Charlotte. What is so unsettling?" He paused, watching her face for any sign of her giving in. "You know I will not leave you alone until I know the truth."

Charlotte walked over to the bed and sat down, looking down at her hands as she played with the fabric of her dress. "Have you noticed something *lacking* in my life?"

"*Something lacking?*" He shook his head, "No, I cannot say I have noticed anything of the sort. What am I missing?"

"I am not married," she stated flatly.

His heart wrenched for her situation and he went to sit beside her, wrapping his arm around his sister's shoulders in an understanding embrace. "Charlotte, whether you ever marry or not, I will still be here for you. I will not force you out of your place in this house when our father dies and this land becomes my own. You will always have a home here."

"Thank you Jonathan, but it is still not the same as being the mistress of my own home." Charlotte stood and left the room.

What am I to do, he thought to himself. *We do not have the funds to send her to Town for the Season. Perhaps fate has some other plan. All I can do is pray Charlotte find what she desires soon.*

He left her room with his mind occupied on his thoughts and ran right into Maria when he stepped into the hall. He caught her elbow to keep her from falling, "I am sorry; are you hurt?"

She answered distractedly, "Oh, I did not think this day would ever come! I am so excited. *BRIGHTON!* I am going to *Brighton!*" Maria enthusiastically ran past him and down the stairs.

Jonathan chuckled and followed after her, eager to be on the road as well.

Darcy knocked on the door frame and peeked into the dressing room to see Elizabeth inspecting her hair.

"I am not certain if I like this style. It seems to be too intricate for just a simple day at home."

Annette, her lady's maid, was assuring her of its suitability when Darcy walked in. "You look exquisite, my love," he said, leaning down from behind to kiss her cheek. Placing his hands lovingly on her shoulders, he nodded to Annette, dismissing her, then asked, "Is there something you need to do before your sisters and the Lucases arrive, or can you spare a few minutes for a stroll in the park?"

Elizabeth placed her hand on top of her husband's and smiled, "They are not expected for at least another hour, and Mrs Tucker has assured me she has things well in hand, so I am at your disposal, sir."

William took her hand to help her stand. "I was able to secure my uncle's box at the Royal Theater for their final showing of *'The Marriage of Figaro'*."

"That will be such fun! Which night?"

"Monday night. I thought by then Sir William and Mr Lucas will have completed their business, and your sister's trousseau should be well on its way to being purchased, so I thought everyone would be ready for a night out."

"Yes, I am certain our purchases will be completed within a few days. Charlotte and I prefer anything to dress fittings, and Jane will want to finish in as timely a manner as is possible to spend some time with Mr Bingley."

"I have a feeling he will be here every minute he can spare this week. If it were not for his intended staying here, I am certain he would be asking to stay. When the Hursts' are not in Town, a room at Darcy House has always been open for his use."

"I do hope he was not offended to not have it available?"

"Absolutely not, my love. He does not wish to overwhelm you with your new duties as mistress by adding being a chaperone at all times. He will be staying with Uncle Hugh and Aunt Helen just three doors down, and I have a feeling we shall only rid ourselves of his presence when it is necessary to sleep this next week!"

Elizabeth smiled, "I am excited for my sister. I imagine she and Mr Bingley will be very happy."

He pulled his wife up from the stool and drew his arms around her, "Are you happy, Elizabeth?"

Nodding her head, she whispered, "Oh, yes—very!"

The two were lost in a fiery kiss until they heard the bell indicating someone had come to call. "Oh, could that be them? Are they here early?" Elizabeth excitedly pulled away from her husband and turned to ensure her hair was still in place.

William stood behind her, resting his large hands on her shoulders. He leaned down to catch her eye in the mirror in front of them. When he did, he winked and smiled broadly, showing his dimples, "You look lovely, my love. Now let us go and see who has come to pay us a call."

As they descended the stairs, they saw their house guests gathering in the front hall, the servants helping them remove their cloaks. Jane and Elizabeth both squealed with glee and embraced as if they had not seen each other in ages, then Elizabeth turned to greet Lydia, Maria, and Charlotte just as eagerly.

Darcy bowed to Sir William and Jonathan Lucas, "Welcome to our home. I see you were able to leave earlier than expected."

Sir William answered with an eager nod, "Yes, yes; the young ladies were eager to be on the way earlier than I anticipated."

Darcy looked over to the ladies and chuckled when he heard Lydia whisper to her friend, "Oh my! Can you imagine it Maria—my sister is mistress of *this grand home!*"

"No, I am in awe. The only thing better would be if it were a castle!" Maria answered in equal admiration.

Darcy saw the two exchange a look of wonderment as they inspected what they could see of the house from the front hall. He and Georgiana had this prospect redone just a few years ago, and he was happy to see that it met with the young ladies' approval. At the time Georgiana showed her dislike of the bright white walls and checkerboard patterned black and white marble tiles, but when it was all put together it was simply lovely and showed off the architecture of the home to its fullest, just as Darcy knew it would. He was not usually privy to the exuberant faces of his visitors as they entered though, so he took pride in seeing their excitement today.

"If you wish to refresh yourselves, our housekeeper will show you to your rooms, then you can meet us in the drawing room," Elizabeth said.

The guests followed Mrs Tucker upstairs, and Darcy looked at his wife. "Your first guests to Darcy House have arrived, *Mrs Darcy*." As he wound his arms around her waist, he whispered into her ear, "I love seeing you perform your duties as the mistress of our home."

Elizabeth smiled and reached for his hand, then stepped back and looked into her husband's eyes. She could see the love he had for her shining in them and it made her weak at the knees.

William saw her weakness and grabbed her elbow, steadying her, then he led her to the drawing room to await the others while he went to get his sister. When he returned, he sat Georgiana next to Elizabeth on the sofa, and the two began to talk of the coming week and how excited they were. Darcy stood watching them and smiling. His sister was such a changed person from just a few months ago, and if it were not for Elizabeth and her family, he knew Georgiana would not be so content now.

Jonathan and Sir William Lucas arrived in the drawing room first, both talking of their travel plans. "We must leave early if the sky today is any indication of the weather tomorrow," Jonathan was saying.

"It would not do to have the girls caught in such inclement weather, so we must arrive in Brighton as soon as may be," Sir William agreed.

The two stepped over to Darcy and nodded in greeting, Jonathan saying, "Thank you for inviting us to stay here while we are in Town."

"Think nothing of it—you are welcome any time."

"I was just saying I believe we should leave early tomorrow. The sky is starting to look a little too dark for my comfort, and I doubt we can make the journey in one day if we have a storm with which to contend," Jonathan repeated.

Darcy walked to the window and drew the curtains back, "Yes, a winter storm may be on its way, and if so, you are correct in leaving early. If you wish to stop for the night in Horley, I can dispatch a footman ahead of you to reserve some rooms at the inn."

"Yes, yes that sounds like a capital plan. Thank you," Sir William replied excitedly. The three men continued to talk of their traveling arrangements and of all the Lucas' needed to accomplish in Town when they returned on Friday. Darcy was writing a note to be dispatched with his footman when the others joined them in the drawing room.

Charlotte gave her best friend a hug. "Oh Lizzy, your home is lovely. I cannot imagine being the mistress of *all this*; you must be very busy."

"My husband's staff are very helpful, Charlotte, so do not think I have no time for other pursuits."

Lydia giggled, "I imagine the people in Town do not know what to think of you walking in the park as early as is your wont."

Elizabeth laughed, "No, I dare say they do not know what to think of me."

They all sat for tea and talked together for another hour before Bingley, having arrived the previous day, joined them, accompanied by Alex and another visitor.

"Lord Ashbourne, it is a surprise to see you in Town."

"It is, and yet a great pleasure to see that you are here as well. Your cousin was just telling me of your recent marriage," and he turned to Bingley, "and Bingley insisted I come with him to meet his intended."

Bingley beamed as he took Jane's hand and introduced her.

"It is a pleasure to make your acquaintance, Miss Bennet."

When Bingley continued to stare at Jane, Darcy spoke up, "Lord Nicholas Stratton, Earl of Ashbourne," he said to his wife, then he turned and said to his friend, "May I present my wife, Mrs Darcy."

"I do apologize for the unexpected intrusion upon your household, madam."

Elizabeth graciously nodded, "It is no intrusion, my lord. You are most welcome."

Darcy went on to introduce the earl to the others, then they all began to discuss the plans for each day of their visit. Darcy invited the earl to join them in his uncle's box at the Royal Theater on Monday, and he gladly accepted before taking his leave.

The others continued to discuss when their dress fittings were scheduled, and Elizabeth mentioned her aunt wanting to host them all for a dinner their last night in town.

Everyone retired early, the two youngest girls excitedly talking late into the night about their adventure in Brighton and all they wished to do while there.

<hr />

Monday, January 20, 1812

"Charlotte, what do you think of this color?" Elizabeth asked, a swatch of rose colored material with tiny white flowers embroidered all over it held in her hand.

Charlotte fingered the delicate material, "Oh, Lizzy! This is so beautiful. I cannot imagine owning a dress made of this. I could never afford something so delicate."

Elizabeth leaned closer to her friend, "I happen to be on good terms with *the supplier* of this clothier," she wiggled her eyebrows, "and you would be surprised just how inexpensive this bolt of fabric is."

"But, Lizzy, I cannot let your uncle lose money! This material is well worth the price, and I would not feel right buying it for anything less."

Elizabeth was about to say something else when her Aunt Maddie came up behind them, "And we would not feel right allowing the best friend of our nieces to pay full price. You are practically like family, Miss Lucas, and as such, you qualify for the *family discount.*"

With tears welling up in her eyes, Charlotte hugged both women, "Thank you. You do not know how this has lifted my spirits."

"Well then, our final objective for the day is accomplished," Elizabeth replied. "Come, we will purchase this and have it sent over to the modiste. Then, since we have extra time, we shall go to the museum. You would love to see the sculptures and paintings, would you not Charlotte?"

Smiling, Charlotte nodded her head, and Elizabeth turned to address the attendant, "We will take nine yards of this, and please have it sent to Madam LeFevre."

"Right away madam," the sales clerk said as she took the sample and left the three women.

"Oh Lizzy, no! It is one thing to purchase such a material for me, but to also have it made into a dress is more than I could bear."

Elizabeth smiled at her friend, "Jane and I have already chosen the pattern and given Madam LeFevre your measurements, so there is not need to say anything more. We are determined."

Charlotte did not know what to say, and the look in her eyes was enough to cause Elizabeth to embrace her friend in a silent exchange. When she let go, she turned to her aunt, "Are you free to join us at the museum, Aunt Maddie?"

"No, I am sorry, but your Uncle is having some associates over tonight for dinner and I must complete my preparations. You two go along, and I will send Jane to join you when I return home."

Elizabeth laughed, "I never thought I would see my sister turn down an opportunity to look at fabrics, but I would guess she and Mr Bingley have enjoyed watching little David in the park this morning."

"Yes, it is amazing what the presence of a good man will make a woman give up, is it not?" Maddie hugged the two, "I will see you both in two days when you join us for dinner. Have fun ladies." She then left them to return home.

Elizabeth linked her arm with her friend's, "Well, shall we go? I have a feeling Jane and Mr Bingley will want to walk very slowly when they arrive at the museum, and there is a certain painting I simply must show you towards the back of the exhibitions."

When they exited the warehouse, they were met by Jack, one of Darcy's most trusted footmen, who nodded and turned to go retrieve the carriage. Just as he turned away, a man ran up to the ladies, grabbing at what Jack thought at first was their packages. When the man's arm went around Mrs Darcy's waist he jumped towards him, knocking him over, but before he could be apprehended the man got away. The two ladies assured him they were well, but he refused to leave their side again, calling for a boy on the street to go find the driver and bring the carriage around from the mews.

They arrived at the museum and Jack informed Darcy of the scuffle, but Elizabeth assured them they were not injured. Still, something did not seem right, so Darcy was determined to talk with his cousin about it.

With a firmer grip than usual on his wife's arm, Darcy led the two ladies through the crowd, looking at the pictures along the gallery walls. They were just about to enter the sculptures gallery when Jane and Bingley caught up with them.

The group walked around for another half hour before Charlotte said she would like to rest for a few minutes. As the two couples walked off, she sat on a bench, watching those in the gallery and thinking.

"May I sit with you," Charlotte was pulled from her reverie by a familiar deep voice. Looking up, she saw Lord Ashbourne. She nearly stumbled in her attempt to stand and felt his hand gently grasp her elbow and steady her. "I did not mean to startle you, Miss Lucas."

"I... I was just... I am sorry I did not greet you properly," Charlotte felt her cheeks flush with embarrassment.

"It is I who must apologize. I saw that you were deep in thought and yet I could not help myself from coming over to say hello."

Looking down, Charlotte felt the pink in her cheeks rise even more. "You are very generous in your solicitations, my lord."

Sweeping to the bench with his hand, he indicated they sit and did not let go of her elbow until she was seated again. He sat beside her, both looking out over the crowd. "Are you enjoying your visit?"

"Yes, very much, but it can be quite overwhelming for a woman from a small town."

He chuckled, "I would say there is more of a crush here at the museum than you would ever see even at an Assembly where you live."

"Yes, we are usually in familiar situations with only about twenty or so families." She was shocked with how much at ease she was when talking with the gentleman beside her.

Looking at his companion, a small smile formed on his lips, "I too prefer the country, but Town does make for a diversion when one is needed. I look forward to visiting where you live for Bingley's wedding."

"Oh? Will you be attending?"

"Bingley has already invited me, and I have assured him of my presence." They sat in silence for a minute before he asked, "Are you here at the museum with your friends and family?"

"Only my friends. My brother and father are about their business today. They will be joining us at the theater this evening.

"I will enjoy seeing them again."

Charlotte looked down at her hands, unsure of what to say to this most amiable gentleman. Was he paying her particular attention, or was he much like Mr Bingley and of a particular bent towards friendly manners?

He seemed to realize her reticence and sat back, gazing out over the crowd. "I come here sometimes just to watch the people. It is amazing what you can learn of society from just sitting back and watching how people interact. Take for instance that group," he indicated a group of young ladies. "They are here for nothing more than to show off their dresses and hats. Now if you ask me, a person should never look like their head is a bowl of fruit or a birds' nest, but I dare say no one ever told them that." Charlotte chuckled, trying not to laugh out loud, as he continued. "The couple right over there," he indicated the direction with a nod, "seems to be forming some sort of attachment right under the noses of their chaperones, and no one is the wiser." Turning to look at the woman beside him, he asked, "Do you like to watch people, Miss Lucas?"

"Not often. In a country neighborhood one moves in a very confined and unvarying society."

"But people themselves alter so much, that there is something new to be observed in them forever," he replied.

"I suppose," Charlotte said. "I am not a good studier of people, my lord."

"On the contrary, I believe you are, you just do not have confidence in the defense of your own opinions."

The two were interrupted by the return of the others from their excursion. "Lord Ashbourne, we did not expect to see you until this evening," Darcy bowed formally to his friend.

He stood and greeted the others. "I was walking by when I saw Miss Lucas, so I stopped to speak with her."

"Yes, we wanted to view one more gallery and Miss Lucas wished to rest for a few minutes," Darcy said.

"I will take my leave of you, until this evening." Bowing to the group, he turned to Charlotte, "It has been a pleasure talking with you, Miss Lucas." Bowing to the others again, he turned and walked away.

"Shall we?" Darcy asked, putting out one arm to his wife and the other to Charlotte. The group made their way to the carriage and was returned to Darcy House, where Darcy made sure a note was dispatched to his cousin with the detailed description of the man who accosted his wife earlier, as well as the name of his footman if the colonel needed to question him further. Unfortunately, the presence of their house guests did not allow for any time to speak with his cousin in person, at least, not without alarming his wife, and that was something he was determined not to do. It was such an odd situation, though, that he dare not take notice of it.

Sarah Johnson

CHAPTER
XII

Elizabeth returned home from their outing and excused herself to rest for a little while. When she sat down to look at her tired and drawn face in the mirror, she noticed a letter sitting on her dressing table. She picked it up and recognized the familiar hand of her Aunt Maddie and smiled as she broke the seal.

> January 20, 1812
> Gracechurch Street, London
>
> My Dearest Lizzy,
>
> I enjoyed our outing today and was very pleased with all we accomplished. I do not wish you to become anxious, but I noticed something about your face today and feel I must ask you something private, thus this letter. I do not want to seem indelicate, so please afford me some leniency in discussing such a subject with you in this manner.

Have you had your courses since you were married?
Could it be that you are with child?

Elizabeth dropped the letter to the tabletop, shock evident on her face as she looked back into the mirror. *Could I be… expecting? My courses—when did I last have my courses?* She frantically searched through her journal for the pages where she kept track of such information. *October… November, yes I remember, it was right before my wedding… December—nothing is written for December… January, again nothing. Come to think of it, I do not believe I have had to adjust our nightly routine at all since getting married.*

Looking back up into the mirror, she inspected her face, turning this way and that way. She noticed a little pudginess that was not there before, and of course, her eyes were a little more inset, evidence of her being tired. She reached for the letter again and continued reading.

If you have had your courses and I am wrong, then
I am sorry to bring on the anxiety I am certain this
letter has done. However, if you have now found I
may be right, I wanted to tell you some signs to look
for other than the ceasing of courses.

She continued to read as her aunt told of things that sounded vaguely familiar, such as being tired and not feeling well, especially in the mornings or late evenings. Aunt Maddie suggested that eating small portions more often would help. She also told of how rich foods were often too harsh and sometimes just some bread would help. Bland foods were easiest for most women, and odd cravings were also a common sign. Her aunt also told of lying flat on her back and feeling her lower abdomen for a firmness. Elizabeth, curious as she was, went over to her bed and lay down. As she felt around, she did notice a firmness that was not there before. Sitting up, she wiped at the tears that poured from her eyes. Looking back down to her aunt's letter, she read of being overly emotional and again burst out crying. *I very well could be with child*, she thought.

I must think logically about this, she thought as she dried her eyes and took a deep breath. Sitting down at her desk, Elizabeth opened her journal to a new page and began making a list from the letter in her hand:

      lack of courses
      unnatural fatigue
      aversion to foods at certain times
      cravings for odd foods
      weight gain, especially evident in the jaw line early on
      firmness in the lower abdomen
      being overly emotional
      differences in skin and hair

Elizabeth then took her list and again sat in front of her mirror. *I must think through all these things in order*, she thought, trying to clear her racing mind.

'Lack of courses'—*I have already determined I have not had any courses since November.*

'Unnatural fatigue'—*William has been most insistent upon my resting every afternoon, and while I would normally balk at so much rest, I have been grateful most days.*

'Aversion to foods at certain times'—*I cannot remember this being a problem so far, but I will keep it in mind.*

'Cravings for odd foods'—*could this be why I have a sudden need for so many sweets? I even started putting honey in my tea, and I have never before been too fond of anything but cream and lemon.*

'Weight gain, especially evident in the jaw line early on'—Elizabeth again examined her face in the mirror, running her hand over her jaw. *There does seem to be some puffiness.*

'Firmness in the lower abdomen'—she rested her hand on her stomach and smiled.

'Being overly emotional'—*I have noticed an unusual amount of tears lately.*

'Differences in skin and hair'—*I have had to wash my hair more often lately, but I thought it might be the change in soap since I married.*

Sarah Johnson

Elizabeth drew in a deep breath and closed her eyes, slowly letting it all sink in. *I fit most of the things here in Aunt Maddie's letter*, she thought. Tears again welled in her eyes, and as she reached for her handkerchief to wipe them away, she had to laugh at herself for such an emotional outburst. *I have many of the symptoms*, she thought. She sat back at her desk, pulled out a piece of paper, and wrote a note back to her aunt of all she discovered.

After she called for a footman to have her letter delivered, she opened her journal to a new page and poured out her feelings, filling many pages with all her thoughts. With her journal in hand, she curled up in the window seat and watched as the world seemed to go by outside. *I must be certain before I tell William*, she thought. *I will wait until the quickening before I reveal anything—I would not wish to raise his hopes and then be wrong.*

William found her asleep with her journal held tightly to her chest and a sweet smile upon her lips. He carefully picked her up and placed her on the bed, putting her journal on the desk before curling up with her for a few minutes until they needed to dress for the theater.

Elizabeth knocked on her sister's door and was bid enter by the familiar soft voice. She saw Jane sitting in front of the mirror, examining the coiffed hair atop her head. "Charlotte said you were nearly finished dressing."

When Jane saw who it was entering, she turned around, tears filling her eyes as her smile exuded the feelings she held on the inside.

"I knew you would look stunning in this dress," Elizabeth said, walking over and taking Jane's hand to have her stand.

Jane ran her fingers delicately down the flowing material of soft pink—so pale it was barely noticeable, but just enough to bring out the slate blue of her eyes in stunning detail. "I think any lady would feel beautiful in a gown such as this. It is exquisite! How, ever, did the modiste complete it so quickly?"

Elizabeth blushed slightly, "I actually ordered this for you before I returned to Hertfordshire for Christmas. I knew you would soon be married and would need a gown such as this if you were to be in Town for the Season."

The two embraced, both trying not to cry, until they heard another knock on the door. Elizabeth walked over to open the door and found Alex standing there with Georgiana in his arms.

"I just wished to see the dress," Georgiana explained with a smile.

Elizabeth stepped out of the way and they entered, Alex giving a smile and nod of approval as Georgiana began to talk of its intricacies and beauty. She made Jane spin around three times in order to see the effect it would have at a dance, even though tonight it would be just to the theater. The three ladies examined Jane's hair in detail as well, as Alex just stood there, his mind wandering to what another Bennet sister would be like if she were in this room now. The thought made him smile, but before it could be noticed by the ladies present, Elizabeth insisted it was time to leave.

"I wish you would come with us this evening," Jane said pleadingly to Georgiana.

"No, it is not time for me to face the Ton in such a situation—not yet." *The Marriage of Figaro* being a favorite of both Georgiana and Jane, the two had discussed the play in detail earlier today. "I promise, when you return for the Season, I will join you in more activities outside of Darcy House."

Jane gave a smile and a nod. "I will hold you to that promise," she said in a sweet, yet firm manner.

Alex replied, "I think it is time I get this young lady to her room. She was already yawning, but insisted we wait to see you all off."

Sarah Johnson

Elizabeth and Jane both kissed Georgiana's cheek, then Alex and Georgiana took their leave as the sisters, cloaks in hand, descended the stairs where the others awaited them.

Bingley watched as his angel came floating down the steps, the movement of her dress making it seem such an ethereal moment. He lifted his hand to take hers for the last few steps, staring into her eyes. He could not look away.

Jane began to blush with the intensity of his gaze, and the opening of the front door broke the moment between the two.

Bingley took the cloak from her arm and wrapped it around her shoulders, his hands staying for just a few seconds longer than propriety allowed. Then he stepped beside her and held out his arm, placing his hand on hers when she wound her arm through his.

In the carriage, the two sat across from one another, neither one able to see in the darkness, but both staring at the shadow they knew was their intended. The others around them were forgotten, and both were startled from their reverie when the door was opened for them to disembark.

The gentlemen exited first, each one taking a lady's hand to help her from the carriage. Bingley's face beamed as he strode slowly towards the doors with his angel on his arm.

Jonathan saw a twinge of sadness in Charlotte's eye, and he leaned down to whisper in her ear, "One day you will meet someone who cares for you just as much as Bingley cares for Miss Bennet."

She blushed at his knowing her thoughts, and looked down at the ground. "I am already seven and twenty, Jonathan. I hold no grand illusions of catching someone's eye at my age."

He squeezed her hand, "You have your own charms, and if they are not seen by another, then that is their loss."

Charlotte had another retort of just how unworthy she was, but it was stopped by a presence that now greeted their group—that of Lord Ashbourne. Greetings were exchanged and they all entered the theater, repairing to the cloak room to remove their outerwear before making their way through the crowds to their box.

Charlotte blushed when she realized the seating situation would have her on a bench right next to Lord Ashbourne. Luckily it was dark enough that the heightened color of her cheeks went unnoticed. No one had affected her as this gentleman did, and it terrified her. He did not offer any more attention than any other acquaintance or friend did, and it was clear he was not one to lead a lady on, so it was a heart wrenching feeling to sit through the play knowing her own fate for her future.

One bright, endearing moment of the evening was being able to watch the engaged couple. The slightest slip of a hand to touch the other's, leaning in just a little too closely when the situation allowed, taking just a moment longer to move away, and the slight sadness in their eye when they did. It was like looking at a well choreographed dance, so elegant and moving, drawing you into the deep emotions that seemed to surround the two in a shroud of elegance.

After the play, they all returned to Darcy House and soon they retired. Charlotte and Jane were both dressed and in bed, but neither was ready for slumber.

Charlotte sank further into the warm bed, and asked her friend, "Was this night all you hoped it would be?"

"Oh, Charlotte, it was simply beautiful!" She began to hum some of the music the orchestra played, and both ladies seemed drifted into a state of peacefulness. When the song ended, she whispered, "Mr Bingley is so solicitous of me that I feel so loved, so cherished, when in his presence. He need not do anything more, anything particular, just be there. I never knew I could feel this way with anyone. I always wished for affection, but this… this feeling… oh Charlotte, it is so much more than love. I cannot describe what it feels like."

Charlotte reached over and squeezed her friend's hand, "I am so happy for you."

Jane returned the sentiment, "I will forever believe that you too will be so happy one day."

She smiled, but shrugged her shoulders, "What you have with Mr Bingley is special—not something everyone can expect. I know already what my future will be, and I am learning to accept that." She turned over and let sleep take her into a world where dreams always come true.

Jane heard the sadness in her friend's words, and did the only thing she could do—offered up a prayer for Charlotte to find such happiness as well.

CHAPTER

XIII

Wednesday, January 22, 1812

L ouisa was going through her recent purchases to see what else was needed from the shops today when a knock came at her door. "Enter," she said, as the young servant girl came into the room.

"Two young ladies are here to see you, madam."

"Thank you Polly, I will be down in just a minute. Have you seen my husband?"

"John called him out to the stables, madam. I have not yet seen him come back from the mews."

Louisa stood and looked at the young girl. "Thank you." Noticing the look on her face, she asked, "Is there something the matter, Polly?"

Head bowed, the servant contemplated how to answer her mistress. *No, I must keep my silence. I promised my cousin the child will be raised in a loving home, and*

I cannot betray my family by speaking of an event that is yet to take place. Decided, she looked up, "No ma'am, it is nothing."

Confused at her answer, Louisa started to ask another question, but knew it was not the time. "Please inform my husband that our guests have arrived and we await him in the drawing room."

Relieved that no further questions were forthcoming, Polly left to do as she was bid.

Louisa, Lydia, and Maria were enjoying tea and cakes when David entered the drawing room. "I am sorry I was delayed, my dear." He turned his attention to the two girls, "Miss Lydia, Miss Maria, it is a pleasure to see you two again."

Pleasantries were exchanged, and soon the group left to visit some local shops, deciding to walk and enjoy the rare sunshine of this afternoon.

After their excursion, Louisa and David escorted the two girls back to their hosts' home and slowly walked back to their own. "I am glad Charles let us know of Miss Lydia and Miss Maria visiting Brighton," Louisa smiled.

David pulled his wife's arm a little closer to his side, "Yes, they are enjoyable to have around." Louisa's words sometimes betrayed her deep want of a child, and this afternoon was one of those times. He heard her sigh and it took everything in him to maintain his composure.

When they neared the front step, Louisa saw something sitting right in front of the door. "What is that, David?"

He looked in the direction his wife pointed and curiously replied, "I cannot tell. The packages you ordered today should not have been left on the doorstep like that."

"No, they should not have been; anyway, I do not think it is them as they are not to be delivered until tomorrow."

Getting closer, they realized it was a pile of muslin. "Who would leave this at our door?" Louisa asked.

Hurst started to step across the bundle to open the door when suddenly he realized it was not just a pile of material. He stooped and pulled back the cloth, revealing a tiny face.

Louisa's breath caught in her chest, "Oh David—*it is a baby!*" She bent down to pick up the delicate bundle, cradling it in her arms.

David looked up and down the street, not noticing anything out of the ordinary. "Who could have left this here?"

"I do not know, but we must get this little one in from the cold," Louisa stated.

Distractedly looking around once more, he replied, "Yes, yes we must." He opened the front door and ushered his wife into the house, calling for the butler, Mr Reeves, who seemed to be away from the front door. When the older man appeared, Hurst said, "Please tell Mrs Lewis that you are both to join us in our private sitting room immediately."

"Yes sir, right away," the old butler replied as he quickly went to find the housekeeper.

When the two servants knocked on the door and were bid enter, they never expected to see the sight before them. The couple stood in the middle of the room with a sleeping baby in their arms. "Sir, Madam, you called for us?" Mrs Lewis asked in a hushed tone, quickly closing the door and rushing to their side.

Hurst answered in an equally quiet tone, "We found this bundle on our doorstep when we returned home."

"I am sorry sir, I stepped away for just a minute due to a commotion in the back," the butler answered.

Hurst waved his hand in a dismissive manner, "No, no, I do not blame you. I looked up and down the street but did not see anything amiss."

Louisa heard the baby start to wake, and knew it would soon need nourishment. "We must find a nurse for this little one or it will have no hope of living."

The butler spoke up quickly, "My niece has just recently weaned her youngest. I can see if she is willing to come and nurse the child."

"Yes, that will do for now. Please take our carriage and go talk to your niece. Let her know we will pay a fair price for her services."

"Yes, sir," Mr Reeves answered as he turned to leave the room.

"And I need not stress enough my confidence in your silence to all others of this occurrence," Hurst said firmly.

"No, sir, I shall speak to no one else," he assured his employer.

Mrs Lewis left the room to locate some articles of clothing that could be used for the small baby, and David and Louisa found themselves facing a situation they could have never imagined.

"What are we to do, David?"

"We need to see if there is a note," he said, leading his wife to the sofa. Louisa carefully laid the baby on her lap as they searched through the layers of muslin. David found a small piece of paper and opened it to read. Tears welled up in his eyes as the few sentences unfolded, the words '*her parents died in a fire and we know of no other relatives*', echoing in his mind. To be so little and have no one—he could not imagine turning this dear child away.

"I must find the local authorities and report this," he said, overwhelmed with the task before him.

With tears in her eyes, Louisa asked, "Will they take the baby away?"

118

He hugged his wife, wishing he could calm her fears, "I do not know, my dear."

Mrs Lewis reentered the room to see them sitting on the sofa cooing at the small bundle on their laps. Touched by the affectionate scene before her, she quietly came up beside them, "I found a sheet that can be used to fashion some clothing for the child, and I am quite handy with a needle, so it should not take much time to come up with something more serviceable than these rags," she indicated the worn cloths the babe was currently wrapped in.. "Polly is cutting it into squares now." The two women soon had the baby in dry clothes and Louisa wrapped her own shawl around the bundle as David stoked the fire to heat up the room.

Mr Reeves knocked, having returned with a young woman, "Sir, Madam, my niece has agreed to nurse the little one for you until another can be found."

Hurst motioned to the two women with the baby. "Thank you. We will leave you to get settled," he said as he and the butler left the room, securing the door to ensure the women's privacy.

"I must speak with the local authorities. Who would that be?" Hurst asked the butler when they exited the bedroom.

"St Nicholas' Church is right down the street; maybe the vicar would be able to assist you?"

"Yes, I will start there."

Hurst was soon standing outside the stone edifice, the tolling of the bell high above in the tower told of the late hour. He shuddered at the chilly wind as it swept along the road, the sun no longer warming the air, and hurried inside to find the vicar.

"May I help you, sir," a man asked when he came through the large wooden door.

Sarah Johnson

As his eyes adjusted to the darkness of the corridor, he saw an older man standing beside the bell rope. "Yes, I hope you can. Who would I talk with about a foundling baby?"

"I am sorry sir, but we cannot take any more babies at this time. My cousin usually takes them to Town twice a month, but he has been sick and is unable to make the trip lately."

"Has there been any word of a missing child?" Hurst asked.

Rubbing his head and thinking, the old man finally answered, "No… no sir, I do not recall hearing of any missing child. Was one found?"

"My wife and I returned from shopping this afternoon and discovered a babe on our doorstep," Hurst replied quietly.

"I am sorry, sir. If I were in a position to help I would be more than willing to do so, however I cannot at this time," the old man said.

"We are willing to take the child in if needed—you see, *we have no children of our own*," Hurst said, emotion gripping his voice. Pulling the note from his pocket, he continued, "We found this inside her blanket."

Taking the note, the vicar replied, "I cannot make this out in the dim light here; please come with me to my office."

Hurst followed him down a dark hallway and into a small room with a desk and two chairs. The walls were lined with bookshelves that could not contain all the bound editions stacked on every surface, including the floor. Motioning to the extra chair, the old man sat at his desk and opened the note, leaning near a candle to better see the words scratched inside. He cleared his throat, "This does not give much information, but it does say she has no other relatives to take her after her parent's tragic deaths."

"Yes; we do not know any more than that," Hurst said.

The vicar smiled, "Well then, it seems the good Lord has seen fit to bless you in a way you could never have imagined."

Tears welled up in his eyes as Hurst answered, "Yes; yes, it seems He has."

"If you do not mind, I would like to enter the child's information into my record book," the old man replied, breaking the emotional tension building in the room.

A small smile forming on his lips, Hurst shook his head, "No, I do not mind at all." His fingers nervously fidgeting, Hurst continued, "We did not know the proper procedure for such an occurrence."

The old man smiled, "The note does help things go more smoothly as we know she was not taken. Without another relation to take her in, she would go to a foundling home where the survival rate of a baby is not good. If you are willing to take her then you might just be saving her life."

It took a few seconds for Hurst to realize what the old man in front of him was saying. As realization dawned, he smiled, "Are you certain we can keep her?"

"There is no one else stepping up to do so, sir" he replied. "Please have a seat and I will find my book." He turned to the desk and dug through a drawer, finally pulling out a small, leather bound journal. He opened it to the last page used, prepared his quill, and began asking questions, "Do you wish to enter your name into the records, or would you prefer to keep this a private affair?"

"As I have yet to speak with my wife, I would prefer this to remain private, for now" Hurst answered.

"Yes sir. If you wish to add your name after speaking with your wife, feel free to come back at any time." He looked down at the book and continued, "Do you know the general age of the child?"

"She must be just a few weeks old." He down at his hands as he held them out in indication of her size, he said, "She was so small I could hold her head in my hand and her feet barely came to my elbow."

"I will put newborn then," the old man answered. "And my next question has already been answered," he smiled as he continued, "it is evidently *a girl*."

With a look of pride on his face, Hurst answered, "Yes, a girl."

"And you have no other information than what was in the note?"

"When we found her I looked up and down the street but nothing seemed out of the ordinary."

He closed the book and returned it to the drawer, "Do you need to find a nurse for the child?"

Hurst stood and replied, "Our butler was able to locate one for now, but if you know of someone who could take on the position permanently, your help would be appreciated."

Thinking for a moment, he then replied, "I may have someone in mind. I will speak with her and find out if she is able to help. Can you come back tomorrow?"

"Yes."

"Good, good; well, if there is anything else I can help you with, please let me know. I am thankful the babe was found and we are not having to bury the poor thing tonight," the elderly man replied.

"Yes, as am I. Thank you for all your help." Hurst followed the man back down the hallway and out to the corridor. He opened the door, a blast of cold air bringing him back to the reality of the moment. He nearly ran back home to tell Louisa they were *finally* to be parents.

I am a father—a FATHER! I never imagined how this would feel, he thought as he took the stairs two at a time to rejoin his wife.

He startled her when he quickly opened the door, finding her sitting with their maid by the fire. The two stood as he walked over to join them, Louisa putting her arm around the young girl's shoulders, "Polly has something she wishes to tell you," Louisa said to her husband. The girl shook with fear and Louisa quietly asked her, "Would you like me to tell to my husband instead?" At Polly's nod, she looked up at David. "Polly's cousin put the baby on our doorstep."

David's eyes met Louisa's, pleading with her to continue.

Louisa urged the frightened girl to sit again and turned to her husband. "Polly's cousin lives on a small tenant farm right outside of Brighton. He came home last week to find his neighbor's house in flames. Their newborn baby was saved, but the parents both died. His wife has been able to nurse the babe, as they have a little one of their own, but they cannot afford to keep her. There are no other relatives to take the child, and in their desperation they asked Polly if she knew of anyone. Knowing we did not have any children of our own, she thought we would love this child the way she deserves."

Understanding dawning on him, he looked at the girl. "She has no other relatives?"

Looking down at her hands, Polly replied, "No sir, she has no one."

Hurst looked at Louisa and quietly replied, "You are incorrect, Polly—*she has us*." Looking back to the girl, he said, "Thank you."

Polly stood and finally looked into his eyes, "Thank you, sir, madam." She turned to leave the room and was stopped by an unexpected question from Hurst.

"Do you know the baby's name, or her parent's names?"

"I do not know the baby's name as I have never seen her until today. Her parent's surname was Addison."

"Thank you," he said, dismissing her.

Hurst crushed Louisa in his arms, "We are parents! Do you hear me, Louisa—we are parents!" They walked over to the basket that held the sleeping child and Hurst carefully picked her up.

When the two were seated again, David holding the baby in his arms, Louisa leaned her head on his shoulder, "We must come up with a name for her."

Looking into the tiny pink face, he quietly answered, "Amelia Grace—for my mother and yours, and Addison for her own parents."

Louisa placed her finger into the small fist and repeated quietly, "*Amelia Grace Addison*—I like that name." Leaning down, she kissed her forehead, "Welcome to our family, *Amelia Grace Addison Hurst*."

CHAPTER

XIV

David quietly moved the baby, curled in his wife's arms, to the waiting arms of the nurse, closed their chamber door behind her retreating form, and wearily climbed into bed with Louisa. She turned and cuddled up against her husband's chest, sleepily saying, "Can you believe we are parents?"

"I think I fully realized it the second time I had to change my shirt tonight," he said with a chuckle.

"She does seem to like soiling your clothing. Perhaps you should keep a blanket with you when she is in your arms."

"Yes, I may just do that." Neither said anything for a minute, then he continued, "I need to go back to the vicar tomorrow as he might have a permanent nurse for us. While I am there I will have the information from Polly added to the record book." Pausing, unsure how she would take his next statement, he drew her a little closer to his chest and added, "I also want to ride out to the area where Polly's cousin lives and find out all I can about this fire."

"You want to know for sure that she has no other family?" Louisa asked quietly.

"Yes." The two lay in silence for a few minutes until David asked, "What made Polly come to you about Amelia?"

"Before we left with Miss Lydia and Miss Maria, I noticed she was acting strangely. I asked if there was something amiss and she answered, '*it is nothing*'. That statement kept bothering me, so after the nurse had Amelia settled back down I asked Mrs Lewis to bring Polly to me. When she came into the room, she was not taken aback at the presence of a baby. I found it odd and asked her about her reaction; that is when she confessed all she knew to me."

"Do you know her cousin's name?"

"No, but I can find out tomorrow. You want to talk with him?"

"Yes; I want to be certain we have done all we can for Amelia, and if she has family it is our job to find them," Hurst replied.

Louisa kissed her husband's cheek and quietly asked, "Is it selfish of me to hope she has no one else?"

David pulled her closer and affectionately said, "I know all you have been through, but I have to know for certain." David felt his nightshirt growing wet under his wife's silent tears. He pulled her closer and kissed the top of her blonde head, emotion gripping his voice, "I have to know she cannot be taken from us, Louisa. Please trust me?"

"I do trust you," she said as she closed her eyes, quickly falling asleep in her husband's loving embrace. For David, sleep did not come as easily, his mind going through the many possibilities of what could happen. The words from the old vicar echoed through his head, '*it seems the good Lord has seen fit to bless you in a way you could never have imagined*'. Silently, he prayed, *I hope he was correct and this truly is a blessing from You*, then David finally found sleep.

Thursday, January 23, 1812

Hurst was up early and nearly dressed when Louisa stirred in the bed. "Good morning," he said, walking over to kiss her cheek.

"Good morning," she sleepily responded, pulling the counterpane higher in the chilled room.

"I plan to leave within the hour," he said, seeing the look on Louisa's face change.

"You wish me to find out Polly's cousin's name?" she asked.

"Yes; the girl seems to be frightened of me and I do not mean to distress her." Hurst pulled on his jacket and again sat beside his wife on the bed. "You know I have to do this."

"I understand," she said quietly. "Do what you feel you must."

He placed his finger under her chin and drew her gaze up to his, "Do not lose hope. If it is truly meant to be, then I will find things exactly as Polly and the note have indicated."

"I will try," she replied. "Please pull the cord and I will talk with her as she helps me dress."

He went downstairs to await his wife, and when she finally appeared they broke their fast together. The maid was forthcoming with her cousin's name and where he lived, and Hurst was soon on his horse riding out of Brighton.

Sarah Johnson

When he approached the area Polly described, he saw the charred remains of a small house. An ominous feeling hung in the air and he stopped to view the scene. The fields behind the small farm were cleared, with only a few cows grazing in the distance. A large tree with its bare branches showed the telltale signs of smoke from the giant blaze. The winter foliage that lay around its base no longer smoldered from the fire that overtook everything in its grasp. The air was heavy with the lingering smell from the fire. The fence around the yard seemed to set it off as a memorial to the lives lost in the small house on that fateful day.

Hurst felt someone come up beside him.

"It is a solemn image indeed, is it not?" a man asked.

"Yes. It tells of such a tragic event," he answered quietly.

"You are here for answers," the man stated.

"How did you know?"

"Your attire tells of your station, and I do not recognize you as being from around here."

Turning to look at the man beside him, he bowed, "David Hurst; and you are?"

He bowed in return, "George Fennimore, at your service."

"Just the man I seek."

"My cousin Polly told you my name?" he asked knowingly.

"Please do not be upset with her, my wife noticed she was in need of some counsel and the girl was forthcoming with the few details she knew."

He shook his head, "No, I am rather relieved. Polly told me you would love the babe as your own, and your being here today is proof of that."

With a somber look on his face, Hurst nodded towards the burned remains and asked, "What can you tell me of the family?"

"My neighbors have been here for just over two years. They were newly married and trying to start their family, but they had a stillborn child last year. It was that situation which bonded my wife to the young woman. She told of their families dying when an illness swept through the county where they grew up. Both were alone and they married so he could take her away from there. Having a little money from his father, he was able to move here and rent this tenant farm. They worked hard to establish the crops, and he hoped to employ some new planting measures that would yield an even better crop this next year."

He paused in his story and looked at the burned house, emotion evident in his voice when he continued. "About two weeks ago she gave birth again. My wife helped her for the first few days, and she and the babe were doing well. When the babe was three days old I had some business in Brighton, and upon my return I saw the entire place ablaze. The father fought his way through the flames and was able to get the baby safely outside to me, but when he went back in to get his wife they did not make it out before the roof and beams collapsed." He looked at the ground and continued, "It is amazing to me that anyone could live through such an event." Taking a moment to look at the house, he finally turned back to Hurst. "My wife took the babe to her breast, but we already have seven of our own and cannot afford to take in an orphan. When Polly told us of you letting the house where she works, and that you were such a loving couple yet had no child of your own, we hoped you would be the babe's savior."

"Why did you not just come and talk with us? Why leave her on the doorstep?"

"I cannot explain why. I would have made a different decision today than I did yesterday." Looking down at his feet, he said, "I watched from the park across the street until you and your wife returned home. Is... is she well?"

Hurst smiled in assurance, "Yes, she is perfect." He looked back to the house, "Can you tell me of her parent's names, or her own name?"

"The parents were Robert and Claire Addison, but they had not named the child yet. They called her *'Poppet'* and refused to speak of the name they had chosen until the christening was to take place. We continued to call her by that nickname; knowing we would not keep her, we did not feel we should give her a name."

Hurst looked at the man and replied, "Thank you, for everything."

The man bowed slightly, "She deserves to be loved, and I can see she already has a special place in your heart."

Tears stung his eyes, "My wife and I have always wanted a child..." He could not finish the statement.

Fennimore nodded his head in understanding, "I thank the Lord we found such devoted arms in which to place the child. Her parents would have wanted that above all else."

Hurst rode back to Brighton in quiet contemplation of all that occurred over the last two days. He found himself, once again, looking up at the large stone church. Pulling open the wooden door, he entered the corridor and looked around for the vicar. Not seeing him, he walked down the long, dark hallway, knocked on the door, and was bid enter by the familiar voice.

"Welcome. I hoped to see you again today," the older man said as he stood to greet his visitor.

"I came to enter more information into the records."

"Sit, sit," he said, pulling out his record book and once again turning to the last page. "What do you wish to add?"

"I found out who left the baby on our doorstep and have also discovered that her parents were Robert and Claire Addison." The vicar scratched the names onto the page, then looked up when he was done.

Hurst then continued, "My name is David Hurst, of Serenity Place in Manchester and Grosvenor Square in London. My wife Louisa and I have named the babe *Amelia Grace Addison Hurst*."

The old man finished filling in the information then closed the book. "I was able to speak with the young lady I told you about last night. Her name is Lucy, and her husband, a local farm hand, was killed while she was with child. She was let go due to the difficulty, and has been staying with me and my wife for a few months. The baby was born last week, but it did not live beyond a few days. As I know you are not from here and would need someone willing to go with you, she came to mind. I have spoken with her and she wishes to have the opportunity to leave this area and be of service to you."

"I am sorry for her loss," Hurst said, his eyes filled with grief for the young woman. Holding out his card, he continued, "We would appreciate meeting her before we offer the position, just to see that she gets along well with Amelia. I trust she can start immediately?"

"Yes, I will bring her by later this afternoon. Thank you."

"No, *thank you*. You have helped make our dream of being parents come true, and you know not how deep a desire that has always been for us."

David could not stop smiling as he left the church to return to his wife *and daughter*.

Sarah Johnson

CHAPTER

XV

Darcy stopped at the doorway and smiled. Elizabeth and Georgiana sat at the pianoforte together playing a tune and laughing at their fumbles. They had been back in Town for nearly a month and he was constantly in awe at what Elizabeth could accomplish with Georgiana. He suspected that before they removed to Pemberley for the summer Elizabeth would have Georgiana at least more amiable to the idea of using her bath chair.

Stepping into the room, he saw movement in the corner as the new footman stood. He had hired Joseph to perform the duty of carrying his sister when he or his cousins were unavailable, and so far he was impressed with the tender care the footman exhibited while still adhering to the strictness necessary to ensure his sister's peace of mind. Waving to Joseph to sit so as not to draw attention to his presence, Darcy sat in a nearby chair to listen.

At the completion of their tune, he clapped and stood, "That was quite enjoyable; excellent, my dear."

Both turned towards him and began to laugh, Elizabeth saying, "I may start to believe you to be tune deaf if you think that was *excellent*."

He kissed her cheek and winked, "It was excellent no matter what notes were hit, because I was referring to the two of you having such fun together."

"Hmmm, yes, I believe you have redeemed yourself adequately," Elizabeth said. She stood and asked, "Have you completed your business letters and meetings already?"

Darcy groaned, "Next time we have guests, remind me I must not let my business affairs get pushed aside. I am sure your sister and friend thought I was urging them out the door a little too eagerly when they left this morning, but I have so much to accomplish, and not being at Pemberley makes it even harder."

"They both understood how busy you are, and I dare say Mr Bingley was eager to be on the road as well," Elizabeth replied. "Are you free now?"

"I still have one last letter to write, but I can do that tomorrow. My steward left a few minutes ago. We have one more issue to clear up with my solicitor tomorrow, and then he can go back up to Pemberley to finish the acquisition of the lands."

"Does he think you will be able to save the watermill along the east bend of the river?" Georgiana asked.

"We have hired some people to examine it, but he will not know for another few months yet what they recommend. Maybe by the time we go to Pemberley he will have some more answers." Darcy kissed the top of her head, "I promise Sweetling, if the structure must be torn down I will have him build another in its place. I know how much it means to you." Elizabeth looked oddly at the pair, so he explained, "Our father used to take Georgiana there to picnic quite often and she has her own walled garden there as well."

Elizabeth nodded in understanding, "I hope it is able to be saved then."

"I hope so too," Georgiana said.

Darcy hugged his sister, "I love you, Georgiana."

She reveled in her big brother's embrace, "I love you too William."

When the two finally separated, Darcy replied, "I have something for you." He turned to the chair to retrieve a package. "I know you will appreciate this gift today," he said as he handed it to her.

Georgiana unwrapped it and smiled, "YOU FOUND IT!" She excitedly turned to Elizabeth, "My father used to sing this song to me when I was little. He could not play, but he had a beautiful voice." Turning back to her brother, she beamed, "Thank you, William, for everything." Looking at the footman in the corner, she declared, "Joseph, I believe I have completed my practice for the day and am ready to go back upstairs to my rooms."

"Are you sure you wish to retire, Georgiana?" Darcy asked.

"Yes, I have some letters to finish and I need to rest tonight as my legs are starting to ache from too much activity," she said. Noticing the worried look on her brother's face, she added, "Do not worry, Mrs Annesley will give me something for the pain. I just hate to take it too early as it makes me tired, so I save it for the end of the day. I think tonight I will have my dinner upstairs and leave you two to your own devices."

The footman came over and tenderly picked up his charge, bowed his head to Mr and Mrs Darcy, then he took Georgiana out of the room.

"I am glad your cousin was able to find someone as trustworthy as Joseph to help with carrying your sister around," Elizabeth said.

"As am I. Is his wife working out well as Annette's assistant?"

"Yes she is, though I do not think I need *two* personal maids," Elizabeth stated.

"You have not come to realize yet what the Season will hold for the newest Mrs Darcy." Kissing her nose in a playful manner, he continued, "I will not have you tiring yourself out by helping Annette as you have been doing lately. She now has an assistant to help with the sewing, and when your sister joins us for the Season, Claire can be assigned as Mary's lady's maid."

Laughing, Elizabeth replied, "Claire *is* very handy with a needle, and she has been able to salvage some of my old gowns to be used in others ways."

William chuckled, "Even with more money than you would be able to spend in a Season, you are still insistent upon reusing things others would have given to a maid months ago."

"You are too generous with my pin money; I cannot imagine spending all of it on myself."

"You are free to spend it on me, my love," Darcy said, drawing her into his arms.

"I do," Elizabeth tried to reach for a gift on the table. "If you will loosen your hold on me, I have something right here for you."

Reluctantly letting her go, he watched as she picked up a small parcel from the side table. "I found this and knew you would love it," she said as she handed him the small gift. He unwrapped it and pulled out a small pin with a sapphire on the tip. "Now when I wear your favorite sapphire necklace, you have something that matches to wear in your cravat."

"It is beautiful," Darcy said, setting it down on the table and pulling her back into his arms. He kissed her soundly, then when she started to lay her head against his chest he pulled away. "As it turns out, I have a gift for you as well, my love."

"Oh? What is the occasion?"

"Do I need an occasion to present my wife with a gift? What was the occasion for the one you just gave to me?"

"Why, because I love you, of course."

"Well, as it so happens, I do have a specific reason for giving this to you," he said as he pulled a small leather box from his pocket. Elizabeth opened it up and saw a ring with two tiny stones. "One is to represent me, and the other is to represent you," Darcy said as he pulled it from the box and lifted her hand. He slid it onto her finger then released it for her to examine.

"It is beautiful, William," Elizabeth said as she fingered the ring. She noticed something etched into the band and asked, "What is this going around?"

"It is a vine with tiny leaves. As you see the two stones here are in places where a flower would be, as in a garden."

She brought it up to examine it more closely, "Oh, how lovely."

"The jeweler said it is meant to have stones added to it over time."

"I do not think it needs anything added, it is lovely as it is," she quietly replied.

"Elizabeth," he said, lifting her chin to look into his eyes, "you are meant to add a stone to it each time you add to the family."

Realization dawning, she smiled, "You know?"

William pulled her back into his arms and replied, "I am very well acquainted with your body, so how could I not notice the changes which have taken place? Aside from that, you require a nap every day, and you have had a few dizzy spells. Mrs Tucker assured me those were all typical signs of increasing."

"You talked with Mrs Tucker about me?"

"She stopped me from calling a doctor when I was out of my mind with worry last week. After all she told me, I began noticing tiny things that were different." Running his hand over the lower part of her abdomen, he asked, "Have you felt the quickening yet?"

She put her hand on top of his, "Not yet, though my Aunt Maddie says it may be another month at least before that happens."

"I am glad she is around to calm your fears," he said as he drew her hand up to his mouth, kissing her palm before he leaned down to kiss her lips. Pulling back, he said, "I say my sister had a good idea in retiring early." Kissing her forehead softly, he continued quietly, "Perhaps we will have our dinner in our rooms as well. Would you care to join me, Mrs Darcy?"

"Anytime you are ready, Mr Darcy."

William reached down to lift his wife into his arms and the two were last seen going up the stairs towards their rooms.

Saturday, January 25, 1812

"COLONEL FITZWILLIAM!" Fitz heard his batman anxiously calling through the closed door. "COLONEL, COME QUICKLY!"

He put his quill aside and swiftly opened the door to find his batman holding up the bruised and bloodied body of his undercover soldier, Lieutenant Denny.

"What happened?" he asked as they led him into his office and to a chair.

"I have no idea how it happened. One minute I was sitting there drinking something at the bar, quietly minding my own business, when someone came up behind me and confronted me. He said he knew who I was and that he wanted to talk with me, so I followed him outside. When I got out there, a group of men were waiting for me, and this is the result."

The colonel cursed and handed him a drink. "I will call for the doctor; wait right here." He stepped out of his office and told his batman to go get the Army surgeon who helped him out sometimes. Returning to his office, he found Lieutenant Denny nodding off to sleep. Fitz spoke loud enough to wake him again, "We cannot have you sleeping until the doctor has checked you over—you might have a concussion. Here, we will walk around the room a bit; I am sure the doctor will be here shortly," he said, helping Lieutenant Denny from his seat and assisting him in staying awake.

Within a few minutes, the doctor arrived and checked over the soldier. "He has a few broken ribs and a banged up face, but no head injury and no need for stitches," he reported. The Lieutenant's ribs were bound and his wounds were bandaged, then he was sent to his room to rest.

Fitz sat at his desk thinking. *If someone does know who Denny is then his mission was compromised. I will have to put another in his place*, he thought. Cursing loudly to the walls, he hit his fist on his desk and stood to flip through the files of all his contacts. One name stood out and he sat back down to go through the papers inside. *Lieutenant Colonel Daniel Russell*—the last time he used him was nigh on two years ago, but it might be worth it to track him down now. He was known for getting results and was an expert at disguise.

Fitz wrote a note and called his batman in to have it sent. If anyone knew how to contact the lieutenant colonel, his father would, and Fitz just happened to be on good terms with the Duke of Hawley.

Upon receiving a note in return, Fitz set out for his home, just south of London, to meet with the duke. He was soon being led through the lavishly decorated halls and into the private study. The older gentleman behind the desk stood in greeting, "Welcome, I have not had the pleasure of your company lately."

Fitz smiled, "Yes, it has been a few months at least, Your Grace."

The duke indicated the two chairs by the fire, "Sit; we have much to discuss." Dismissing the servants, he continued, "Now, I know you have not come to see me for my own sake, so let us dispense with formalities and get down to business. What can I do for you?"

"Your keen insight is admirable, Your Grace." Fitz sat on the edge of his seat and continued, "I need your assistance in locating your youngest son."

"I see. I take it you are in a tight spot in your investigation?" At the shocked look on the colonel's face, he answered, "Oh yes, I am well aware of your investigation into the murder of two of your soldiers. I have been kept up to date on the particulars from your superiors. I may be old, but I still have quite a bit of influence in certain arenas, especially when it comes to *my godson's* career."

"I should not be surprised, Your Grace." Fitz smiled. Sitting back, he continued, "Since you have been kept up to date on the particulars, I will inform you of our newest predicament. My undercover soldier came back today with a bloodied face and broken ribs. He said someone has found out who he is, but he could give no more information than that."

"And I take it this is why you wish for my son's assistance?"

"Yes, Daniel is the only one I could think of who has the ability to blend into certain situations without being found out. I cannot use Denny for such after this, especially if he has been identified."

The Duke stood and walked over to the sideboard, poured two drinks, then held one out to Fitz, "I will tell him you are in need of him. When and where do you want to meet?"

"It cannot be here in Town," Fitz answered. "I fear there are too many eyes watching what goes on around here right now. In three days I will be in Brighton delivering some papers for the General; do you think he will have enough time to arrive there?"

"Yes, I can assure you of his presence in Brighton in three days' time," the Duke said confidently. The meeting place and time was set and the two men were soon embroiled in a battle over the chess board that sat between them. "How is it you taught me all I know of this game, and yet I can never win against you?" Fitz asked jokingly.

Smiling conspiratorially, the Duke answered, "You are correct in that I have taught you all *you* know, but I have not taught you all *I* know."

Fitz laughed hardily, "I have always appreciated your candor, Your Grace."

Sarah Johnson

CHAPTER XVI

Monday, January 27, 1812

Mary smiled when Hill brought the letter with the familiar Darcy seal in to her. She sat down in her window seat, Beatrice in her lap, and she opened the letter from her dear friend.

> January 23, 1812
> Darcy House, London
>
> Dear Mary,
>
> You have missed quite an adventurous time with your eldest sister and Miss Lucas staying here. I am sorry you were unable to join them, but I look forward to your coming for the Season. Just think

of all the fun we had at Netherfield Park, plus all the diversions of Town added to our daily routines. I cannot wait!

William and Elizabeth were so busy with our guests they did not have much time alone, so now that the house is quiet again I have not seen very much of them the last few days. I do not mind a bit, as it has given me more opportunities to practice my music. One problem I am finding is that without use of my legs, I have to hold the keys down to sustain them. It is proving to be quite a challenge to relearn the music I mastered years ago, but I am determined to one day play as eloquently as I could before.

My eldest cousin came over a few days ago and I beat him in a game of chess. You can imagine my excitement as I have never won against him before. He said he was distracted, but I cannot imagine what would weigh so heavily on his mind as to cause him to lose to me at a game I do not boast of even fully comprehending. I asked Aunt Helen if she knew what was causing Alex such distress lately, but all she said was his birthday is coming up soon and he may be thinking of finally settling down and putting his wild ways behind him. If that is truly the reason, then I hope he is successful in finding what he desires this next Season.

I am sorry to change the subject so abruptly, but I was called away by Mrs Annesley for my lessons, then Elizabeth and I spent some time playing together on the pianoforte. I am now back, and I cannot wait to tell you of my newest acquisition. William surprised me with a piece of music I have wanted for ages. Can you guess which one it is...

Mary could almost hear the excitement in Georgiana's voice as she told of her gift. *He is such a solicitous brother*, she thought. After reading through the letter again, Mary sat down in the window seat with her cat on her lap. "Why can I not forget *him*, Beatrice? I thought I was finally getting past the reactions I had to his presence, but one mention in Georgiana's letter brings those feelings right back again." Looking intently at the letter, she quietly asked, "What does this line mean about his *wild ways*? Is he really as Miss Bingley says? I cannot imagine that what she has told me is wrong if his own mother would comment about his character in such a manner as this," she held up the letter to the cat. Yawning, Beatrice stretched and jumped down to curl up in front of the fireplace. "Yes, I imagine this does not interest you in the least."

Mary sighed and stood to put her letter away, then sat at her desk to write back to her friend, telling of all the wedding preparations they were inundated with during these cold winter days. After sealing the missive, she curled up in the window seat again, looking out to the grey sky and once again pondering what was revealed to her over the last few months about a *certain someone*. Hours later after the sun had set, she crawled into bed more confused than ever. Beatrice curled up beside her and the two were soon fast asleep.

Tuesday, January 28, 1812

"Colonel, fancy meeting you here," Fitz was interrupted by the familiar voice of David Hurst.

He stood and bowed, "It is good to see you again."

Hurst nodded towards the table at which his wife, Maria Lucas, and Lydia Bennet sat, "We were just sitting down to tea and cakes when I saw you over here alone. You are welcome to join us if you are not otherwise engaged."

Pulling out his watch to check the time, he replied, "Thank you, but I was just finishing my tea and have another appointment soon."

"We will not keep you then. If you have a chance while you are in Brighton, feel free to stop by and visit. I have someone I wish you to meet," Hurst said, indicating the small bundle his wife cradled in her arms.

A smile overtook Fitz's face, "I will do that." He took the card Hurst held out to him with the address on it. He noticed a man who sat alone on the other side of the room, watching the Hursts' table intently. *I wonder what he is up to?*

Hurst returned to his wife and Fitz soon left for his appointment. The man in the corner had now disappeared, but Fitz had a bad feeling about the stranger and was determined to find out why he was watching his friend's table so intently.

Bingley was just sitting down at his desk to go over the particulars of the yearly business review in front of him when Smyth came into the room. "Your mail, sir," the butler said, holding out a tray.

"Thank you. Please have Mrs Benson bring some tea," Bingley said in dismissal.

He rifled through the contents of the tray then stacked a few letters of business on the corner of the desk and put the ones from friends and family in front of him. He did not wish to hear more of Caroline's whining about her '*dreadful situation in Scarborough with their aunt*', so he set her letter aside and opened the one from Louisa instead.

Mrs Benson nearly dropped the tea tray when Mr Bingley came dashing out of the door, calling out that he would be at Longbourn if he was needed. He rushed through the halls, slamming the door in his haste to reach the stables. *What has happened*, the housekeeper wondered.

Bingley was soon galloping over the cold Hertfordshire landscape, the three miles between the two estates passing below his horse's feet at such speed that he was taken aback when he arrived at Longbourn so quickly. Jumping from his mount, he threw the reins to the lad who came rushing from the stables.

He stood at the door and tried to calm his racing heart as he waited for Mr Hill to answer the door. When the butler finally came, Bingley quickly asked, "Where is Miss Bennet?"

"She is in the drawing room with the rest of the family, sir. Do you wish me to announce you?"

Anxiously removing his greatcoat, Bingley answered, "Yes, yes, with haste, please."

The aging butler led the way as fast as he could, and upon opening the door to the drawing room he did not get out a word before Bingley was eagerly pushing his way into the room.

"Mr Bingley, we did not expect to see you this afternoon."

"I received a letter from my sister Louisa and wished to convey some news, sir," he anxiously replied.

Indicating the chair next to his eldest daughter, Mr Bennet said, "Please have a seat and tell us your news, sir."

Bingley was beaming as he sat down and proudly replied, "I am an uncle!"

Gasps of excitement and joyous effusions were heard all around, and the story of Amelia Grace Addison Hurst was soon told to all.

When the excitement subsided, Bingley said, "My sister wishes to come back to Netherfield earlier than they initially intended, and was wondering if you would like Miss Lydia and Miss Maria to ride with them? They will be leaving on Monday the third, and will be staying the night in Horley and again at their house in Town, arriving here on Wednesday the fifth." He turned to his intended and squeezed her hand, "Then they will stay until after we are wed."

"I see no problems with such arrangements. I will write a note to Sir William and ask his opinion, though I doubt he will mind the change in plans. I know my friend was not looking forward to such a journey in this winter weather to convey the girls back here and was talking of letting his son go alone," Mr Bennet said.

Seeing that his two youngest daughters were eagerly working, once again, on the bonnets laid out on the table in front of them, and that his eldest daughter was clearly not interested in anyone but her intended now that he was here, he thought it would be best if he rest. "If you will excuse me, I will be in my study," He stood and stretched his aching leg before he slowly left the room, leaning heavily on his cane.

Mrs Bennet watched her husband leave, worried over his slow movements. She soon excused herself from the drawing room to join him, stopping first at the back sitting room, where Mary was practicing her music, to give her the news Mr Bingley came to convey. She then continued on to her husband's study while Mary went to give her well-wishes to Bingley.

After knocking, Susannah was bid enter. "Are you feeling well, Henry?" He tried to put on a smile, but his wife was not fooled. "Now, now, do not give me that look. I know you are in a tremendous amount of pain, my dear."

"I will be well," he assured her. "This cold weather is just getting to me today."

Susannah sat next to him on the sofa, urging him to put his leg up on her lap and lay his head on a pillow while she rubbed his sore muscles. "I am delighted for Mr and Mrs Hurst," Mrs Bennet said with a wistful smile.

"Yes, a baby is such a blessing to have around. I have a feeling little Amelia will be well cossetted."

"Do you think our daughters will make us grandparents soon?" Susannah asked dreamily.

"It is a great possibility that before next Christmas we may have more than just son-in-laws added to our family gatherings," Henry replied.

"Do you really think so?"

"Yes, I do. Elizabeth had *that look* about her when she and Darcy were here for Christmas, and I would not be a bit surprised if they announce soon that they are expecting."

Continuing to rub his leg, she replied, "Oh, I hope you are right, Henry. You were always able to tell when I was expecting, sometimes even before I knew myself."

Henry stopped his wife's hand and drew it to his lips, "It seems like no time at all has passed since we were preparing for our first child, and now here we sit about to give her hand away in marriage, having already done so with our second child. Where does the time go?"

A nostalgic look came over Susannah's features, "I have wondered that often lately. The nights when we walked the halls or rocked a cranky baby for hours, thinking it would never end. I am ever grateful for your mother encouraging us to be so involved with them from such a young age, unlike others who leave the care fully in the hands of the nursemaids. I thought time was surely standing still then, yet in only a moment our girls are grown." She stood and turned toward her husband, holding out her hand to him, "Come dear; I think you need to rest above stairs for a few hours."

Slowly standing, he grasped his wife's hand in his own, lifting them both to look at them. "I remember the first time I took your hand in mine. I thought it was the most lovely sight I could imagine, and I wondered often in the first few years of our marriage what made you trust me so much when I hardly trusted myself. Our hands are now a little more wrinkled than that day so long ago, but I still feel such a deep connection when I hold your hand in mine."

She smiled. "When you had your accident and the doctor had to give you laudanum for the pain, I would sit beside you for hours. Often you would wake and reach for my hand, then settle again until it began to wear off and the pain would come back." Tears filled her eyes at the painful memories of their past.

"I regret the pain it caused you, but I do not regret what we have gained through my accident."

"Nor do I," She leaned into his embrace where she remained for a few minutes until he let her go.

"Come," he said, "we will repair to our rooms to rest." They left the room, giving the note for Sir William to a nearby footman.

CHAPTER
XVII

Thursday, January 30, 1812

Fitz stepped out of the inn so caught up in his thoughts he nearly ran into the man passing in front of him. "Oh, excuse me, I am dreadfully sorry," he said with a short bow.

He gave a nod, "No harm has come to me. I see you are a part of our fine military."

"Yes, I am." Recognizing the man as the one he had seen watching Hursts' table so intently yesterday, Fitz hoped the man did not remember him.

Spellbound by the uniform the colonel wore, and seeming not to recognize him, the man said, "I have always dreamed of one day wearing a bright red jacket and traveling to faraway lands, but I have never been given such an opening to join. Have you traveled the world in your career?"

Unsure why the man was continuing the conversation, he thought he may be able to garner some information from him. "There were quite a few years when I saw other shores more often than I did our own, but lately I have been lucky enough to stay here in England."

With a flash of intrigue, the man asked, "Have you ever seen India, or Africa?"

"My regiment traveled to India twice, and I spent the best part of a year in Africa."

The man had a far-away look to his eye, "I always dreamed of one day going to the great western frontier of America."

"I have never had the opportunity to set foot in that particular land."

"If *I* did, I would never want to leave. They say you can see for miles across the plains, with no mountains or hills in sight. If I ever came into a bit of money, I would leave everything here to live in such a place."

"Would you not miss your family?" Fitz asked, trying to see what information this man would offer.

A dark look came across the man's face as he suddenly said, "My parents have been dead for many years. I must be going." Turning around, he disappeared into the crowd.

Fitz returned to his room to write down the odd conversation, and once again set out to visit his friends, soon finding the house and knocking on the door.

"May I help you, sir," the butler answered.

"Colonel Fitzwilliam to see Mr Hurst," he said as he gave his card.

"Right this way Colonel." The butler took his hat and led the way to a drawing room.

He smiled when he saw David Hurst with a small bundle in his hands, sitting in a chair by the fire. The butler quietly knocked on the open door, and Hurst nodded his acknowledgement at the visitor, dismissing the servant.

"Welcome, Colonel," he said quietly. "Please pardon me for not standing to greet you properly."

Shaking his head, he replied, "No, no, I believe we are good enough friends to do away with such formalities, especially for such an angelic creature as you hold in your arms now." He walked over to the fireside sofa and sat down, leaning over to see the baby.

He gently readjusted the blanket and lifted the babe a little, "Colonel, may I introduce to you my daughter, Amelia."

Fitz could see tears of joy forming in his friend's eyes. "She is beautiful." Settling back in his chair, he urged, "So, tell me how this came about so suddenly. As I was just in your company not two months ago, I think I would have known if you were expecting a child."

Not put off by the tone of his comment, Hurst carefully stood and pulled the servant's cord. "Come with me and I will gladly explain all that has happened," he said as Lucy entered to take Amelia from him.

The two men removed to a small private study and sat, a drink for each in their hands.

"A week ago we came home from a shopping excursion to find Amelia on our doorstep."

"Just abandoned?" Fitz asked worriedly

"Yes—the note wrapped inside her blanket indicated her parents died in a fire and that she had no other relatives."

"You are only visitors here in Brighton and cannot be known by many locals."

"That was my first thought as well. As I soon learned, it was a cousin of our maid. Mr Fennimore returned home one evening to find his neighbor's house in flames. The father was able to deliver the baby into his hands. Mr Addison then returned inside for his wife, but they were trapped beneath a fallen beam and neither one survived. There are no other relatives and Mr Fennimore has seven of his own to look after. When Polly, our maid, assured him we would love her, he knew he had to give her to us. Having her well cared for was all he could do for her himself.

Fitz sat back, the drink in his hand forgotten. "What is to be done in such a situation?"

"I went to speak with the local vicar and he said his cousin usually takes the foundlings to London twice a month, but he has been sick and is unable to do so right now. There is no foundling home closer."

"I take it your wife is attached?"

Hurst's face beamed as he said, "We both fell in love with her at first sight. As you know from our past discussions, my wife has been unable to have a baby in the ten years we have been married. We think this is due to an accident she had as a child, but we do not know for certain. What you might not be aware of it that the first few years of our marriage our families put such pressure on us to have a child that it nearly tore us apart. We tried every potion and elixir out there and even spent a Season in Bath. Nothing helped. I finally had enough of seeing my wife cry with every letter she received and I had a few choice words for them all. I do not blame Louisa for our troubles, and it hurt me that they did. I finally put my foot down and told them they would not hear from us again if they did not desist with berating my wife."

Fitz sat back in his chair and just let his friend talk. Tears pricked at his eyes as he watched his friend's demeanor. He had known of their lack of progeny, but never of the struggles they faced, nor just how deeply Hurst wanted to be a father, though it clearly showed on his face now.

"After all these years we were finally resigned to never having a child. It is not something we would have chosen, but we were coming to terms with this conclusion. This trip for us was the final realization that we would be the end of the Hurst line." Tears started to fall down his cheeks as he continued, "Then we came home to this gift from God delivered right to our doorstop. You can imagine the joy we both felt immediately, and the dread of not knowing what would happen. Our butler's niece was easily persuaded to be our nurse until another could be found, and I went in search of answers. I cannot tell you how my heart swelled when the vicar said she was evidently left for us to raise. I felt I could have floated home to tell Louisa of all I learned. When I saw my wife holding our daughter, I knew my life would never be the same. In an instant I had more love for two people than I ever thought possible." Hurst took a drink then continued. "Our maid eventually confessed to us about her cousin's part and I was able to meet with him to learn all I could of her parents. They are truly the last of her family, as both of them were the sole survivors in each of their families in a county-wide illness a few years ago. They married and moved here to start their own family. Amelia was only three days old when their home caught fire."

Hurst took a drink and sat up in his chair, drying his eyes. Chuckling, he continued, "Louisa says Amelia resembles a portrait of me as a baby which she has seen often at Serenity Place, but I do not see the resemblance. I think she looks like Louisa with her golden hair and deep blue eyes." Hurst became teary again and his voice cracked as he quietly added, "I have always loved those eyes and knew if we ever had a child they would have them also. It is as if God knew my heart's deepest desire, one I have voiced to no one until now, and He saw fit to give me that in our daughter."

The two men sat in silence for a few minutes before a knock at the door indicated their private tête-à-tête was over. They abandoned their solitude and returned to the drawing room to visit with Louisa, Lydia, and Maria. The three were quite proud of all their recent purchases for Amelia and could not help showing them off to the two gentlemen.

"When do you return to Town?" Fitz asked Hurst.

"We planned to stay in Brighton until the wedding then go straight to Netherfield Park, returning to Town for the Season, but we have now amended our plans to leave on Monday for Hertfordshire. I have already sent ahead for horses to be ready at the stops. We extended the invitation to Miss Maria and Miss Lydia to join us on our journey, but we have yet to hear if it is confirmed."

Lydia spoke up, "I heard from my father just today, and he and Sir William are happy to allow us to travel with you."

Hurst smiled, "Capital, capital. Then our plans are to leave at first light Monday, and be at Netherfield Park on Wednesday."

Lydia leaned over towards Louisa and added, "My father also says he will make it up to me for having to cut my trip short. He is to give me a party for my sixteenth birthday!"

"What a grand idea," Louisa replied.

Nodding his head, Fitz said, "I too will leave on Monday. If it is acceptable to you, I may ride along beside your carriage as far as London."

"That is a good plan, Colonel. I may join you on horseback and leave the ladies to deal with the joys of traveling with a baby."

Fitz laughed, "Oh believe me, I have heard many a tale of the lungs of a little one in a carriage."

"I believe we shall have no issues with Amelia," Louisa stated confidently. "She loves to be jostled about, and we have bought enough to keep her warm. Lucy, our new nurse, seems to have a special way with Amelia and I do not see an issue arising that we are not already well prepared to face."

"We shall see, my dear, we shall see," Hurst smirked.

Fitz soon took his leave, hiding in the park across the street to see if he would again spot the man he had seen watching the Hursts' table yesterday. He was rewarded within the hour when he saw the familiar form following Hurst and the two girls as he escorted them back to their hosts' home. Fitz was confused when the man did not follow Hurst as he returned home, but instead continued to watch the house where Lydia and Maria were staying.

What could he possibly be up to in following two young girls who were not yet out? Fitz decided he would not let this man out of his sight until they left Brighton on Monday.

Monday, February 3, 1812

With eyes bleary from his late night watching the stranger, Fitz rode up to the front of the Hursts' house. The footmen were packing the last of the trunks onto the carriage while other servants prepared the inside of the equipage for the women's comfort.

Seeing the butler, he tipped his hat, "I see the preparations are well under way."

"Yes sir, Colonel Fitzwilliam. Mr Hurst will be down shortly and gave instructions that he will meet you in the dining room. Would you like anything to eat while you wait?"

"One thing I learned long ago is to never turn down food, as a soldier never knows what his future will hold," Fitz said honestly, following the butler into the dining room.

He was joined by two very tired girls, neither of whom wished to talk. The girls stayed the night with the Hursts due to their early departure and were up late talking of all they had experienced while in Brighton. Lydia smeared some jam on a piece of bread she had clearly held in the fire a little too long while Maria quietly drank a cup of warm chocolate, both ignoring their red coated visitor.

The Hursts entered the dining room before Fitz finished his heaping plate of food. "Colonel, it is good to see you." Indicating the plate, he joked, "I see our cook has been paid a compliment by how high you have piled her food."

"As you see," he said, returning to his fare.

"We were just discussing our plans," he said, pulling out a seat for his wife and sitting beside her. Louisa toasted a piece of bread for her husband as he began to speak of the particulars of their travel with the colonel.

When they were finished, Louisa picked up the basket of food provided by the housekeeper. "Mrs Lewis has packed us quite the fare, with cheeses, boiled eggs, several crusty rolls, and an assortment of cold meats and fruit. I do not anticipate having to stop for more than just a change of horses." Turning to Lydia and Maria, she continued, "Come girls, we will get settled in the carriage with Lucy and Amelia, then you can both go back to sleep."

She led them out to the foyer where they each put on their pelisse, gloves, and bonnet, and stumbled out to the carriage. Within ten minutes of being on the road, the two were leaning into their respective corners and were fast asleep again.

Louisa proved to be right in her assertions that Amelia would travel well, and the weather was nice enough that they made good time. Fitz and Hurst rode behind the carriage.

"I have a rather odd question for you Hurst," Fitz said. "Have you noticed anyone following Miss Lydia and Miss Maria while you were in Brighton?"

Thinking for a minute, he replied, "No, I did not notice anything out of the ordinary, but I have been rather distracted lately."

"I saw a man several times over the last few days, and I was disturbed enough by his demeanor that I decided to keep a watchful eye on him. He followed them several times, though I never did see him try to interact with them. I learned last night from the barmaid where he stayed that he was throwing money around, saying his *patroness* could well afford a few drinks for his comrades. The name he gave was *George Wilson*, though I doubt it is his real name. I have a sketch I made here," Fitz said as he pulled out the rough drawing from his pocket and showed it to Hurst. "I am sorry it is not very realistic, but my art tutor was never impressed with my attempts at portraits. Are you certain you have not seen this man before?"

Hurst studied it for a minute, then said, "Now that I see this, I did notice him around a few times, but he never caught my particular attention. What could he want with Miss Maria and Miss Lydia?"

"I do not know, but it cannot be anything good." Fitz pocketed the sketch and the two men continued on behind the carriage. Fitz stayed with them until they reached the Hursts' house in Grosvenor's Square, then he made his way to his parent's house in Cavendish Square, falling asleep almost as soon as he laid his head upon his pillow.

Sarah Johnson

CHAPTER

XVIII

Tuesday, February 4, 1812

Bingley found himself once again trying to go over the business reports from last year, but he could not focus. Early this morning, he received a note from Hurst saying they made excellent time and expected to be at Netherfield Park later today. Putting the stack of papers aside, Bingley pulled out two clean sheets, writing notes to Longbourn and to Lucas Lodge inviting the respective families to join him for dinner when they came to retrieve their daughters. He had the notes sent, then sat daydreaming of the day he had looked forward to for years—*the day he would meet his niece.*

Finally getting back to the dreaded reports after having put them off too many times already, he called for coffee and tried to get through all his solicitor had sent. Wanting all the time he could spare for his new niece and his intended was just the motivation he needed, and within a few hours the task was finally completed.

Now to wait, he thought as he nervously shuffled things around on his desk. Finding the most recent letter from Caroline he had yet to open, Bingley sighed and reached for his letter opener. Heating it in the candle then sliding it under the wax seal and straightening the pages, he sighed loudly and began to read.

> January 21, 1812
> Scarborough
>
> Dearest Brother,
>
> When can I expect you to rescue me from the ramblings and wild emotional outbursts of our most silly relation?

Hmmmm, most silly indeed, he thought.

> This harsh winter here in the north is beginning to chafe my skin, and I do not see how this could be good for my next Season in Town.
>
> I cannot imagine that you left me here to endure all of this simply because of one small incident that cannot even be proven to be my fault. How do you know it was not one of the servants rattling Lord Primrose's door handle? I feel I have been utterly failed by my brother who was meant to protect me after our dear parents' untimely deaths. How could you treat me as an unwanted member of the family, abandoning me as you have?

Angered by her selfishness, he balled the missive up and threw it into the fire, watching as it was quickly consumed by the flames. *What am I to do with her*, he thought. *I cannot subject my sweet Jane to Caroline's temper. Hurst and I have some business to discuss when he arrives, as I doubt they will want her around either, especially with a new baby. Caroline may just have to endure more time with Aunt Hamilton, whether she likes it or not.*

After pacing around his study for a few more minutes, Bingley repaired to the billiard room to work on his shots. An hour later his solo game was interrupted by Smyth, who announced visitors nearing the house. He quickly made his way to the front steps to welcome his newest family member.

Upon the Bennets' arrival at Netherfield Park, they were shown into the drawing room to await their host. Within a few minutes, a beaming Charles Bingley walked through the door with a tiny bundle in his hands.

Jane's heart caught in her chest when she saw him. *I can picture him holding our own baby,* she thought, blushing when she realized he was staring at her. His wink made her think he knew what was going through her own mind, and she blushed even more and looked to the floor.

Bingley introduced Amelia to the guests then walked over to Jane, pulling back the blanket for her to see the tiny angelic face better.

"She is beautiful," Jane whispered.

Bingley gently reached for her fingers and squeezed them, "She is all I have ever hoped for in a niece." When Jane looked up into his eyes, he quietly said, "I look forward to one day holding our own babe in my arms just like this as well."

He was soon leading Jane across the room to sit on the sofa. "My sister and brother were in need of rest, as was Amelia's nurse, so it seems I am on duty for the next hour."

Mr Bennet quipped, "Somehow, I doubt Uncle Charles minds a bit."

He chuckled and shook his head, "No, I do not mind at all." He gently kissed the forehead of the baby curled in his arms.

They all sat amicably chatting for a few minutes before Maria and Lydia joined them. Greetings were exchanged and the conversation was then turned to all the delights Brighton held for the two young travelers. The next hour easily passed with all listening to the two discuss the fashions and shops, what wonderful music they heard while walking on the promenade beside the Styne, and the young ladies' descriptions of the stops they made along the road at the posting inns. Lydia was especially excited to report on the food served in such places, saying she acquired a new recipe for their cook of the most delightful cake she had ever eaten.

The Hursts' arrival in the drawing room changed the conversation back to Amelia. When the Lucas' were announced a few minutes later, the stories were retold for all. Soon the drawing room was host to three distinct groups—the younger people, the women, and the men.

After having heard Lydia's stories three times already, Kitty slowly eased out of the group and was soon sitting alone, her drawing pad sitting open on her lap. Jonathan saw her and leaned over to Mr Bennet, quietly asking permission to go sit with her for a minute. At the older man's stern reproof that he would be watching, Jonathan walked over to the corner where she sat.

"What are you drawing Miss Kathryn?"

"Oh, Mr Lucas, you startled me!" Putting her hand on her chest, she jumped in her seat.

"I am truly sorry," he said with a small bow. "May I sit?" he indicated the chair next to her.

A small smile played on her lips as she nodded.

"What are you doing hiding over here in the corner?"

She looked back to the group of young people, Lydia enthusiastically describing something from her trip once again. "I am happy my sister is home, but…" she sighed.

"Miss Lydia is retelling, yet again, of their adventures in Brighton?"

"Yes," she answered. "I have heard the tales three times already, and a fourth is more than I can bear today."

"You always were more of a quiet person than she and Maria," he said. Wanting to break the tension he felt building, he asked, "What are you drawing?"

Kitty held up her sketch pad, "I have not had many opportunities to sketch a baby, so I was testing out my abilities."

"May I?" he asked, indicating the pad. At her nod he took it from her hands. Jonathan looked over the rough outline, regarding the mouth she was currently working on. Handing it back, he said, "You have captured the babe's mouth perfectly."

"I was hoping to give this to Mr and Mrs Hurst as a gift, if it is nice enough when I am finished that is."

He smiled and looked over to the happy father holding his daughter in his arms. "I think they will love it." Catching Mr Bennet's eye, he knew his time was over, so he stood and bowed, "I will not keep you from your activity any longer," then he went back to join the group of men on the other side of the room.

Kitty sighed and tried to return to her sketch, but her inspiration had faltered. Turning to a new page, she quickly sketched out the group on the other side of the room, focusing on the gentleman to whom she was quickly losing her young heart.

Sarah Johnson

Wednesday, February 5, 1812

The sudden banging on the front door startled her from her sleep. She had not rested well the last few nights and it was taking its toll as she found herself unable to stay awake late in the afternoon. Straightening her dress and pinching her cheeks, she went downstairs to find out who had come.

She opened the door to the drawing room and smiled at her accomplice, "I have not seen *you* in a while."

He rounded on her, fire in his eyes, as he loudly cursed and pounded his fist on the nearby table, "I was unable to carry out my plan as *the girl* left Brighton unexpectedly. From what she told me a few weeks ago, they were to stay until at least next week, but I spent all day yesterday waiting for our appointed meeting, only to learn from a maid in the house that she and her friend left already."

Sitting in the chair, Mrs Younge calmly stated, "I did not have much faith in your plan, so it is of no consequence. We have more important things to discuss right now, like our plans for her sister, *Mrs Darcy*. Please sit and I will tell you what it is I need you to do."

He continued to pace until he heard her clear her throat, then he quickly sat down, "What are we doing now?"

"We need to know what the area is like so we can plan the best options for an accident," she replied. The next part of her plan for him was laid out, and he soon found himself downing drinks in a nearby pub, angry that he was unable to carry out his design once again. *Lydia Bennet, you will pay dearly for your treatment of me*, he said to himself. *You cannot push me aside and assume I will forgo my intentions. I will find a way to ruin you and your family, and there is nothing your rich brother-in-law can do about it this time.*

Thursday, February 6, 1812

Fitz knocked on his brother's door, and, upon being bid enter, he saw Alex standing in front of the mirror fussing with his already straightened cravat. "If you keep playing with it you will have to call John back in to undo the mess you are bound to make of that cravat."

Turning, Alex gestured to his clothes and asked, "Does this look… fashionable?"

"I am sure the horse will not care whether your waistcoat matches or not," he joked.

After giving him a stern look, Alex turned back to the mirror. "I will be riding in the carriage with Darcy, Elizabeth, and Georgiana, and we are to go to Longbourn this evening for Miss Lydia's birthday celebration."

"Ahhh, yes, Miss Lydia did say her father promised her a birthday dinner because of her early return home from Brighton. That explains why you have dinner attire on so early in the morning. I take it this is what you plan to wear?"

"Yes, that was my intention. I just received these from the tailor," he indicted the new breeches and coat. "I am not certain if I like this new knot John has put in my cravat though," he said, once again fussing with it.

Raising his eyebrow, Fitz replied, "I am sure you will be the talk of every parlor in Meryton, big brother!"

"Ha, ha, Fitz. If I were not in my new jacket I would whip you for that statement."

"It might be a good fight, but you would never win against me," he smirked, quickly putting his older brother at ease with his teasing.

Alex smiled and turned back around, "Help me off with this jacket. We are to leave in an hour and I have too much left to do before then."

"Do you have a plan yet?"

"Yes, but I may need your help in holding back from what I truly wish to do," Alex replied.

"And what would that be?"

He smirked, "I am sure you can well imagine."

The ride to Meryton was cold, but at least he was distracted with Georgiana's nearly constant chatter of all Bingley had written of the week leading up to the wedding.

Bingley was not one to do anything without much aplomb, and his wedding was no exception. He had invited so many that every room at the local inn was taken while a few of his closest friends, as well as some of his intended's family, would be staying at Netherfield Park, filling the guest and family rooms there as well.

They arrived and Bingley immediately met them at the door with a warm welcome, his niece in his arms. After showing her off to his dearest friends, he let Alex take Georgiana upstairs to get settled. Elizabeth joined them as well in hopes of resting for a little while before they would need to dress for the evening ahead.

"I hope you brought your hounds, Darcy, as we are to have a fox hunt in a few days."

"I did not see much of a point in bringing them all the way from Derbyshire in the middle of winter, but my cousin did insist we bring our firearms."

"Yes, yes, good point. Perhaps the pups Mr Bennet's dog had a few months ago will be ready to train?"

Darcy chuckled at his friend. Obviously he was so distracted with the preparations for his wedding that he was not thinking properly. A pup of such a young age as the ones born in the autumn would not be old enough to do anything but get under the horses feet and cause an accident. He knew his friend was well aware of this fact, but it was clear he was not thinking clearly at the moment. He decided not to bring it up though, so he followed along after him silently as Bingley continued to tell of the other activities they were to partake of this next week.

"So let me see… we will have a fox hunt and some shooting for the men, and of course a ball for my most cherished angel."

"Of course," Darcy nodded.

"Louisa suggested an evening musicale. You will never guess who she has found to come all the way from London just to regale us with their talents?"

Bingley did not even stop for Darcy to give an answer, but he would have guessed correctly if given the chance. His friend had been a fan of the troupe for years and used them at several gatherings in Town.

Alex walked in just in time to hear Bingley say, "One evening we are to enjoy games. I especially look forward to the game we played at the Bennets' a few months ago. Do you remember? It was quite a sensation, was it not?"

"Yes, it was! I even won a handkerchief," Alex said as he patted his pocket, where he happened to have his prized handkerchief right now.

"Only because you are as big as a giant," Darcy smirked.

"I am shocked you remember anything of that night other than your own happiness."

Bingley turned to his friend with a big smile, "That is right—that is the night you became engaged."

He smiled in remembrance, then joked, "Well, I do try to keep abreast of varying topics of interest. I doubt I will ever forget your impression of

Jack the Giant Killer, including how much you resembled a giant next to the notably petite Miss Mary Long." He laughed, "I dare say you will treasure that handkerchief for many years."

"Yes, it is quite a memorable day—for all of us." Alex's memories tended towards the details of the moment he met the lady who had since stolen his heart, though she in turn did not yet return the sentiment. *One day*, he thought, *one day she will love me.*

The friendly banter continued until it was time to begin preparations for the evening. They were just coming into the hall to go upstairs when Mr Bennet was announced. He greeted them and said he needed to speak with Darcy.

CHAPTER

XIX

At exactly four o'clock in the afternoon a curricle pulled up in front of Longbourn and a man of average size descended. His trunk was taken from the back of the carriage by one of Longbourn's footmen, and the man was escorted to the sitting room by the butler.

"Reverend William Collins to see you, sir," Hill said and then left the room.

Bennet was surprised to hear who had come to visit, and on such a day as today! He stood and bowed, welcoming their guest and introducing his wife to his cousin.

Mr Collins immediately began speaking, almost as if he were quoting a well thought out speech. "I thank you, sir. The disagreement subsisting between yourself and my late honoured father always gave me much uneasiness, and since I have had the misfortune to lose him I have frequently wished to heal the breach; but for some time I was kept back by my own doubts, fearing lest it might seem disrespectful to his memory for me to be on good terms with any one with whom it had always pleased him to be at variance.

My mind however is now made up on the subject, for having received ordination at Easter, I have been so fortunate as to be distinguished by the patronage of the Right Honourable Lady Catherine de Bourgh, widow of Sir Lewis de Bourgh, whose bounty and beneficence has preferred me to the valuable rectory of this parish, where it shall be my earnest endeavor to demean myself with grateful respect towards her Ladyship, and be ever ready to perform those rites and ceremonies which are instituted by the Church of England."

When he stopped to take a breath, Bennet tried to interrupt, but the man continued on as if he did not hear him.

"As a clergyman, moreover, I feel it my duty to promote and establish the blessing of peace in all families within the reach of my influence; and on these grounds I flatter myself that my present overtures of good-will are highly commendable, and that the circumstance of my being next in the entail of Longbourn estate will be kindly overlooked on your side, and not lead you to reject the offered olive branch. I cannot be otherwise than concerned at being the means of injuring your amiable daughters, and beg leave to apologize for it, as well as to assure you of my readiness to make them every possible amends. I am very sensible of the hardship to my fair cousins, and could say much on the subject, but that I am cautious of appearing forward and precipitate. But I can assure the young ladies that I come prepared to admire them. At present I will not say more, but perhaps when we are better acquainted..."

"Mr Collins," Bennet was finally about to interrupted, "my daughters are not at home presently, and since you have not been formally introduced, I would prefer if you would refrain from discussing them. We are to have a gathering this evening and you are welcome to join us and our neighbors in celebration. I am certain you would like to rest now, so I will have Mr Hill show you to your room."

A little confused after being interrupted in his practiced soliloquy, he replied, "Yes, I thank you."

Before he could start again, Bennet called the butler and had his cousin led from the room.

He had wondered for years if William Collins was anything like his father, and it was clear from just their introduction that he was every bit as inept. But there was something else about the man that bothered him. He was glad Jane and Mary would be staying at Netherfield Park this week. *I will have to keep a close eye on Kitty and Lydia and make sure he is not often in their presence.*

He expressed a need to speak with his wife in private, and she said she would join him in his study after she went to inform the cook of their added guest.

Susannah soon entered his study. He was in a chair by the fire, reading. "Henry, dear, what is it you needed to see me about?"

"Please close the door and sit here with me; I have something of import to discuss with you."

She did as he bid, patiently waiting on her husband to begin.

He did not want to frighten her, and he was not sure how to bring this up. He finally decided to just come right out with his suspicions. "There is something about that man I do not trust."

"Oh, Henry, I am so glad you brought this up; I do not trust him either."

"I do not wish him to be around our girls. We are fortunate in that Jane and Mary will be away this week, but I do not want him exposed to Kitty or Lydia either without one of us present.

"With so many others around, surely he would not have a chance to be solely in their presence. Perhaps you should go to Netherfield and speak with William?"

"Yes, I will do just that."

Susannah stood and kissed his cheek. "I will have the girls all dress in Jane's room when they return from Meryton. Oh, I do hope the shop has shoe roses! I cannot imagine what a fuss it will be if they do not."

Bennet stood to find the letter from his cousin on his desk and read through it once again. He did not remember any mention of him visiting, but perhaps he missed it? The letter was a bit ridiculous and he had skimmed parts of it in his haste to get through the eight pages the man had written. The man was a pompous sycophant who constantly spoke of his love for his patroness. Bennet thought to himself, *how could I be related to this idiotic man?*

After reading the letter again, assured he had not missed the announcement of his arrival, he left to speak with Darcy.

"Welcome, welcome," Mr Bennet said as he opened the door. He reached out to hug Elizabeth, then bowed to Georgiana in Alex's arms, "Miss Darcy, it is a pleasure to see you again. Lord Primrose, always nice to have you join our family as well." Then he turned to his son-in-law, "Darcy, I am pleased you could make it in time for our gathering."

"I am sorry my business kept us from arriving earlier in the week, sir," he replied.

"I am sure we will have plenty of time to catch up over the next few weeks. You are still to stay on at Netherfield Park after Mr Bingley and Jane are wed?"

"Yes, we are to stay until after Easter, then we will return to Town for the Season."

He smiled and looked to his daughter, "I am happy to hear you will be here for a time." He turned to the others, "Follow me and I will forge a way through the crowd to Miss Darcy's chair."

Alex looked around at the many familiar faces as he followed Mr Bennet to the drawing room. As he came around a doorway, he nearly dropped Georgiana when he saw Mary on the other side of the room smiling and talking with a young gentleman he did not recognize.

"Alex?" Georgiana said when he stopped. "Are you well?"

Shaking his head, he looked back at his cousin, "W...what was that? Did you say something?"

"Are you well?" she asked again.

"Oh… y-yes." He continued on to the chair Mr Bennet now stood beside. When Georgiana was settled, he excused himself from the room. Not knowing where to go, he wandered around for half an hour until the announcement was made for everyone to gather in the drawing room. As he stood at the back of the crowd, he saw Mary standing next to the unknown young man once again.

Mr Bennet stood in the front of the room, his family all around him, and welcomed all to the evening's celebrations. Then he invited everyone to join the dance floor, saying Darcy and Elizabeth had agreed to lead the first.

Music could be heard throughout the house as the musicians began warming up and the floor was cleared for the dancers. Alex slowly made his way around the perimeter of the room, drawn into the scene before him of Mary partnering this same unknown gentleman on the dance floor. His heart dropped and he made his way outside for some air. He walked around the garden, but could still see the dancers through the windows. He was unsure if she was truly enjoying herself or not, but one thing was for certain—she was much more at ease with this young man than she ever was in his company.

He soon found Darcy, informed him he did not feel well and returned to Netherfield. He was determined to get through this next week for his friend's sake, then he would leave for London at the first opportunity.

Bennet was trying to enjoy himself, but his cousin was a constant at his side and told so many plays in his chess games that he lost four times. He finally decided to give up playing this evening and decided to walk around. When he saw his daughter standing by her friend and talking, he sighed heavily. An introduction must be made, so he might as well dispense with it now. He led his cousin over to the ladies.

"Miss Lucas, it is good to see you this evening. Elizabeth," he smiled and kissed her cheek.

She eyed the man standing by her father's side.

"Mr Collins, may I present my second daughter and her dear friend Miss Lucas. Standing by my daughter's side of course is her husband, Mr Fitzwilliam Darcy."

Bowing with each introduction made, Mr Collins stopped abruptly with the last one. "Mr Darcy, I am especially pleased to make your acquaintance. I have had the privilege since the spring to be well acquainted with your family. Your aunt, Lady Catherine de Bourgh, has become my patroness…"

As Mr Collins continued to speak, Darcy's ears began to ring with the nasally voice. *Does this fool think I will be impressed? I have not met someone as conceited, pompous, narrow-minded, and dare I say, silly, before now. I think you have outdone yourself with this choice, Aunt Catherine.*

Bennet saw that his cousin would not stop speaking, so he interrupted him and led the man away. It would not do to annoy Darcy after just traveling here today. More introductions were made to the other neighbors, but Mr Collins continued to fawn over the nephew of his patroness at every opportunity.

Friday, February 7, 1812

Most of the locals would be visiting Netherfield Park for some of the activities, but a few, Jane and Mary, as well as Charlotte and Jonathan Lucas, would be staying there for the week. Charlotte was to share a room with Jane, and Mary, once again, would be with Georgiana.

Bingley took on the task of ensuring their stay was perfect by outfitting their rooms to fulfill their every need and insisting flowers from the hot house be placed within daily.

With great anticipation, the two sisters' trunks were loaded and they were on their way early that morning. They both looked forward to spending more time with Elizabeth, and Mary was excited to stay with Georgiana again, though she was a bit apprehensive about the viscount once again visiting at the same time.

The first thing Jane noticed about the room was the pale lilac color of the wallpaper. It was such a lovely color—one of her favorite colors actually, though she had never told Charles. *How did he know?*

Jane's thoughts were interrupted with a familiar knock to the open door and immediately she knew who chose this room—*Elizabeth. Of course she would know which room would make me most comfortable during the upcoming week.*

The two greeted each other with great affection, then they settled onto the fainting couch to discuss what letters could not convey since Jane's return from London a month ago.

They were interrupted by a knock at the door and a servant entering with another trunk, followed by the person to whom it belonged.

"Charlotte! Oh I am so pleased you decided to stay here this week."

"I feel rather odd staying when I am not that close a friend to Mr Bingley," she said with trepidation.

Elizabeth waited until the footman left the room, then she closed the door and ushered her friend over to the sofa, "Mr Bingley is such a solicitous gentleman that he could not fathom refusing such a simple request from me."

Jane sighed, "Yes, he is very solicitous."

"Oh my—now we are to come to the fawning over Mr Bingley part of our morning," Elizabeth joked. "Well, let us get it over with. Tell us Jane, what is it you love most about Mr Bingley?"

Jane blushed and looked at Charlotte, who returned the inquisitive look Elizabeth had. She knew they would never leave her alone until their curiosity was assuaged, so she sighed and began. "I know he is considered by many to be a handsome man, but that is not what first drew me to him. If I had to say one thing, it is the way in which he cherishes every word I speak. I do not speak my mind as easily as either of you, and yet he esteems what I say above all others. It is like no other feeling to have someone treat you as if their world is brightened just by your smile."

Charlotte sighed and leaned back on the couch, her hand dramatically held up to her forehead, "Oh my! If it were not for Lizzy's hatred of poetry, I would say we should begin quoting their common lines of love conquering all right now."

The three laughed and continued talking until Charlotte gave the excuse of needing to speak with her brother and left the two sisters alone once again.

"I think she is lonely, Lizzy."

"Yes, I saw it in her eyes as well. First I marry and move away, and now you are to marry as well. She despairs that being the oldest single female in the area, and her family's lack of connections and opportunity to travel to find a husband, has burdened her with spinsterhood."

"We must do something about it. Will you promise to help me find Charlotte a nice gentleman this coming Season in London?"

"I will try, but I have already invited her to stay with us and she refuses, saying she does not wish to add such a burden to my first Season as Mrs Darcy, especially with Mary's visit already determined." She turned back to the door, "We must do something though."

"Yes, we simply must. Perhaps she will accept an invitation from me?"

Elizabeth hugged her sister, "Oh Jane, you are too good. No one would wish to intrude upon you just a few weeks into your marriage. We will find a way though. Perhaps it is time we speak with Jonathan about it and see if he has anything to add to our arguments to tip the scales in our favor."

Jane smiled, "Yes, I hope he does. I will speak with Charles as well—he may have an idea."

Sarah Johnson

CHAPTER

XX

After seeing to the needs of her two daughters that had left for Netherfield this morning, Susannah spent the remainder of the day trying to avoid her husband's cousin, choosing instead to walk to Meryton with Kitty and Lydia and visit a few of the shops.

While in the milliner's shop they saw her sister enter, and, true to form, they felt her staring at them immediately. She never said a word, but she did not need to—her glares spoke volumes. Miranda was still upset over not receiving an invitation to Elizabeth's private wedding ceremony and had been belittling Susannah to all who would listen ever since.

Now with Jane about to be married as well, the old grudges were renewed and Miranda was spreading her lies once again. It was too much for Susannah's frayed nerves, so she and her girls returned home without making any purchases. She would much rather listen to the never-ending prattle of Mr Collins than have to put up with her sister today.

Sarah Johnson

Bennet held out his hand for Susannah to step down from the carriage and he nearly tripped over his cousin when he stepped back. Why does the man stand so close to me? Susannah drew his attention when she wrapped her arm around his, and he looked down to smile at his wife. Just as his presence had a calming effect on Susannah's nerves, he found she made his patience for Mr Collins stretch just a little more than was his wont.

When I first read his letter, I thought I would enjoy the diversions of this fool, but he is quickly growing burdensome. I pray this week passes quickly and I am able to present the papers and usher him out my door with haste. If he sneezes one more time, I may just go mad.

Just as Bennet was thinking it, Mr Collins sneezed and very loudly blew his nose, then wiped his forehead and stuffed the handkerchief back into his pocket.

"Are we ready then?" At their nod, Bennet led them into the house and began the required introductions.

That evening after dinner, the guests were entertained by Bingley's favorite musical troupe. As Charlotte closed her eyes and listened to the music sweep over the room, she felt someone watching her. When she opened her eyes, she did not notice anyone. Ignoring the uneasiness, she closed her eyes again and listened again to the lilting tunes.

Lucas saw a familiar gentleman on the other side of the room observing his eldest sister. *Hmmm… I wonder…* As he continued to observe the crowd, another set of eyes often found his sister's form as well. His stomach knotted with the leering way the second man looked at her. There was something about him that unsettled Jonathan greatly.

When the singing ended and everyone ambled about, Lucas made his way over to Darcy. "I have not had the pleasure of being introduced to all in attendance here this evening."

Darcy watched as Lucas eyed Collins standing on the other side of the room. "Believe me when I say, you do not wish for the acquaintance."

"Oh? And why is that?"

He nodded in the man's direction and quietly replied, "*That* is Mr Bennet's cousin."

"Ahhh, the one to whom he must present his case for Longbourn? I did not know he would be in attendance this week."

"He showed up unannounced and has been fawning all over my family since his arrival. It seems his patroness is my aunt, so he is determined to pass on her well-wishes with every breath that escapes his lips." He watched the man for a minute, then added, "There is something unnerving about him. I just do not trust this feeling."

"I thought the same when I saw him observing my eldest sister during the performance."

Darcy looked straight at his friend, "Lucas, you must do anything you can to keep him away from your sister."

"I will do just that. Thank you." He noticed Elizabeth staring at the two and he smiled, "I think your wife is trying to garner your attention."

"*That* she always has," he said.

Lucas chuckled, "I imagine so. I will leave you to her then." He walked around the room and eventually made his way to Lord Ashbourne.

"Welcome to the neighborhood, my lord."

"I thank you, sir."

"Are you enjoying your stay so far?"

"I arrived just before the dinner hour, but I can assure you I am sufficiently diverted. When Bingley said he would have a fox hunt, I could not pass up the opportunity, especially with a ball and a wedding as well."

"I did not take you for a sentimental type, my lord."

He chuckled, "Neither did I, but as I have grown older I see things a little differently than when I was a decade younger."

The evening soon came to an end and everyone retired speaking of the superb music they had listened to and the new acquaintances they had met.

***

Saturday, February 8, 1812

The sun shone bright through the dining room windows. Jane was met at the door by Bingley, who immediately offered to escort her to a seat, retrieving a plate of food from the sideboard for each of them. She and Charlotte stayed up for hours speaking of all that happened over the last few months, and Charlotte opened up about her personal struggles with still being single. Jane was determined she would find someone for her friend, and the sooner the better as Charlotte's disposition could use some cheering.

Jane carefully watched the newcomers as they came in the door, asking Bingley about each of them. Two were married and came with their wives and young children, and the rest were single gentlemen whom he had known for years; a few brought their sisters with them also. Bingley told her of their families and their estates, but was curious as to why she would want to know.

Upon his questioning her, she told him of her desire to see her friend Charlotte meet someone, and Bingley's face brightened. He knew just the person, but assured his intended that the two were already acquainted from Charlotte's stay in London—his longtime friend Lord Ashbourne. He was engaged six years ago, but, before they could marry, his intended died of scarlet fever. He had since distanced himself from the marriage market. While his duty to Parliament kept him in Town, he rarely attended social functions. Bingley only managed to convince him to come to Netherfield Park because of Ash's love for fox hunting and his own wedding.

Jane and Bingley decided that offending the earl would not do, so they set out only to encourage the two silently and see where it led from there. If it was meant to be, then it would be up to them, but they would offer as many opportunities as possible for the two to become friends.

As Charlotte came through the door, Bingley rose and offered to escort her to a seat. He strategically placed her near Lord Ashbourne. When he again took his seat beside Jane, the two were cordially speaking. Bingley looked to his cohort and they both shared a smile at their seeming success.

The morning was meant to be one for relaxing out of doors, but for Henry Bennet it had already proven to be headache producing. He now rode his horse to Netherfield Park to join Bingley's guests and the gentlemen of the neighborhood on a shooting expedition. Unfortunately, he had been awakened rather early with his dogs barking at something unknown outside. Their noise woke the entire household, including Mr Collins, and as a result Mr Bennet's ears were assaulted with the nasally sounds he had come to associate with the sycophantic man much too early. Oh if only his brother Gardiner were already here, then they would laugh about the man and all would be more easily forgotten, but the Gardiners were not to arrive until later today.

Arriving at Netherfield Park, he was greeted by the group already forming in the front yard, and introductions were made for his cousin once again.

Darcy leaned over slightly and quietly said, "I see he is still attached firmly to your side."

He gave a wry grin, "If you cared for my sanity, you would divert his attentions in some way today." When Darcy chuckled, he continued, "For now you can be counted as my favorite son-in-law, but whether you continue to be held in such esteem after this week is yet to be determined."

Darcy raised his eyebrow, "I believe my cousin would divert Mr Collins' attention adequately."

"Now *that* might just keep you in good standing with me. I am happy to be on the proper end of your offer and I cannot but feel sorry for your cousin."

When Charlotte came down the stairs to join the other ladies who gathered, Mr Collins pushed himself through the crowd to greet her.

"Miss Lucas, I am pleased to see you again. It has been my greatest pleasure to remember the conversation we shared just last evening. I have even worked what we spoke of into three sermons and greatly look forward to delivering such inspiring words when I return to my patroness, the Right Honourable Lady Catherine de Bourgh…"

Jonathan and Darcy were able to rescue Charlotte from the clutching hands of the parson, and Charlotte blushed as Jonathan led her through the crowd of gentlemen assembled. Her eyes met those of Lord Ashbourne as they passed near where he stood, and he bowed in greeting, a small smile on his face. She returned the greeting and soon found herself inside with Elizabeth, her cheeks glowing in embarrassment.

Alex saw the young gentleman he recognized as being Mary's dance partner from the other night. He was standing near Jonathan Lucas, so Alex made his way over to his friend, "Mr Lucas, I was hoping you were to join us for grouse shooting today." He then looked to the other man, hoping an introduction would be offered.

Bowing in greeting, Jonathan replied, "Lord Primrose, it is always a pleasure to see you." Noticing where his eyes trailed, Jonathan offered,

"May I present my brother, Mr James Lucas." He turned to his brother announcing, "Mr Darcy's cousin, Viscount Primrose."

Bowing deeply, just as his father Sir William Lucas always did, James' face flushed and he excitedly replied, "It is a great pleasure to meet such an honored and distinguished gentleman such as yourself, my lord."

Alex tried not to laugh at the younger man's ridiculous reaction to his being a viscount, "Yes, thank you." James excused himself, then turned around and walked away, and Alex quietly asked Jonathan, "I take it your brother has not been exposed to many peers before?"

"Unlike me, he has never been to Town with our father, nor has he had the opportunity to travel outside the small society here and the few friends he has made at Oxford," Jonathan answered.

With a mischievous look to his eye, Alex said, "I wonder how his introduction to one of higher rank than I would go. Do you care to find out?"

Jonathan smirked as he quickly turned around to catch up with his brother, "Let me introduce you to the others you might not know in this crowd," he said as they walked over to Ash. "Lord Ashbourne, may I introduce my younger brother, Mr James Lucas." Gesturing with his hand, he said to James, "This is Lord Nicholas Stratton, Earl of Ashbourne."

James was mid-bow when the realization hit of what his brother had said. His face immediately went white and he would have fallen over if not for his brother's strong hand helping him stand up straight again. James excused himself to sit down for a minute, leaving the three others to laugh at his response.

"I have never before seen such an interesting display when I was introduced to someone," Ash said, smiling at the two others.

"He was stumbling all over himself when he found out I was a viscount, so I just could not resist it, what with your being an earl and all," Alex replied.

Ash chuckled, "I believe this shall be quite an excursion. Between the parson who cannot stop talking of his noble patroness, and your brother who cannot seem to breathe in the presence of a peer, I think we shall have at least a few diverting displays today."

Alex was grateful for the distraction today held, even if he did have to share it with the ridiculous parson and the younger Lucas. As he mounted his horse he determined he would just have to shoot more grouse than Mr James Lucas—at least that he could win fair and square.

"So why have I not heard of your brother before now," Alex asked Jonathan as they rode beside each other.

"Well, my brother is… how shall I put this… he does not hold our family in much esteem. So when a holiday from school arrives, he seeks out other opportunities than coming back home. He is here this time only because my father insisted on his presence as he is taking a semester off from his studies."

"So he is not particularly attached to the neighborhood? Or anyone in it?"

Jonathan understood exactly what he was asking, and laughed heartily, "Goodness, no! My brother is in no way ready to give up his bachelorhood and settle down. Honestly, I doubt he will be ready even a decade from now. He still does not even know what field he wishes to go into, thus his break from school. I thought perhaps your brother might offer some advice towards the military."

He chuckled, "With his reaction to the earl, I doubt he would do well, what with all the younger sons of peers taking many officers positions." The unease he had felt for day vanished and his confidence rose. Perhaps he still did have a chance with Miss Mary.

CHAPTER

XXI

Hurst was certain he was wrong… *no, it could not have been the same man,* he thought. Feeling a sense of foreboding, he knew he needed to find out for certain. He told Bingley he was not feeling well and would meet them back at Netherfield, then he distanced himself from the hunting party to better see the wood in the distance. Far to the right he could just make out Longbourn, and the trees among which he had seen the movements were abutted against the estate's back garden. If it truly was who he thought, word would need to be sent to Colonel Fitzwilliam immediately.

He kept a close watch on the wood and was rewarded with another glimpse of activity. Slowing his horse, he watched the eerily familiar outline of the man as he went from tree to tree, obviously watching Longbourn.

Not wanting to alert the man to his presence, Hurst quietly turned around and rode back to Netherfield, quickly made his way to his brother's study, and wrote a note for Colonel Fitzwilliam. Then he found the butler to have it dispatched immediately. *Do I need to alert Mr Bennet of what I have seen? Maybe I am just overreacting and should wait on a response from Colonel Fitzwilliam first.* He thought of his little daughter and knew how he would feel as a father if someone kept such news from him. So instead of waiting, he wrote another note, sent a footman to catch up with the shooting party, and left to again follow the man he had seen.

Mr Henry Bennet was having a hard time keeping up with the younger men, the stiffness in his leg starting to bother him. When a footman arrived with a note for him, he was grateful for the rest, until he opened it and read the words within.

> Mr Bennet,
>
> Please do not cause alarm, but I need you to immediately join me at the convergence of Netherfield Park and Longbourn along the line of the wood. Make haste, but as I said, do not cause alarm. Come alone.
>
> Sincerely,
> David Hurst

Curious as to what it could be, and immediately wondering if it had something to do with the noise his dogs alerted them to early that morning, he excused himself from the party claiming fatigue and made his way back towards Longbourn. When he saw Hurst waiting at the wood, he quickly rode over to join him. "What is wrong?"

Hurst stepped down from his horse and replied, "I cannot go into all the details now, but come with me… quietly."

The two tied their horses to a tree and Bennet followed until they were deep in the wood, very close to Longbourn's back garden. Hurst stopped and placed a finger over his mouth indicating they should remain silent. They slowly crept through the wood, careful of stepping on twigs. As they got closer to the garden wall another figure came into focus. Hurst again stopped and indicated this was who they were following. They watched the man for a few minutes, but as he was just sitting there, Hurst saw no point in remaining any longer. Quietly, he led the older man back out of the wood and to their horses. "Come with me and I will explain," he said as they mounted, then rode off towards Netherfield Park.

Mr Bennet followed, still not sure what was going on, but determined to find out what he could. As they made their way through the house to Mr Bingley's study, he tried to calm his racing heart. As soon as the door closed, he demanded, "Tell me what is going on!"

Hurst turned to the older man and replied, "Colonel Fitzwilliam was in Brighton the last few days we were there, and he rode back with us as far as London. As we rode beside the carriage, he alerted me to the fact that he had seen a man following Miss Lydia and Miss Maria. I did not remember seeing anything out of the ordinary, but the sketch he showed me of the man was someone I did recognize seeing about the city. It is the same man I now see scoping out the wood behind Longbourn. I thought I saw his familiar figure earlier, and I left the shooting party to see if I was correct. I followed him through the trees and when I noticed how close to Longbourn he was, I knew I needed to alert someone to his presence. So I came back here and dispatched an express to Colonel Fitzwilliam, then wrote the note to you."

"What could he want?" Mr Bennet asked, fear gripping his heart as his hands began to shake.

Hurst led the older man to a chair and answered, "I do not know, but we will find out. The name he bandied around Brighton was that of George Wilson, though the colonel does not think it is his real name."

"George Wilson... *George Wilson*...," he said out loud while he thought. "I do not recognize that name."

Hurst sat down at the desk and pulled out a piece of paper. "I am going to make note of everything we saw and perhaps the colonel will know what to do next."

"I need to let Sir William Lucas know, as you say he was following his daughter in Brighton also."

"I would prefer to keep this between us until the colonel arrives. I cannot know for sure if he was following Miss Lydia, Miss Maria, or both, but for now he seems to be focusing on Longbourn."

Nodding his head, Mr Bennet distractedly replied, "Yes, that does seem to be his focus today."

Hurst asked if he saw anything unusual the last few days.

"We were awakened rather early this morning with a commotion in the wood—my dogs were quite determined something was there. When we searched though, nothing was found, so we returned home. Now I am convinced it was this man."

Hurst wrote that detail down on the paper, then handed it to Mr Bennet asking if he had anything else to add. Upon the older gentleman's response that he did not, Hurst rose and fixed two drinks, handing one to Mr Bennet. The two sat in silence until an hour later when the shooting party returned.

As they were going out of the room to join the others, Mr Bennet said, "When I return home I will alert my staff to keep watch of the wood, and I will keep my daughters in the company of others, either at home or here at Netherfield Park, until we know why this man is here."

"That is a good idea." Hurst answered.

"Fitz!" Hugh called as he saw his youngest son come in and start up the stairs.

Turning, he answered, "Yes Father?"

"Here," Hugh said, handing him a letter, "this came express for you about an hour ago."

Looking at the address, he was curious—it said Netherfield Park, but he did not recognize the writing as that of Alex, Darcy, or Bingley. Addressing his father again, he asked, "It came by express, you say?"

"Yes; I knew you would be here within the hour so I did not have it sent over to your office."

Waving it in the air, he replied, "I was not there anyway. Well, I shall never know what it is about until I open it. Thank you." He again started up the stairs, tearing into the missive.

> Saturday, February 8, 1812
> Netherfield Park, Hertfordshire
>
> Colonel Fitzwilliam,
>
> While out with a shooting party today, my eye was caught by some movement in the wood. After investigating what it could be, I saw the familiar form of the man from your sketch. He was in the wood that abuts the back garden of Longbourn. Please hasten your return to Netherfield, as I have a bad feeling about this situation.
>
> Sincerely,
> David Hurst

Cursing loudly, he grabbed a small valise and started throwing a change of clothes into it, calling for his valet. When the man came into the room he replied, "I must leave immediately. Finish packing my trunk and have it sent to Netherfield Park." When the man did not start fast enough he cried, "Make haste man! Make haste!" Finishing his own packing, he left to tell his father of his early departure.

He knocked abruptly and was bid enter. While putting on his greatcoat, he replied, "I have business to which I must attend immediately. I am having my trunk sent on to Netherfield Park as we planned to be there in two days time anyway."

Standing, Hugh asked, "Is everything well?"

"Yes, why would it not be?" Fitz answered with practiced ease.

"The express letter was from Netherfield Park, though I did not recognize the writing," Hugh replied.

With a hug, Fitz said, "Everything will be well; I promise. I must go now."

Hugh responded with a hug in return and said, "Stay safe, son."

"I always do," Fitz assured him as he donned his hat and grabbed his valise. "I will see you Monday when you arrive."

On his way out of Town he stopped to check on Lieutenant Denny in hopes that he was well enough to take on this new assignment.

"Are you certain you are healed enough for this? If not, I will find someone else."

"Sir, I am well enough to take on such a lush assignment as following someone around. Believe me, a few bruised ribs is nothing compared to other injuries I have sustained in my service to the Crown. There is only so much of lying around a soldier can take."

Fitz chuckled, "Yes, I understand your sentiment." He sat to write down where he would be, giving it to the officer, "George Wilson is the name he was going by when I ran into him in Brighton, though it might not be the same in Meryton. I will have to keep my distance, as I am certain he would recognize me. If you need me however, you can send a note to Netherfield Park," he said, indicating what he wrote.

Denny winced when he straightened his back to salute.

The colonel looked questioningly at him and queried, "Are you certain you are ready for duty?"

"Yes sir, I am ready."

He shook his head, mumbling to himself as he readied the necessary papers. When the task was completed, he handed them to the lieutenant, "I think it best you take a well-sprung carriage instead of riding."

"Yes sir."

He gave a nod, though he still felt it might be too much so soon after his injuries. With a salute, he dismissed the lieutenant and left for Meryton.

Upon his arrival at Netherfield Park, Fitz assured Hurst of assigning his best soldier to follow the scoundrel. A note was sent to Mr Bennet, and while it did slightly ease his fears, he was still on edge.

Sarah Johnson

CHAPTER

XXII

Monday, February 10, 1812

B ingley was coming out of the drawing room, where some of his house guests were gathered, when he heard a commotion at the front entrance. Hoping it was nothing major, he walked that direction. He came around the corner to a tirade he did not expect.

"CHARLES! I do not know WHAT I have done to deserve such treatment, but I *refuse* to return anywhere with *that woman*!" Caroline shouted, pointing outside to their elderly aunt.

Bingley turned around to see their Aunt Hamilton directing the footman as to which trunk was hers. He turned back, imploring his sister, "Be quiet Caroline; she will hear you!"

"I do not care *who* hears me," she yelled back. "I *never* want to be left to her *nerves* again!"

Standing taller, Bingley sternly addressed his obviously less than repentant sister, "Whether you would prefer it or not, you will have to find somewhere else to live when I am married as I will not have you turning my wife into a puppet for your own fancies." He turned around and walked outside to welcome his newest visitor. Bowing, he smiled at her, "Aunt Hamilton, it is good to see you again. Welcome to Netherfield Park."

"Oh, Charlie, how I have missed you," she said as she hugged him. Tears were seen in her eyes as she pulled away, her ever present handkerchief waving already as she said, "I was so happy to hear of your engagement. I hope you have chosen a lady who will cherish your love just as you deserve. Oh my nerves are on edge with all this traveling; please tell me you are happy?"

Smiling, he replied, "I am more than happy, Aunt Hamilton. In fact I can honestly say it is not difficult to love Jane, and you will see for yourself soon enough."

She heaved a big sigh of relief, "With what Caroline said of your intended, I was not certain what she would be like." Leaning in as if she were telling a secret, but not lowering her voice any, she continued, "I have heard tales the likes of which you would not believe about her mother's nervous condition. Why Caroline says it would even put me to shame. Then there were stories about a father who cannot be bothered to rein in his wild daughters. It is difficult to determine what is truth and what is fiction. I cannot imagine you connecting yourself to such a family."

With a stern look at his sister, who was haranguing a footman in the foyer, he replied, "I cannot imagine why Caroline has told you such lies, but let me assure you Aunt Hamilton, the Bennets are all wonderful people and I dare say you will get along famously with all of them, especially Mrs Bennet. My dear Jane is a model of comportment and dignity—she is an angel."

With her hand on her heart, she replied in an exaggerated manner, "Oh I am so glad you have made such a match! Oh, my! Where are my salts?"

Bingley sagely took her arm and led her inside to a seat. "When you catch your breath, maybe you would prefer to retire for a little while? We will have some entertainments later today, and I am certain you will wish to be well rested."

Nodding her head in agreement, with her handkerchief still waving through the air, she replied, "Yes, yes, that is just what we need." Standing, she loudly pronounced, "Come Caroline, you will sit with me and read for an hour while we rest from that long trek through our lovely country. Then we will seek out this new grandniece of mine and will enjoy getting to know her."

Caroline started to say something when she was stopped by Bingley, "I have placed you in adjoining green rooms. Mrs Benson will lead the way."

"Wh… what of my room before?" Caroline cried.

"That has been given to Lucy, Amelia's nurse. We could not have her so far away when the baby needs her, so Louisa placed her in the room nearest theirs."

"B… bu… but, she is a SERVANT!"

Taking his sister's arm, he turned her around and started to lead her up the stairs himself, "Yes, but Amelia is very much a part of this family, and Lucy, being her nurse, is naturally an extension of Amelia at this time. Louisa and David do not want their daughter too far from them as they are quite attached."

Caroline's face turned a shade of red Bingley had never before seen and he was glad he thought to have all breakable items removed from her room.

When he descended the stairs the last of their visitors arrived—the Earl and Countess of Rosebery. "Welcome! I am so very glad you could make it for my wedding," he said to them as they were ushered into the front hall.

"How could we miss such an event as this?" Lady Rosebery said, taking Bingley's hand in hers. She smiled, "You have been almost as a son to us at times, and I am extremely satisfied with who you have chosen. She is your perfect match."

"Now, now, dearest," the earl said, taking his wife's hand while also giving her his handkerchief. He turned to Bingley, "She has been emotional since we left London."

"Perhaps you would like to rest?"

"Yes, I am certain my wife would, I however would like to speak to my son. Can you tell me where I can find Fitz?"

Bingley put his arm out to lead Lady Rosebery up the stairs, "I believe he is in the study with Darcy." His attention focused back on the lady beside him, "I thought you would not mind being placed in the family wing—it may give you a bit more privacy as well."

She smiled and patted his hand, "Thank you."

"My Aunt Hamilton has just arrived as well, and in a little over an hour we are all to meet in the hall for an excursion to some castle ruins. It will be quite the tour…"

Hugh watched his wife's retreating form, smiling at the gentle way in which Bingley dealt with her tears, then he turned to make his way to the study to speak with Fitz. He was determined to find out what had brought him here so urgently two days ago.

<hr>

Today they would tour the countryside on horseback and in carriages, making their way to some nearby castle ruins where there would be a large bonfire to keep them warm, food and drinks, tents, chairs, and rugs. Before dark, they would return to Netherfield Park to rest, have dinner, and enjoy an evening of parlour games.

Elizabeth was speaking with Jane, Mary, and Charlotte when she heard Mr Collins' voice over the chatter around them. He was soon bowing low in front of the group, asking if he could have a moment of their time.

"What is it you need, Mr Collins?" she asked.

"My dear cousins, I am esteemed with my patroness, Lady Catherine de Bourgh, and twice she has condescended to give me her opinion on the subject of balls; and it was but the very Sunday night before I left Hunsford that she said, 'Mr Collins, if given the opportunity, you must dance. A clergyman like you must dance—choose properly, choose a gentlewoman and let her be an active sort of person,' she said to me. So it is with great delight," he turned to face Jane, "that I offer my own services in partnering you for the first dance of the ball, Miss Bennet."

"I am sorry, sir, but Mr Bingley has already asked for my hand during that dance," Jane answered.

Turning to Elizabeth, he replied, "Then I offer my services to you, for you hold the distinction of being the second born and also the wife of my grand patroness' nephew."

Smirking, Elizabeth replied, "My *husband* will be leading me out onto the floor for that dance, sir."

"I am sorry to have come too late to ask you first," Mr Collins said. He bowed to Mary, "It seems I am meant to ask for your hand then, my dear cousin, for you are the next in line of age and I would conjecture to say Lady Catherine de Bourgh would approve of my asking you."

Glaring at the hand he held out to her, Mary was saved from answering when the Fitzwilliam brothers joined the group.

Alex stepped up to her side and replied, "Mr Collins, I have already asked for Miss Mary's hand for that set. I doubt my aunt would condone your overstepping my own superior position in society for you to dance with your cousin?"

Taken aback, he replied, "Oh, no… no my lord, I shan't offend her by stepping in where you have already asked. Please accept my apologies for the implied insult."

Turning to the last female of the group, Mr Collins continued, "Miss Lucas, if you are free, I would be honoured to partner you for the first?"

Charlotte answered without any emotion showing on her face, "Yes, I am free, thank you Mr Collins."

As Collins walked away, Darcy, Bingley, Ash, and Lucas joined the group. Fitz said to Darcy, "You are always just a bit too late. You have missed one of the most discomposing conversations I have had the pleasure of witnessing."

Darcy took Elizabeth's hand, "What did I miss?"

"Mr Collins thought to condescend in asking us for our hands for the first dance of the ball."

Darcy raised his eyebrow, "All of you?"

"Yes, all of us," Elizabeth answered. "It is fortunate we were asked previously and could deny him the privilege."

Mary knew the viscount had not previously asked for her hand, but did not say anything to the others. Instead she began to inwardly fume over his assertive way of forcing her hand.

"Not all of us," Charlotte said quietly.

"I am sorry, Charlotte. Maybe he will not be too trying a partner."

Lifting her chin, she replied, "Do not pity me, Lizzy. I look forward to the ball and will dance with whoever asks for my hand as that is the purpose of a ball, is it not?"

Stepping up, Fitz bowed, "I feel I must try to save your feet from what I fear will be a mighty trampling. If you are free for the second, Miss Lucas, may I have the honour?"

"Yes you may, Colonel." Charlotte answered with a smile.

"I believe I am free for the third, if you are also available?" Alex asked with a bow.

"My dance card is filling up nicely it seems." She smiled and answered, "I would be honoured, my lord."

Ash then stepped in front of her and bowed, "If your card is not too full, would you be available for the supper dance?"

Blushing slightly, she answered, "I am available and would be glad to join you on the dance floor, my lord."

Before the group dispersed, Charlotte's dance card was sufficiently filled as to not allow Mr Collins another opportunity to dance with her. She was flattered at the attention she received from the gentlemen around her, but she was not as opposed to dancing with him as they might have thought. Mr Collins would provide a comfortable living as the parson of such a grand lady, and would one day become a part of the landed gentry, so to her, being the oldest single female in the area, his attentions were well received.

While all the others were gathering around choosing their mounts for the ride, Alex looked over to the fence and saw Mary watching a group of horses out in the field. He decided to go speak to her. He walked up to the fence, "They are gorgeous creatures, are they not?"

Startled to hear a voice beside her, Mary said, "From far away, yes, they are lovely." She turned and realized who was beside her.

He smiled and placed his hand on the railing, "Are they truly so terrifying for you?"

Remembering the mortifying way in which they met, she turned and once again looked out over the field of horses, determined to avoid him if he was just going to make fun of her.

Alex looked back to the others gathered around and leaned against the fence, his arms resting on the top and his foot cocked up on one of the lower rungs. He looked sideways at her, watching her eyes as they strenuously tried to avoid looking his direction.

Mary continued to ignore him.

Turning to face her while he still leaned on the fence, he continued, "My personal favorites are the champagnes; I have bred a few of those at Dalmeny over the years, including my mount today."

Gripping her parasol handle tighter, she closed her eyes, hoping he would take the hint and leave her alone.

Alex looked over his shoulder as the riders slowly started out on the trails. Bingley and Jane were on a pair of bays and were following closely behind a group of some friends from Town. Darcy talked Elizabeth into riding his horse Whitie while he rode beside her on another horse. Kitty and Lydia chose a pair of black and white horses, and both were in a large group of the local young people. He recognized Lord Ashbourne riding beside Jonathan Lucas, and he thought one of the ladies with them was Miss Lucas. Looking around, he caught sight of the open carriages the older ladies and Georgiana decided to put to use on this crisp day. Bingley's aunt, his own mother, and Mrs Bennet carried on speaking in an excited manner—he could only guess they were discussing details of the impending wedding. Mr Bennet and Mr Collins were close to the carriages, speaking with a group of men. *Now that is an odd individual*, Alex thought as he remembered his introduction to Mr Collins.

He looked back to Mary, "Are you not riding in the carriages with the other ladies? I am certain Georgiana would appreciate your company."

Mary put her chin higher into the air, and turned slightly away from the gentleman she was set to avoid.

He decided he would change tactics and throw out a challenge, hoping she would meet it. "It is amazing to me you have such courage, for I do not believe I have met someone with more than you, and yet you will not get anywhere near a horse."

Exasperated at his persistence, she said, "I have no desire to be near horses."

"But if you did desire it, you would find the strength to face your fears?"

She turned to him, "Yes, as you well know, my lord. I have always found that, as my sister says, *'my courage always rises with every attempt to intimidate me'*, though, unlike Elizabeth, I do not like to tempt fate by chasing after such diversions on a regular basis."

Standing straight again and towering over her much smaller frame, Alex asked, "Do I intimidate you?"

Looking him in the eyes, she answered, "No, my lord, you do not. If you will excuse me…" Mary quickly turned around and walked away to join the ladies in the last carriage. Sitting down next to Georgiana, she glanced over at Alex and turned away abruptly when he winked at her.

Alex smiled—he was successful in getting her to speak to him, even if it was dripping with disdain. He was determined to break through the stone walls erected around her heart. He walked over to his horse and patted his nose, "I think one of these days she will appreciate my fortitude in pursuing her good opinion." The horse neighed in response, and Alex jumped onto his back with practiced ease and quickly rode out to catch up to Jonathan Lucas and the group of people with him.

CHAPTER

XXIII

Lucas and Charlotte were speaking with Lord Ashbourne about the trails they would be traveling today when Alex joined them, so Jonathan asked him, "Have you seen the castle ruins we are to visit today in your previous visit to our neighborhood, my lord?"

"I was mostly at the mercy of my host and my cousin, and they rarely showed much interest in anything but Longbourn and its surrounding gardens," Alex joked. "I did venture into Meryton once on my own, but with my wonderful ability to get lost anywhere, I confined my outings mostly to places others went as well."

Ash replied, "Yes, your penchant for getting lost has generated many a tale over the years, has it not?"

Alex added with a smile, "Of course, but some of those tales are exaggerated a bit."

"Oh, I doubt that, my friend." Ash said. "So, tell me, when were you last lost, and what came of it?" Turning to Charlotte, he smiled, "I dare say this will be quite a story, Miss Lucas. I am certain it shall keep us well entertained on our ride."

"I would really rather not say," Alex replied.

"Oh no, we will have none of that; I am certain we need to hear it if you are refusing our request. Your stories are always quite diverting."

Alex knew his friend would not let him get out of this, so he finally gave in. "Well, I believe the last time I got lost was the day I left London for Netherfield Park the first time I rode this way. My carriage had a last minute repair to be made, so I decided to ride out on my own. A simple three-hour trip turned into over five hours. I became turned around twice and had to ask for directions, once from a young child who looked quite oddly at my hat."

Ash laughed, "I would think he had never seen one formed quite like Lock's forms yours for you."

Alex adjusted the hat on his head and continued, "Yes, well, my fashionable choices aside, I shall continue. Let's see, where was I—oh yes. I stopped to get something to eat, and while I was inside filling my belly, someone outside was alleviating my horse of his saddlebag. Then, while I was in the stable trying to speak with an irate stable master, a horse relieved itself while I was a bit too close; unfortunately, as my saddlebag had been stolen, I could not clean up very well."

All those listening to his tale were laughing by now and he continued in a lighthearted manner, "When I finally made it close enough to see signs pointing me in the right direction, I came upon a local individual in need of assistance, and being the kind and caring person I am, I stopped to help. I ended up with mud all over me from sliding down a hillside. You should have seen the looks I received from the butler when I finally arrived at Netherfield Park."

Ash doubled over laughing. When he was finally able to speak again, he said, "See, Miss Lucas, what did I tell you? Somehow, my friend here gets lost more often than anyone I know. It does not just stop there though, he tends to find trouble, or it finds him, on a regular basis. I am surprised his story did not include a tale of his horse throwing him, for that happens often enough, too."

The group continued to laugh and talk all the way to the ruins. Lucas could tell Charlotte was a bit uneasy about something at first, but he was not sure what it could be. By the time they arrived at their destination, she settled into a cordial countenance, so he decided to put off speaking with her about it until later when he could be assured of their privacy.

Sir William Lucas and Henry Bennet were trying to speak with William Collins, but getting anything intelligent from the man was wearing on Bennet's resolve to involve his cousin in the discussion. When they saw a group of men inspecting a horse's leg, Bennet said, "I wonder what is wrong?"

"Hmm, maybe we should go find out," Sir William replied. The three men joined the group, listening to what was being said as they walked up.

"I think his leg will be well." Ash said. "I would wrap it and not allow him to be ridden for a few weeks, but I think he will heal nicely."

"Are you certain?" Hurst asked.

Alex spoke up, "I have never known Lord Ashbourne to be wrong when it comes to horses. I believe he has more knowledge of horses than any other man I know. Personally, I would trust his judgment in this matter."

"Then I will trust him as well and have my horse sent back to the stables," Bingley said.

Bennet spoke up, "What has happened?"

"It seems one of the horses has stepped into a hole and injured his leg," Darcy explained.

Bennet winced at the perceived pain, "*Ouch*. Well, I know all about leg pain. If you think the horse can survive the walk back, you can stable him at my house. We have an extra stall, and Longbourn is less than a mile from here. Netherfield, I believe, is closer to four miles, and that might be a little much on his leg at this time."

"Thank you, Mr Bennet. I believe I will take you up on your offer," Bingley said. "I will have one of the servants take him there immediately. I only wish it was not my own horse that has gone lame, as I enjoyed riding along the trails with your daughter."

Alex spoke up, "You can ride my mount, Bingley, and I will just catch a ride back on one of the carriages." He smiled, "I am certain Georgiana would enjoy my company."

"Yes, that will work, thank you, my lord" Bingley's face brightened at the prospect of once again riding with his angel.

When it was time to return to Netherfield Park, Alex settled Georgiana into the carriage, turned to help Mary in as well, then climbed in himself to sit with them.

"I do not need a chaperone, Alex," Georgiana replied.

"As it turns out, Bingley was in need of my mount so I volunteered to ride back with you," he explained.

Some of the other ladies they rode with earlier had already returned to Netherfield Park, including Mrs Bennet, Aunt Hamilton, Lady Rosebery and Mrs Gardiner, so Mary found herself in the uncomfortable situation of sitting between Georgiana and the viscount and across from two ladies she did not know. They looked at her haughtily and whispered something to each other, then put their noses in the air and refused to even glance her direction. Her own gaze went to her lap where she tried not to worry the fabric clutched tightly in her grip.

Alex noticed her comportment and her paled complexion and became concerned when she would not speak. When they finally arrived, he let the footman assist the other two ladies down then he jumped down, reaching his hand out to help her on the step. Alex picked up his cousin, asking, "Miss Mary, I was wondering if I might have a word with you after I take my cousin to her room?"

"Yes, of course," she quietly answered, following the two up the stairs and to their shared room. She removed her bonnet, spencer, and gloves and stepped out into the hall, watching as Alex sat Georgiana down on the bed, kissed her forehead, and knocked on Mrs Annesley's door, speaking with the nurse for a minute before he also returned to the hall, closing the door behind him.

"I just wanted to say," he looked away and nervously ran his hand through his hair, "Miss Mary, I feel I owe you an apology. When you clearly did not wish for my presence, it was forced upon you for the carriage ride back." Mary looked down, but he continued on quietly, "The other ladies were wrong to treat you as they did. Although I cannot apologize for them, I must apologize if my own actions led to your discomfort." He saw her start to look up at him, so he joked, "I would kneel and ask your forgiveness, but I fear others may perceive my actions as something else you would not wish."

Mary could not keep the chuckle from escaping her lips, "William Shakespeare— *When thou dost ask my blessing, I'll kneel down and ask of thee forgiveness'*. King Lear is not my personal favorite of the Bard's work, but I did always like that line," she admitted.

"I truly do apologize, Miss Mary."

"How can I do anything but accept an apology made with such sincerity, my lord." She looked up into his smiling face, her eyes alighting on his bright green orbs, mesmerized by their intensity. She thought for sure he could see to the depths of her soul, and she almost wanted him to. It would end this war within herself over what he wanted with someone as insignificant as she.

He knew that was not all for which he must apologize, so he continued on, "I fear our harsh words earlier were due to my own rather assertive actions as well, as I had no right to say we were to dance the first set together without first garnering your approval."

She looked away, the feeling of anger rising within her once again.

He reached, barely touching her glove-encased hand and quietly said with great sincerity, "I would never wish to force your hand in anything. Please accent my apologies, and if you wish it of me, I will release you from the set."

Mary looked down at her hand, so very close to his, and felt her heart beat more loudly than it had in months. She could not understand her own reaction to this man. The far-off sounds of the other guests broke the moment that held them both captive. She knew she could not deny him the dance. "I feel you have saved me from my cousin, so for that I must be grateful. I do accept your hand for the set, my lord."

He was visibly relieved.

"I must warn you though, I do not take kindly to such forceful actions and will refuse if you try such a tactic again."

He nodded, "I understand completely. Are you returning downstairs to join the others?"

"Yes."

He put his arm out, "Then may I escort you?"

She smiled at the simple request and gently placed her hand on his arm, walking beside him as he led her down the stairs and to the drawing room.

Alex made his way over to a fireside chair, then left her side to mingle among the other guests, leaving Mary's mind reeling from her own reactions to him. She looked across the room and caught him winking at her again. Unlike earlier today, she blushed at his deed, then looked away only to see Miss Bingley and the other two ladies from the carriage watching her intently.

Fitz watched as Mr Collins stayed near Mr Bennet most of the day. Twice he overheard the man speaking with anyone around about his lovely patroness, and Fitz had to suppress a laugh. *Aunt Catherine, I believe you have an admirer,* he thought. After a few hours of watching with a keen eye, Fitz decided he did not trust this man. *I do not know what you are up to, but I may just stick around until you go home,* he thought to himself.

<hr>

Tuesday, February 11, 1812

"I am sorry, my lord," Charlotte said, "but I do not understand the fascination with chasing a fox around while you jump fences and ride through all manner of terrain, nearly killing yourself on a horse."

"The fascination is in the thrill of the chase and in the win," Ash answered.

"I do not think I could ever do such a thing to one of God's creatures," Charlotte said with conviction.

"I believe I would have to agree with you, Miss Lucas," Mr Collins cut in when he walked up to the two. "I doubt my patroness would allow such atrocities to be performed on her lands, and I cannot see the purpose in it myself."

"The purpose is to flush out the scoundrels before they kill the livestock and local game that will get the residents and tenants of such an estate through these winter months. If the foxes are left to have their way the results could be disastrous to a lot of people."

"As a clergyman, I cannot condone violence and must openly oppose such brutality," Mr Collins vehemently replied.

Turning to look at the pompous man, Ash patted his horse's neck, "Will you not be joining us today? As a peer, I always feel it is my duty to lead by example. Certainly you are familiar with that charge as well Mr Collins, especially with your being a parson."

Realizing too late that he may offend the earl with a refusal, he stammered, "I… well… I had thought to…"

"We are leaving very soon, so would it not be best if you found your mount?"

He bowed, "Yes… yes I will do just that, my lord. Thank you." Then he turned and hurried off to speak to a groom about a horse.

Chuckling at the ridiculous man, Ash turned back to Charlotte. "As I was saying, Miss Lucas, it is a necessary evil at times."

"It is possible I shall never understand, my lord. My father's estate is very small."

 "I would imagine you do not have much experience in dealing with foxes then, Miss Lucas."

"No, I do not. I will pray for your safety, and hope you find the fox in record time today."

"Thank you, your prayers are very much appreciated. While I love the thrill of the ride, it is a very dangerous sport, and I have seen many accidents that left tragic results." He bowed and mounted his horse as Charlotte turned to join her friends.

"You look a bit flushed," Elizabeth said. "Maybe we should get you inside to a fire. It would not do to have you sniffling through Jane's wedding ceremony tomorrow."

Jane wrapped her arm through Charlotte's, "Yes, we cannot have you catching a cold."

"I would not wish to miss the ceremony for anything in the world, Jane. I am so pleased you have both found someone who will love you as you deserve."

"You will have that one day as well," Elizabeth said with confidence.

"I would just hope for a comfortable union. I am not as romantic as you, Lizzy."

"I refuse to believe you will not find love. It might just be, as you say, the romantic in me, but I will continue to believe it until my dying breath," Elizabeth said as they returned inside to join Georgiana and Mary in the music room.

Sarah Johnson

CHAPTER

XXIV

Wednesday, February 12, 1812

J ane sat in front of the mirror, the nervousness that was making her stomach knot on the inside could not be seen on her calm demeanor, but her aunt knew—she always knew.

She leaned over Jane's shoulder and placed a cup of tea on the dressing table in front of her, saying in her ear, "This should calm you, my dear."

"Thank you, Aunt Maddie."

She smiled and excused herself from the room, saying, "I will see you in a little while at the church."

Jane sat in the silent room remembering the ball the night before. It was so beautiful! The moment she descended the staircase and saw her intended standing there staring at her would forever be a memory ingrained in her heart. His hand reached for hers, his fingers squeezing hers as he led her down the last two steps. Then he placed her arm around his and the two entered the ballroom where everyone else was awaiting them.

Jane was not one to delight in the idea of being the center of attention, but it felt so wonderful to have such effusions heaped upon them. She lifted the dance card from the table top and read the somewhat messy, yet masculine script of her intended—he insisted on writing his name in for four dances, though they were only allowed to dance three.

During the time for the fourth the two escaped away to the snow covered garden to catch their breath. As they walked side-by-side, the chilly air escaping their mouths in soft white puffs, Jane felt such peace.

Sitting here now she drew her hands up to her heart and closed her eyes as the feelings within her nearly exploded with the love she felt for him. They shared the most glorious kiss, his warm lips almost seeming to give life to her on the inside when they met hers. It only lasted a moment, then they had to return back inside, but the warmth she felt on the inside was still glowing this morning as she prepared for her wedding.

Everyone who came into the room said something of her being the most beautiful bride, but it was Elizabeth who understood more than anyone else that it was the glow of love that made her so beautiful.

Today she felt so full of life and passion—*and so cherished.*

She looked again into the mirror and hardly recognized herself under the lace her mother insisted upon, but none of that mattered. She was ready to stand beside her intended and recite the vows that would tie them together for life.

Once again Susannah entered her eldest daughter's room, a ribbon flying through the air as she talked of its color being the perfect shade to offset the beautiful dress Jane was to wear today. She tied it around her daughter, then made her stand and stepped back to fuss over the tiny details no one else would see.

Jane stilled her mother's hand, "Mama, it is time."

Susannah's eyes filled with tears and she embraced her eldest daughter, happy to find a handkerchief being placed into her hand by her husband, who was there to escort them to the church.

The happiness Jane felt during the ball was nothing compared to the tranquility that overtook her the moment Charles Bingley placed the ring onto her finger. His words of devotion and the crack of his voice as he vowed his life to her made her heart fill even more. How she could keep from bursting, she knew not. She was ever so grateful for the moment when her husband led her through those gathered at the door and into the waiting carriage that would return them to Netherfield Park, after making a winding way through the neighborhood of course, allowing the others to arrive there first and giving the newlyweds a few minutes of peace before the wedding breakfast was to begin.

Charles beamed at his bride. "You are so lovely."

"My mother insisted we use every scrap of lace she could find in the house on this dress. I can only thank my father he allowed me to purchase my trousseau in Town without her presence, as I can imagine just how much it could have been."

He chuckled and reached for her hand, holding it as he looked longingly into her eyes.

The intensity between the two built until finally Charles could take it no longer and he slowly eased closer to her, capturing her lips in a soft and sensual kiss. Their lips moved slowly, each taking great pleasure in the new emotions they both had welling within them.

Charles moved his hands up to Jane's neck, urging her into the kiss that he wished would never end. When finally the two separated, he leaned his forehead against hers, his eyes closed, as he whispered, "I thought I knew what love was, but this is something so new, so enormous, I cannot describe it."

"I understand," she whispered back.

He opened his eyes, "You feel it as well?"

"Yes."

He smiled as he turned to look out the window, then back to her, "We have a few more minutes before we are to arrive. Would you…"

She did not allow him to finish his question before she brazenly moved closer to him, capturing his lips with her own.

Elizabeth found herself being pulled into the music room away from those gathered at Netherfield Park for the wedding breakfast. Her husband's arms wound around her, drawing her to his chest.

"I have missed you these last few days," he said.

"I have been right here."

"Yes, and so has every other person we know." He pulled her tighter and kissed the top of her head, "Are you certain you wish to stay here until Easter? If we return to Town we could have a few weeks alone before the start of the Season."

"What about Georgiana? We cannot just ignore your sister."

"We can ask your father if she can stay at Longbourn. Your family will be joining us in London just over four weeks after we leave, and Georgiana now has her own staff that can accommodate her private needs," Darcy said, referring to the footman he hired to carry her around when he or their cousins were not available. "We can come back for Easter then accompany everyone else to Town. That would still give us three weeks at least on our own."

Elizabeth leaned back to look her husband in the face, "I have to admit that does sound nice, but I simply cannot choose to be so selfish. Georgiana needs us right now, and I know my mother will have a difficult time now that Jane is going away until Easter, and would you truly wish to have my mother fussing over Georgiana? You know it is what will occur if we leave early."

Pulling her back into his chest he said, "I will not apologize for wishing you would take the selfish route, but I understand why you cannot. You are right—you are needed here, and my sister does not need to bear such a burden. Alex cannot stay this time like he did when we were first married, so it would be best if we remain here for now."

His lips descended upon hers and the two were lost to the noises filtering through the closed door. Eventually though they knew they would need to return to the others.

"As much as I love being here with you, I want to speak with my sister before they leave," Elizabeth said.

Grumbling, Darcy replied, "Only because I know you will miss her over the next few weeks."

Elizabeth pulled away and turned to leave the room. Peeking back in from the doorway, "When all the others are finally gone we can find a few places to hide around here. How would you like that?"

William winked at her, "Go find your sister, you minx."

Elizabeth soon saw Jane on the other side of the room in a group of the neighborhood matrons. *Oh no*, she thought, *I best go and rescue her before they completely embarrass her maidenly sensibilities.* She came up beside her sister and wound her arm around her, whispering in her ear, "Do you want me to rescue you?" At Jane's subtle nod, she turned to the group and said, "I require my sister's assistance for a minute, if you all do not mind?" At their agreement to the plan, the two stole away into the corner.

Elizabeth hugged her tight, "Oh, Jane—you are a married woman! Can you believe it?"

"Lizzy, it is more than I can bear!" Tears threatened to spill out at the pronouncement.

"Now, now, we must not cry; what would your dear husband say about your red rimmed eyes." Elizabeth led them over to a nearby sofa. "Your ceremony was perfect. I thought for sure Mama would go overboard with all the lace and flowers, but there is something to be said for being married in winter. I am sure she would have had it decorated even more so if she had more time."

Jane covered her mouth with her hand and chuckled, "Yes, it did save me quite a few rows with her over the decorations."

In exaggerated exasperation, Elizabeth put her hand to her chest, "You? My dear sweet Jane, have a row with someone? I cannot even imagine such a thing!"

"Now Lizzy, you know I have my own opinions about some things. After all, I have dreamed about this day since Granny Bennet used to read us stories of a prince carrying off his lady fair."

"Was it all you hoped?"

"All I hoped, and so much more. I will cherish every moment of this last week, and greatly look forward to this coming time with just Charles," she answered dreamily then blushed when she realized just what could be implied by her words. "Now tell me Lizzy, are you happy as well?"

Elizabeth smiled, "I do not think happy is a strong enough term to describe my feelings." Settling back into the seat, Elizabeth continued, "William is so solicitous of my needs. It seems nothing escapes his notice. Why, even last month he surprised me with a private dinner in a beautiful orangery. I had forgotten the date, but my husband was busy all that week preparing for our two month celebration. The staff provided the most luxurious setting, and everything from the wine to the food and even the atmosphere in the room was hand selected by him. He had Georgiana talk me into wearing his favorite necklace so he could regale me with the story of his mother being presented it for her debut ball. She caught the eye of his father while wearing it." Sighing, she wound her arm through her sister's, "If Mr Bingley is half as inventive as William, I would say he will keep you more than happy for many years."

"Oh Lizzy, when I return for Easter we will have so much to talk about!"

Jane reached over to hug her sister. "But I will miss you in the upcoming weeks."

"I will miss you as well." Pulling back, she said, "Now, now, did we not already say no more tears?"

Jane dried her eyes and chuckled at Elizabeth. "Charles will not tell me where he is taking me, but has promised it to be a wonderful six weeks."

"Well, I shall not spoil the surprise for you. I know you will love it though. Now let us go and find our husbands and see if we can talk them into one last country dance before you leave."

Charlotte was looking for Elizabeth when she saw the two sisters sitting alone in the corner. Not wanting to disturb them, she sighed and turned to walk away. As she was about to enter another room she heard her brothers talking on the other side of the doorway, the subject of their conversation making her stop immediately.

"I do not see why you want to defend her," James said.

Jonathan quipped, "Defend her? You make our sister sound as if she is pushing towards the grave at any moment! She is but seven and twenty, not ninety."

"I am just saying it is a good thing for her that you are the eldest and will inherit from our father, as I would force her out into her own establishment."

Jonathan gave his younger brother a stern look, "As the heir, I will gladly take on the responsibility of our sisters, *both of them*, and I will not mind one bit if I have to provide for them for the rest of their lives. With your attitudes towards women it is a wonder anyone would even condescend to dance with you."

"Mary Bennet was nothing more than a diversion," he said, referring to his dance partner from the opening set at Lydia's birthday celebration. "I would bet that one day she and Charlotte will both be known as the town's old spinster maids."

"I do not know what makes you think you can speak of gentlewomen in such a manner," he said hotly. "I thought you put your previous condescending attitudes behind you when you asked Miss Mary to dance, but it seems you have not. Your arrogance and disdain for the feeling of others may cause you more pain in the future if you do not mind your tongue," Jonathan warned.

"I do not see how it is any of your concern," James replied with a snort.

"You will find out just what concerns me if I ever hear you voice such foolishness as I have just heard escape your mouth in the presence of our sisters or Miss Mary," Jonathan nearly growled in response before he turned and stormed away.

Charlotte was frozen in place. Not only did she feel out of place being the oldest single female in the area, but she could do nothing about her dilemma. She sunk into a nearby chair and did not move until it was time for the newly wedded couple to leave. She joined the others, standing at the back of the crowd.

Jonathan saw his sister's downtrodden demeanor and went to stand beside her. "Are you well?"

She answered back quietly, "I know not how to adequately answer how I feel in this moment." She then turned and walked back inside and up to her room to rest alone until it was time for them to return home.

Sarah Johnson

CHAPTER

XXV

Thursday, February 13, 1812

L ord Ashbourne, it is good to see you up early this morning," Alex said as the earl came into the otherwise deserted dining room.

"I must leave this morning and thought I would try to avoid a certain person who is known to be a late riser," Ash replied

"Ahhhh, yes, I know what you mean." Alex chuckled at his friend. "It is lucky for me I am needed in London, especially with Bingley not being here to help keep his sister in check over the next few weeks." He took a sip of his tea, savoring the rich flavor. "Bingley finds some of the best products; I wonder where he gets this tea?"

"I asked him just the other day and he said Mr Gardiner found this blend for him," Ash answered. "When I return to Town I have already decided I will have to visit his establishments and see what else he may have."

Alex nodded, "I have been many times and was quite impressed. So where are you off to this morning?"

"I am needed in Northamptonshire for a few weeks. There is some business I cannot put off until summer."

"Were you not just there last month?"

"Yes," he sighed. "I am fortunate it is not as great a distance as Derbyshire is for you or your cousin."

"Yes, it is quite the distance. Unfortunately, I may find myself having to go to Dalmeny before the Season starts also," Alex replied.

"I heard a rumor you are taking over the running of your father's estate. Is it true?" Ash asked.

Alex drank down the remainder of the liquid in his cup and sat back in his seat. "My father has not been feeling well for a number of years. To ease my mother's nerves, he and I came up with a plan that I upon my marriage or my thirtieth birthday, whichever came first, I would take on the majority of the running of the estate, leaving my father free of that burden and the travel it requires."

"And your birthday is fast approaching," Ash said in understanding.

"Yes," Alex answered. "I just hope this will allow my father to rest more. The three day journey to Dalmeny is quite arduous, and to have to go back and forth at least four or five times in a year, plus all the times he is needed in Town because of Parliament—I just hope my taking over early will relieve some of the burden that has weighed on him the last few years." Looking down at his empty cup, he said with much emotion, "I do not wish to have to take over the earldom too soon."

"If anyone understands, it would be me," Ash replied. "It was thrust upon my shoulders at the ripe old age of five, though I did not have the duties of Parliament until I turned one and twenty."

"You have been lucky to have a wonderful example in the Duke of Hawley as your guide."

Ash chuckled, "Sometimes I think that old man will never die."

Darcy entered the dining room and sat, putting the folded newspaper on the table, "I see you two are up early. Both of you are leaving us today?"

"Yes," Alex answered. "I must return to London to take care of more business, and Ash is needed in Northamptonshire."

Looking at the earl, Darcy asked, "When will you return?"

"I hope to only be gone a few weeks at most. Maybe I will stop back through on my way to Town—if you and your lovely wife will still be in the area, that is."

"Feel free to," Darcy said. "Bingley has offered to let us have use of Netherfield anytime, so we will remain until Easter, then will return to Town for the Season."

Standing, Ash said, "If I complete my tasks before I must be back in London, I will certainly stop here for a few days."

Alex stood also, "As much as I would love to stay around and visit with your family more, I have too much to go over with my solicitor. If you need anything, you know where to find me."

Darcy offered, "When your papers are written up, I will read through them for you if you wish."

Alex agreed, "I would like that; thank you Darcy. I will be in touch."

The two said their goodbyes and both rode away from Netherfield Park in opposite directions.

The last of the guests would leave later this morning, so Darcy's plans for the morning centered on meeting with his father-in-law again to once more go over the papers they were to present to Mr Collins. Then later this afternoon the task would be completed and everything would be left in the hands of the parson.

The three gentlemen were seated in Bennet's study awaiting Mr Collins. Bennet held Mary's cat Beatrice in his lap and was running his hands through the thick, white fur. The knock on the door interrupted their conversation, and he called for the person to enter, setting the cat down on the floor. Seeing his cousin at the door Bennet said, "Mr Collins, come in. Have a seat, sir."

"I hope I am not late. My patroness, *the Right Honourable Lady Catherine de Bourgh*, has told me often, *'Mr. Collins, you mustn't be late. Punctuality is a noble trait, and not often found in the lower classes of society. As a parson, it is your responsibility to set an example to those under your tutelage.'*"

When he took a breath, Bennet cut in, "No, you are not late. I have asked you here to discuss some business with you, and if you do not mind, I have asked my brother, Mr Gardiner, and Mr Darcy to join us." Henry indicated the other two gentlemen.

"I do not mind at all." His response was interrupted when he sneezed.

"God bless you, sir," Bennet said.

"Thank you, thank you," he answered, trying to bow his head as he wiped his nose.

Once again taking the silent moment to further the cause of this meeting, Bennet picked up the stack of papers from his desk. "As you know, due to an entail on this estate and its land, when I die it is to go to you. I have a proposition to bring up to you though, and I hope you will give me the time to explain it fully before you form an opinion."

His interest garnered, Mr. Collins nodded his head in agreement, "Yes, that I can grant you sir." Again, he sneezed, apologizing profusely for such behavior.""

"Maybe the Hertfordshire air does not agree with you," Gardiner said.

Or it could be the many animals you have all around. Why, I cannot turn around in this house without a horse or a dog or a cat being in my face, Mr Collins thought, but dared not give voice to his true opinion. He reminded himself quickly what he was here to accomplish. He feigned a look of shock and said, "Oh, I had not thought of that. I hope it is not the case, as it would be a wonderful county in which to one day settle."

"That is precisely what I wished to speak with you about," Bennet said, handing the papers to his cousin. "Here are some papers I have had drawn up, and I wish to explain them to you. If you have any questions we will be able to answer them for you, as these two gentlemen are both privy to all that is in this contract.

Bennet stood and began pacing as he laid out his case before his cousin. "The Bennet family has had the privilege of being master over these lands and house for over two hundred years. However, with no son of my own, this is set to end upon my death. I have been making my own investments for many years hoping they would pay off, and they have. I am proposing to you, sir, that in lieu of this estate, you be well compensated monetarily. You could then purchase your own estate and become a master immediately, or invest the money and see what will become of it as you continue on with your patroness."

He was quite intrigued. *This may just be another way for me to get out of this dreadful situation,* he thought, *if it comes to it that is.* "Yes, yes, I see what you are saying, sir. Just what is this amount you are willing to pay me for relinquishing my rights to this fine estate?"

Bennet walked over asked, "May I?" as he held his hand out.

Collins handed him the contract and watched as his cousin flipped through to the appropriate page, then handed it back, pointing to the figure written. He had never seen such a figure, nor imagined someone would offer to give such to him just for a signature and a promise to leave. His head began to spin and the next thing he knew everything around him went black.

"Mr Collins… Mr Collins, can you hear me?"

He started to come to and realized he was laying on the floor with the three gentlemen and the butler staring down at him.

"Mr Collins? Can you sit up?"

He did, with some help from the others, but his head now had a knot on the back of it and he knew he would need to lie down a little longer.

"Come with me," the butler said as he helped him stand. "I will help you to your room and we will get you something to help the headache you are sure to have."

When the three men were left in the study alone again, Bennet smirked, "Well, that was not quite the reaction I expected."

<hr>

Saturday, February 15, 1812

Fitz saw Denny sitting on the other side of the room at a table in the dark corner. He stepped up to the bar and ordered a drink, then stood there while he drank it, giving Denny enough time to sneak out into the back alley where they were to meet.

When he was nearly done with his drink, a brawl nearly started on the other side of the room, so he used this opportunity to sneak out as well.

"Pssst… over here," he heard Denny say.

Fitz felt along the rough stone wall further into the darkened alley and was glad to finally be face to face with his undercover soldier once again. They had exchanged a few notes, but he felt it was time they meet again to discuss what they would do next.

"Are you well?"

Denny chuckled, "How often will our every encounter begin with you asking me just that question? As I have assured you, I am healing well enough. This is not so arduous a duty."

The colonel sighed in relief, "I know you have written of your health, but as important as you are to this investigation, I find I must be reassured. You are one of the few who has been with me from the start, and this investigation would be nowhere without your influence. For that I am eternally grateful. Now, what of the scoundrel?"

Denny told of all he had seen George Wilson do, and that he could find very little information on him from the locals. He was still not sure why he was following Miss Lydia Bennet, but he was certain she was his target.

The two decided it would be best if Fitz returned to Town to pursue a new lead on their other suspect, and Denny would remain in Meryton, keeping a close eye on Miss Lydia, and all the Bennets, until the man left the neighborhood once again.

Fitz reminded Denny to stay safe, and the two parted ways to continue their investigation, both hoping they would find the information necessary and this would all come to an end soon.

Sarah Johnson

Jane awoke to the soft touch of her husband beside her, his fingers running through her now unbraided hair. She opened her eyes and slowly stretched.

"I did not mean to wake you," he said.

She smiled coyly, "I think you did mean it, but I do not mind."

He leaned over his wife, looking into her eyes and could not help the smile that beamed on his face. "How did I manage to marry such a beautiful wife?"

She blushed, but before she could say anything his lips were on hers. She wound her arms slowly around his shoulders, drawing him closer as the passionate exchange deepened.

When the two finally did separate and both lay next to each other on the bed, Charles asked, "What shall we do today?"

"Oh, I know not what to do! What do you suggest?"

"Well, Brighton has many beautiful sights, but they all pale in comparison to staying right here with you."

She giggled, "We cannot remain in our rooms for another day—what will the servants say?"

"Believe me, they would talk more if we ignored each other. It is expected that newly wedded couples be left to their own devices."

"And just how do you know this?"

He smiled and touched her nose with his finger, "I just do. I happen to be well acquainted with the servant's quarters. My father was not so well off as I am now, and Pemberley was where I spent most of my school holidays. Darcy and I would explore the hidden passageways used by the servants, and sometimes we would catch a few words as they passed each other in the corridors."

"Oh my! I cannot imagine my personal business being bandied about so freely!" She was mortified that the servants would speak so of such intimate and private goings-on.

He leaned in and kissed her cheek, "Fret not, my lovely wife—I shall never allow such freedom with our own servants."

Worried for her sister, she asked, "Does William allow his servants to speak so?"

"Absolutely not! He has Mrs Reynolds at Pemberley and Mrs Tucker at Darcy House. Neither one would allow such frivolous gossip from the servants. The few times we heard any of them speaking, they were dismissed within just a few short days. If anything is said of us, it will be that we are absolutely," he kissed her forehead, "completely," then he kissed her nose, "unequivocally," he kissed one cheek, "irrevocably," then the other cheek, "in love," finally his lips descended upon hers and the two were again lost again in a passionate embrace.

Eventually they escaped their chambers to enjoy the beauties the city of Brighton held. Jane enjoyed several of the sights Lydia told her about, and one special tea room Louisa said they must visit. Mostly though, the weeks were passed with the two sharing as much time together as they could, as one would expect from any newly wedded couple so passionately in love.

Sarah Johnson

CHAPTER

XXVI

Monday, February 24, 1812

T he weather was nice enough this morning for Charlotte to go for a stroll. She found herself rambling about quite a bit these last few weeks as her brother's words rolled around in her head. *I am grateful for Jonathan's understanding, but I do not wish to be an encumbrance on him,* she thought. *What can I do about my situation though? Who would possibly want to marry someone of my age with no dowry and no connections except a father knighted because of his success in business? I must find someone. I cannot put such a burden on Jonathan for the rest of his life.*

"Oh, I am sorry," she cried out when she walked right into someone. Looking up, she saw Mr Collins. "I am so very sorry, sir. I was not attending and did not see you there."

Standing and dusting off his pants, he replied in his nasally voice, "Miss Lucas, I was not attending either, and it seems our inattentiveness has caused quite the scene, has it not?" With a gleam in his eye he asked, "Do you often walk alone around these parts?"

"I am not as familiar with the land as Mrs Darcy, but I have spent many an afternoon wandering about over the years," Charlotte answered.

Looking around, he seemed agitated, "If you do not mind, would you tell me some things about the area that an outsider like myself might not know?"

Puzzled, she replied, "If you wish it of me, sir."

Excitedly he replied, "Oh yes, I do wish you would. I want to know as much as I can about the area in which I will one day settle, once my cousin has passed on and the entailed land is mine, that is. May I escort you, madam?"

Charlotte took his arm and the two walked most of the way to Netherfield Park, the parson unusually quiet and listening to Charlotte as she pointed out all the local landmarks along the way.

"Well, I see your destination is within sight, so I must leave you now," he said when they were close to Netherfield Park. He bowed and turned around and was gone immediately.

Continuing on alone, she was bid entrance by the butler and was soon was announced to her friend who sat in solitude in the library reading a book.

"Charlotte! I did not expect to see you today," Elizabeth said.

"Am I disturbing you?"

"No, no, I am alone here for a while. Miss Darcy is resting; Mrs Hurst, Mrs Hamilton, and Miss Bingley all went into Meryton to do some shopping; and William is out riding with my father."

"I believe my father and brother are with them," Charlotte added.

"I would not be surprised; my husband misses riding when we are in Town, so he goes nearly every day when we are in the country. Did you walk all the way here? Alone?" Elizabeth asked in surprise.

"Yes I did walk, but not alone."

"Oh? Who came with you?"

"It is just me now. I ran into your cousin, Mr Collins, on my way," Charlotte explained. "He escorted me the rest of the way, wanting to know about the local area. He is such an odd sort. I do not understand him sometimes, but he is solicitous of the needs of those around him."

"Yes," Elizabeth answered with a sly look to her eye, "only if his patroness would approve of his actions. My husband's aunt holds much power in that man's mind."

"His patroness is your husband's aunt? What a coincidence that is," Charlotte smiled.

"It was not planned, I can assure you," Elizabeth answered. "From all I have heard about Lady Catherine de Bourgh from her most esteemed parson, I do not wish to meet her anytime soon. I doubt she will condescend to acknowledge me anyway as I have stolen her nephew with my arts and allurements."

Charlotte laughed sat next to her friend when Elizabeth offered a seat, "Thank you; I needed a bit of joviality today."

"What is wrong, my friend?"

"Nothing of significance," Charlotte replied. Smiling, she turned, "Now, yesterday after church you said you have some news you wish to tell the family, but you are waiting on your sister's return from her honeymoon. I refuse to be put off until Easter, so you must tell me now—are you with child?"

Elizabeth's smile was answer enough and the two hugged and cried, talking of all their hopes and dreams for the next hour, Elizabeth encouraging her friend to not be too downtrodden about not being married yet, that her time would come soon enough. Charlotte dared not contradict her, but she still had her doubts.

Thursday, February 27, 1812

Georgiana, Elizabeth and Louisa were seated in the drawing room, Amelia asleep in Louisa's arms as the three ladies talked. "You have become a good friend over the last few months Mrs Darcy," Louisa said. "When we are both in Town next, Amelia and I will have to come visit you."

Elizabeth smiled, running her finger down the baby's soft cheek, "I would like that very much."

Georgiana spoke up, "Oh, must you leave so soon? I have quite enjoyed having a baby around to spoil."

Squeezing the younger girl's hand beside her, Louisa replied, "Unfortunately, we must. My family has had the opportunity to meet Amelia, but David's family has not. They eagerly await our return to Serenity Place." She turned to address Elizabeth, "David's mother was so very appreciative of the drawing your sister made. She said she has it hung on the wall, and already has an artist coming to paint a family portrait once we arrive."

She smiled, "My sister has a natural ability in that area. I will tell her how much it is loved though—she would appreciate that."

"Speaking of sisters, you will have a full Season right from the start with your recent marriage, as well as Jane, and Miss Mary joining you in Town as well," Louisa said. "I only wish I could be there to see you all take on society with such grace as I know you all will."

"You will not be returning for the Season?" Georgiana asked Mrs Hurst.

"No, we want to get this little one settled in one place for a while, so we will miss the festivities in Town this year."

Georgiana smiled, "While I like the diversions London offers, I cannot wait until we are able to go back to Pemberley in a few months."

"I agree completely," Louisa affirmed. "Our family has waited a long time for this little one, and they wish to pamper her as soon as possible."

"My brother has promised to throw a small birthday dinner for me this year," Georgiana said. "I wish you could be there, but I understand your desire to visit family."

Louisa smiled at the younger girl, "Thank you. Our plans are quite fixed."

The butler came in the room, interrupting the conversation to say, "Lord Primrose and Colonel Fitzwilliam to see you, ma'am."

The two brothers stepped into the room and came over to greet the ladies. Fitz bowed, "It is always a pleasure to see my cousin's beautiful and lively wife." Taking Georgiana's hand he kissed the back with all gallantry, "My dear cousin, you are looking lovely as ever." Turning with a bow, he continued, "And Mrs Hurst, it is always a delight. May I?" he asked, holding out his hands to Amelia.

"I was just about to take Amelia upstairs to her nurse, Colonel," Louisa answered.

"I will not hold her long—I promise," he said. Louisa handed the baby over to him and marveled at how small she looked in his massive hands.

"How are you?" he asked Amelia as he sat down. "I see you are growing quite nicely. Before long I will need two hands to hold you properly."

Alex chimed in, "My brother always did chase after the prettiest young ladies."

They all laughed, and Elizabeth asked if either of them would like something to drink.

"I, for one, would just like to refresh myself," Alex replied. "Did your husband tell you I was coming?"

"No, he never said anything to me," Elizabeth said, "but he has been gone all day—he and my father have a weekly routine of playing chess on Thursdays."

"Ahhh, he finally found someone who can challenge him," Fitz said.

"My father feels the same way," Elizabeth replied.

"Well I hope my unexpected presence does not put you out?" Alex asked.

"Absolutely not; you are welcome any time, my lord—as I am certain my brother has already stated," Louisa assured him.

"I will only be here for a day or two," Alex explained. "I am on my way to Dalmeny, but my cousin offered to look over some papers before we send them to the solicitor."

"I will accept your benevolence for the same amount of time it seems," Fitz added. "I have some business to take care of in the area and would much rather stay here than at an inn."

"Well you are both welcome to stay as long as you need. Lord Ashbourne has just arrived as well on his way back to London from his home. He went with my husband this morning," Elizabeth said.

"Capital, capital," Fitz replied as he stood carefully, gently handing the baby back to her mother, "Thank you for allowing me to hold her for a few minutes. Now if you do not mind, I must change from these clothes and make myself more presentable."

"Right this way," Louisa said, leading the two men out the door and up the stairs.

Caroline was about to descend when she saw the two visitors walking up the stairs behind her sister. "Lord Primrose, I did not expect to see you here in my home again so soon."

"Your home, madam? I am a bit confused—I thought this was the home of Mr and Mrs Bingley?" Alex quipped.

Taken aback, Caroline's face flushed, "Well, of course it is, but as he is my brother it is also my own home." Louisa cleared her throat, making Caroline rethink her words, "I mean… it is… generally accepted that an unmarried sister lives with her other male relatives… until she marries."

"Right this way, my lord," Louisa interrupted. When the two brothers passed her, she turned to Caroline and whispered sternly, "Meet me in your room. I will be there momentarily."

Louisa showed their guests to their rooms, telling them what time dinner was to be served, then went to her sister's room to have a talk with Caroline.

"I will not have you disturb our guests," Louisa said firmly when the door was closed.

A false shock was apparent on Caroline's face, "I would not dream of doing so, dear sister."

"You will leave the earl, the viscount, and the colonel all alone. If I hear of your doing otherwise, I will have you removed from the house to the inn until such time as Aunt Hamilton is ready to leave for London, *dear sister,*" Louisa warned. Not waiting for Caroline's reaction, she left the room.

CHAPTER

XXVII

F itz quietly knocked on Alex's door.

"Come in," he called

He opened it to find his brother sitting in a chair reading through some papers.

"Do you need something, Fitz?"

"Nothing of much import; I was just going to take a ride and see where I end up. I may stop off and say hello to some in the local neighborhood; say, at Longbourn? Care to join me?"

Alex folded the papers, placing them back in his trunk. "I think I can spare a few hours. It is not as if I am going to know what else needs to change in these until Darcy takes a look at them anyway."

The two rode in silence and as they dismounted, Alex saw someone sitting in the garden. Recognizing her familiar visage, he told his brother, "I think I will take a stroll first and will join you inside in a few minutes."

Looking the direction Alex's gaze was fixed upon, he replied, "Good luck."

"Thanks—I might need it."

He wound his way through the bare shrubs, then stood behind Mary for a full minute before he made his presence known. "Good afternoon Miss Bennet."

Mary turned around, a confused look on her face. "Oh, Lord Primrose, I did not know you were visiting the neighborhood."

"I am traveling through on business and needed to speak with my cousin on my way north," he answered. "May I sit?" he asked, coming up to the bench on which she sat.

"Oh, yes, please do," she folded the letters from Caroline Bingley, placing them back into her journal and slid down to one end of the bench.

"I did not mean to disturb you."

"I was just going through my correspondence." She was outside thinking about all she knew and had been told of the man who now sat beside her. A little embarrassed of his unexpectedly showing up, her face flushed.

"Are you feeling well, Miss Bennet?" Alex asked.

"What? Oh, yes I am well," Mary answered. "I am sorry, but I am not used to being referred to as *Miss Bennet* yet. My sister has always been *Miss Bennet*, and I almost expect her to be behind me when someone says that name."

With a lift of his brow, Alex replied, "If it would not offend you, I could still call you *Miss Mary*. We are, after all, nearly family."

246

Mary's face flushed an even deeper shade of red when she heard her name roll from his tongue. Quietly she answered, "I know in the past I have been insistent upon keeping with formalities, but I would like it if you called me by my name."

"Then *Miss Mary* it is," he smiled at having been given such an honour from her. Feeling he should not pressure her any further, he asked, "I have yet to greet your family; would you like to join me?"

"Yes, thank you," she said. Mary secured her letters back inside the journal and put it in her pocket before she stood. Seeing his outstretched arm, she wound her arm around his, gently placing her hand on top. Closing her eyes at the sensation it caused in her stomach, she took a deep breath. When she opened her eyes again, she noticed he was staring at her, his bright green eyes boring into hers. With a blink, the moment was broken and Alex led them inside.

Mary went to her bedroom, not sure what to think of such an interaction. Within a half an hour she saw the four men leaving through her window, and she found herself watching the man on the champagne colored horse as he rode away.

Turning to the page in her journal where she had penned the hurt feelings of a few weeks ago, she read.

> February 12, 1812
>
> Why am I so affected by his hardly approaching me all week? I did not want him to approach me—or so I thought. I have dreaded this last week for nearly two months, and yet, now that it is over and I know he is gone, I am torn apart inside. I do not even like this man at times, and yet I cannot help but yearn for his attentions. Is this how others of my sex have been drawn in by him as well? Is this normal or is he in control and playing a well laid out game with me? How can I possibly determine what his true intentions are? At first he acted the part of

the knight ready to save his lady fair from whatever beset her. Then he insulted me behind my back to his cousin, nearly at the first of our acquaintance, and set about on a two month journey of what I can only describe as trying to gain my attentions, even asking me for the first dance at the ball. That is until the last two weeks he was here, when he barely acknowledged me, leaving the country with hardly a civil goodbye.

His return for Jane's wedding was definitely not that of a knight wishing to win his lady fair's heart. The man hardly spoke three words to me, and those were stilted at best and only spoken because the presence of others around us necessitated our interaction. He insisted to others we were to dance together, without even giving me the decency to ask. Although, truly, he did apologize for such actions and explained that his only intention was to save me from having to dance with my cousin. The dance itself was so awkward though. I have never before danced a full set with someone in complete silence.

Once again he left, this time without taking his leave of me at all. I do not know what to think. Does he have someone waiting for him back in London? Is that why he left so suddenly after the wedding when the other guests stayed a little longer? So many questions, and yet no answers are at my disposal.

Mary closed her eyes. She could not imagine the words she had written being said about the same man who sought her out in the garden today. *I know not what to think. I wish I knew just what he thought of me, but more importantly, I wish I knew what he is really like. Is he the charming gentleman from this afternoon, or is he the man others warn me about. Am I ever to know the real Alexander Fitzwilliam?*

Friday, February 28, 1812

Darcy, Alex, and Fitz were having one last late night drink in the library. Alex sighed and closed his eyes, savoring the flavor of the liquid as it slid across his tongue.

Fitz looked at him, "Not a good week I take it?"

"You could say that," Alex said as he sat down heavily in the chair.

"How did your business go?" Darcy asked.

"My father was able to alleviate part of the problem, but we will be quite busy for the next few weeks." He sighed loudly, "Sometimes I wish you were the heir, Fitz."

He smirked, "I doubt you would have made such a stellar soldier."

"No, if I were not meant to take over Father's position, I would have probably chosen the law or medicine," Alex said.

"I cannot see you as a doctor either," Fitz said. "Now, a solicitor? That is a good possibility."

"Well, as arduous as it is sometimes, you *are* the heir," Darcy reminded him.

"I know, and whether I like it or not, this business must be completed before my thirtieth birthday or my mother will have my neck. I promised to allow her to have the largest ball she could plan for my birthday, so I must be in Town by then."

"Do you think Father will miss Dalmeny?"

"He will always be welcome there, Fitz. It is not as if I will forbid him entry," Alex said. "They will still be living on the grounds, just at the dower house instead."

"Yes, I know, but he will not be making the decisions any longer."

"I think Father will miss it more than Mother. She has never liked the manor as much as he does," Alex said, "but, the decision was made ages ago that I would take over upon my thirtieth birthday or my wedding, whichever came first, and this seems to be coming upon us rather quickly now." Alex took a drink and sank back further in the chair. "I think Mother will appreciate having Father around more instead of off every few months to deal with one problem or another up there. With his age, the travel is difficult for him. I did not want to have to go right now in the middle of winter, but this visit is necessary to make sure the changes are going along smoothly. Mother has already chosen which servants will go to the dower house with them, and she wishes to have their chambers emptied before we return to the north for summer," Alex said.

"Will you be moving into the master's chambers yet?" Darcy asked.

"No, I am perfectly happy with my own rooms for now. Maybe I will move when I marry," Alex shrugged his shoulders, then downed the last of his drink.

Lifting his eyebrow, Fitz asked, "And when will that be?"

He was saved from answering when a knock came at the door and the butler entered, followed by Lord Ashbourne.

"Colonel Fitzwilliam, a letter has come for you," Smyth said, holding out a silver tray upon which the letter was placed.

"Thank you Smyth," he said, dismissing the butler. "Good evening, Ash."

"I came in search of a drink," the earl answered.

"Then you have come to the right place," Darcy answered, standing to pour a drink for the earl. "We are trying our best to empty Bingley's supply while he is away."

"Well gentlemen, it seems I have business to which I must attend," Fitz said, holding up the letter in his hand. "If I do not see you before I go, I take my leave of you now. Darcy, Alex, I will see you when you return to London." He bowed to the others and left the room.

Darcy stood, "I think I will retire also." The others said their goodnights and he was soon on his way upstairs to his wife, leaving the other two men alone in the library.

Alex joked with the earl, "I was surprised he lasted as long as he did. I thought for sure Darcy would have retired along with Hurst an hour ago."

The two laughed, then sat in companionable silence for a few minutes before Alex asked, "Are you returning to Town tomorrow?"

"No, I think I may stay around here for a few more days; enjoy riding around the countryside a little longer before I have to be in Town," Ash answered. "You?"

"Yes, I leave for Dalmeny in the morning."

"Good luck, old man," Ash said. "Tomorrow the maidens will be out in force wreaking havoc on all unassuming single gentlemen."

Alex groaned, "Then it is best I retire now so I am up and gone before Miss Bingley rises."

Ash laughed, "I take it she has set her sights on you after your cousin was taken off the market?"

Alex rubbed his eyes in frustration, "Yes, unfortunately."

"You know, there is but one solution to such a conundrum."

"And what is that?"

"Just get married," Ash replied.

Alex sighed, "If only life were as simple as that sentence implies."

A look of sadness stretched across Ash's face, "Yes… unfortunately."

Realizing what he said, Alex quickly apologized, "I am sorry; I forgot about your past and all you went through when your intended died. Please forgive my slip of the tongue."

"Think nothing of it," he said. "At the time, I could not fathom going on with life as usual without her by my side, and yet I have for over six years now. I determined I would never again propose to a woman, but over the last few months I have once again found myself growing weary of being alone."

"I think she would have wanted you to find someone else and marry," Alex said.

"Yes; she told me as much before the fever took her," Ash whispered.

"Then why have you shied away from society all these years?"

He leaned back in the chair and looked towards the ceiling, "I grew weary of the machinations of the Ton. I do not wish to be a pawn in someone's game, married off for political gain, connections, or financial increase. Yet that seems to be all the ladies in London care about." He whispered, barely audible, "My Sophie was different. She cared not for my rank and position, nor my money. It mattered not to her whether I lived in a castle or a small farm house."

"May I ask you a rather intrusive question?" At the earl's nod, Alex continued, "Being a daughter of a simple country gentleman, can you truly say your intended would have been able to withstand all the Ton was prepared to throw at her?"

He thought for a minute, then answered quietly, "At the time I would have said yes, but now I am not so sure. She was quite young and naïve. If I had it to do all over again, I would have wished she be older than just nineteen and I would have let her have at least one full Season in Town before I pursued her interest. I think age can teach some lessons I overlooked in my search for a wife, but what can I say—I was young myself. If I were to look at marrying again, I would prefer it be to someone older."

"Anyone *specific* in mind for the position?" Alex quipped.

"I refuse to answer that question." Eyeing his friend, he asked, "Is there a *specific* reason you wanted to know?"

Alex smirked and raised his glass, "Yes, but that is all I will say." He drank the last of his drink then stood, "And with that, I think it is time I retire. Good night my friend," he said as he left the room.

Alex went to bed thinking of all his friend said. *Maybe it would be best if I do not pursue Mary until she has been through at least part of the Season? It is a good thought, though I do not know how I will hold myself back; if I do not make my intentions known, she is likely to have several suitors before she leaves London.* He nearly cried out in frustration. *If only I could talk to someone else who could guide me in what I should do.*

Maria and Lydia were each cuddled beneath the counterpane, giggling about the events of their day. Maria laughed loudly causing Lydia to say, "Shhhh, your sister is sleeping!"

"Charlotte? Oh do not worry. She sleeps so soundly that nothing can rouse her," Maria assured.

"Good—I have a bit of gossip I would not want to go any further than you!" Lydia said excitedly.

Settling down again, Maria urged her friend, "Well, do tell. What could it possibly be?"

"It seems Miss Cynthia Long has fixed her sights upon a certain Tom Lewis in a town ten or so miles away, though I do not know in which direction so I cannot say which town it is. Her sister Emma told me today that Cynthia has decided to set out early tomorrow morning to acquaint herself with his neighborhood, thus affording her the opportunity to propose to the man!"

"NO! Oh it cannot be! Has she no shame?" Maria cried.

"She told her sister that tomorrow is Leap Day and she intends to do as she pleases because she is ever so tired of waiting on him to make up his own mind about her."

The two laughed heartily, continuing to talk of how they would never have the nerve to do such a thing.

Charlotte stayed quiet, listening to all they said. While she had heard of the tradition of a lady having the right to propose on Leap Day, she never thought of using it to her advantage. *I am so desperate, this may be the only way I will ever find a husband,* she thought, *and I cannot put it off for four more years. Who could I possibly ask who would agree to marry me, for it would do no good setting myself out there in such a way if the man refused.*

Going through the local gentlemen in her mind, she determined no one on her list would accept. *Who visiting the neighborhood might accept my hand? Hmmmm… there is but one man I can think of—Mr Bennet's cousin, Reverend Collins, seems nice enough. I think he might even accept me, after all, he has gone out of his way to escort me, and even asked me to dance. Could I really set myself up for such a marriage? Now Charlotte,* she scolded herself, *you never did have as many romantic sensibilities to fulfill in a marriage partner as Lizzy. Mr Collins has a comfortable living now and will one day inherit Longbourn. With no connections or dowry to speak of from me, he may be the best option available.* Charlotte finally found sleep after convincing herself of what she would set out to do on the morrow.

CHAPTER
XXVIII

Saturday, February 29, 1812

hen she came into the dining room she found everyone else already at the table. "I am sorry for being late," Charlotte said, sitting down between Jonathan and James.

"What are your plans today?" her father asked.

"I was thinking of visiting Longbourn," Charlotte answered. "Maybe I can go with Miss Lydia when she returns home?"

"Oh, must you go home today?" Maria asked her friend.

"Yes, my father insists upon it. I have fallen behind on my studies and must focus on them again, otherwise I fear he shall not grant me permission to go to London when the Season begins," Lydia replied.

Maria said dreamily, "Oh I dearly wish I could go to Lord Primrose's ball!"

"I would not say I am going to it exactly," Lydia explained, "but Kitty and I have made plans with Miss Darcy to have our own entertainments." She looked over to see that the others were paying them no mind, then she whispered to her friend, "Perhaps I could talk my father into you joining us while we are there. It will only be a short while, then we will be back home."

"Oh, what fun that would be!" She nearly squealed, then the two turned their focus back to the others as the conversation continued on.

"Father and I have some business to attend in Meryton, so maybe we can drop you both off on our way," Jonathan offered. "How soon can you be ready?"

"I will be ready to go directly after our meal," Lydia replied.

"As will I," Charlotte agreed, pushing the food around her plate and contemplating what she already determined to do today.

"Capital, capital" Sir William stood. "I will call for the carriage directly."

They all finished breaking their fast then left, Charlotte soon finding herself nervously standing in front of Longbourn. "You go ahead, Lydia," she said, "I wish to sit in the garden for a few minutes before I go inside." Looking up at the sky, she replied, "Who could resist this rare sunshine?"

Looking up, Lydia shrugged, "If it is what you wish," and went inside.

Charlotte was trying to calm her nerves when she saw some movement at the back of the garden. Recognizing the person she came to speak with walking towards her, seemingly in his own world, she called out "Mr Collins, what a pleasure to see you again."

Surprised at being addressed, he stumbled over his words, "Miss... Miss Lucas... er, what a... a pleasure," he nervously looked over his shoulder, then back at her, "to… to see you today. What brings you to… er… Longbourn?"

Charlotte closed her eyes and swallowed the lump in her throat, deciding to proceed with her plans quickly. "Mr Collins, my reason for coming to Longbourn today was to…," taking a deep breath, she continued, "to speak with you about something of import."

"Yes, what is it?" he asked impatiently.

She nearly stumbled over her words as she said, "Today being what it is, I thought to secure my future, and I came to ask if you will marry me."

The man's face turned ashen as he stood planted to the spot, obviously taken aback at her proposal. Sudden his face flushed to a deep red and his eyes showed great offense at such an offer, "Madam, I would not marry you even if you were the last woman on earth!" He spat the words out vehemently and quickly strode away.

Dejected, Charlotte sat down on the cold stone bench, not certain where her plan had gone wrong. After a few minutes she heard someone come outside. Not wanting to be in company at the moment, she stood and quickly made her way out of the walled enclosure. Tears welled in her eyes as the reality of what he said cut into her heart. *I would not marry you even if you were the last woman on earth.* She dried her eyes only to have them fill again. Not knowing where to go, she began walking away from the main road and soon found herself at the bridge which led across the river. She was lost in her grief as she sat overlooking the river below. The water flowed swiftly along, dragging mud and branches in its wake. *How very much like my own life,* she thought. *I have no way out and have no control of where life is taking me. I cannot even propose properly or turn the head of any worthy gentleman.* Her body shook as she cried like never before. She failed to hear the rider crossing the bridge.

Seeing a familiar face in such distress, Ash quickly dismounted and tied off his horse, then went to her side, "Miss Lucas? Are you well?" Realizing she did not hear him, he put his hand on her shoulder, "Miss Lucas?"

Startled, her breath caught in her chest and she turned to see the worried face of Lord Ashbourne. Nearly clawing at the tears that refused to stop coming, she said, "I am sorry for disturbing you, my lord."

"May I sit," he asked, indicating the ground next to her.

Looking around, she said, "I suppose… if you wish it." She again tried to calm the flow of tears, but they seemed to have a life of their own.

Ash pulled out a handkerchief and handed it to his companion. "Do you care to tell me why you are sitting here by the river, crying?"

Wiping her eyes, she shook her head and replied in gasps, "It… it is too… embarrassing… to tell… anyone."

Trying to lighten her melancholy, he said, "If you will not tell me, then I must guess. Let me see… your favorite hat has been caught up in the wind and you came in search of it, barely missing it as the river swept it away beneath its forceful flow?"

A small smile just touched the corners of her lips as she said, "No, sir, my hat is still firmly attached to my head."

"Oh, yes, I do see that now, and quite lovely it is," he said with a smile. "Well, if it is not your hat, then perhaps you found yourself so lost you did not know your own way home again and were waiting on me to come to your rescue?"

Shaking her head, she let out a small giggle, "No, my lord, I know exactly where I am."

"Are you not going to help me?" he asked. "I could go on like this all day if need be, but I fear without some assistance we shall never get to the truth of the matter."

Charlotte looked down at her hands worrying the handkerchief in her lap, unsure what to say. After a minute of silence, she asked, "Have you ever found yourself truly alone?"

Ash looked down to the rushing river below, "More alone with each year that passes since…," clearing his throat, he continued, "well, never mind that. We were talking about you, were we not?"

She shyly looked down at her lap, "Must we talk of me?"

Turning to look at her, he was struck by the slight blush that overtook her cheeks. "What has upset you so very much, Miss Lucas? Please tell me? I promise I shall not jest at your expense, no matter how silly it may seem."

Closing her eyes once again, she tried to calm her racing heart. "I… I… well, today… you see, I was so… desperate… I had to at least try."

Ash reached over and gently took her trembling hand in his. When she looked up at him, he said, "I promise you, I will understand and not judge whatever it is you have done too harshly."

Charlotte once again tried to calm her heart, closing her eyes and taking a deep breath. The gentle pressure of her hand in his gave her the confidence to finally say, "I find myself in the position of being the eldest single female in the area, and, today being what it is, I undertook the task of trying to secure my future."

"Today being what it is?" he asked, then suddenly he understood. "Oh, right; I understand your meaning."

"Yes, well, my attempts to secure my own future were rebuffed quite vehemently," she said, looking once again to the raging river below.

Ash's heart beat rapidly as he realized what her words meant. "You proposed and the man refused you?"

"Yes," she said quietly.

He gripped her hand harder as he felt rage building inside. "What man in his right mind would refuse one such as you?" he asked.

259

Taken aback at his words, she turned to face him, "I am seven and twenty, have no connections or dowry to speak of, and have little beauty. It seems my best days are behind me, my lord."

Looking at her he asked, "Who refused you?"

"I would rather not say—I do have my dignity to protect, after all."

Smiling, he said, "If you do not tell me, I shall, once again, have to guess."

Looking to the sky she sighed loudly. "It was Mr Collins."

"That buffoon? Surely your heart is not touched by such a man?"

"No my heart is not touched by him, but there is no one else in the neighborhood who would even think of accepting my offer," she said.

"You did not ask everyone though, did you?"

"No"

"Then how do you know every gentleman would deny you?"

"I just know," she said, slipping her hand out of his and looking down at her lap. "I do not want a husband simply for the position. I said for years I had no romantic sensibilities, but that is simply not true—I wish to be affected by his presence, just like every other lady would wish it. Yet it is not to be." Barely audible she continued, "The one man who affects my heart would never offer for me."

"Your heart has been touched by someone, and yet he has not approached you for your hand?" Ash asked.

"No, he has not," she answered. "I do not know if he even knows of my feelings, but it matters not as I do not deserve such a husband."

His heart jumped and he knew he must pursue this matter further. "It would be an honour for any man to be approached by one such as yourself, Miss Lucas."

"And yet I have been denied already today," she answered.

Gazing to the river below, he quietly said, "*I could deny you nothing.*"

Tears once again stinging her eyes, Charlotte said, "Yet somehow I doubt that is true."

Reaching out for her chin, he gently turned her face towards him, "Miss Lucas, please look at me. I do not make a habit of being deceitful, and I speak the absolute truth to you now. If you but ask, I could deny you nothing."

"My lord, I cannot," she choked out.

"Why?"

"Did you not hear me tell of my lack of connections and no dowry?"

"Yet you are affected by my presence?" he asked boldly.

Swallowing hard, she closed her eyes, tears spilling down her cheeks, she quietly answered, "Yes."

"I have not searched for all these years because my desire is to marry for affection and not for my position in society or what I own."

Pulling back a little, she looked down and replied, "I do not know what you own, my lord, and your position means little to me. I have no political aspirations."

"What if I told you I owned but one hundred acres of wood and a small cabin?"

Shrugging her shoulders, she replied, "It matters not to me."

He smiled, "That is exactly what I mean. To you, worth is seen more in character than in money and possessions."

"But you do not own such as you have said, and your wife deserves to be someone who can attend to the job of mistress of your home in the proper way. I have not been educated to be such a lady, but a parson's wife I could easily attain."

"Actually I do own one hundred acres and a cabin," he said. "I told you I do not make a habit of deceiving."

"If you are so set on marrying me, why have you not approached me yourself?" Charlotte asked.

He looked up to the clouds and took a deep breath, then began. "Six years ago the lady I was to marry passed away from scarlet fever before we were wed. With everything I went through, I promised myself I would never again ask a lady to marry me. It is only recently I have begun to wish I had the courage to do so again, but my courage has failed me." His eyes were teary as he again put his hand under her chin and turned her face towards him. "Please, Miss Lucas, help end this misery I have succumbed to these many years. I beg of you to have courage where I do not."

Tears once again spilling from her own eyes, this time for a different reason, Charlotte swallowed hard and whispered, "Lord Ashbourne, will you marry me?"

"Yes," he answered just as quietly. The two sat in silence staring at each other until finally his mouth slowly descended to join hers in a short but sweet kiss. When he pulled away to look at her face again, he said, "Thank you for making today the best day of my life."

"I doubt that is true."

Hurt evident in his eyes, he asked, "Why do you doubt me so easily?"

"Because I know you have not been completely honest with me," she answered.

"About what?" he countered.

"About your property; I doubt you own but one hundred acres and a cabin."

"Actually I do own one hundred acres and a cabin… in Ireland. I must apologize for leaving out a few other properties: a small estate about the size of Longbourn located in Scotland, a house in Bath and another in London, an estate in Italy, though I have not seen it since I was eight, and a sizeable estate with a castle in Northamptonshire."

Looking askance at him, she replied, "And you ask me why I doubt you, sir?"

Turning to face her again, he took her hand in his, "Please do not doubt this—I have wanted to ask for your hand since I saw you sitting on that bench at the museum, but I did not have the courage. I did not even know you, and yet I felt so drawn to you—more drawn than I have ever felt to another. Then my own past hurts weighed so heavily on me that I could not bring myself to approach you. So, you see, your asking me today has made me very happy. I accepted you not out of obligation or to make you feel better, but because I truly think you are the best woman I know."

Charlotte looked down, thought quietly for a minute, then replied, "I thank you. I did set out today to ask someone because my own situation caused such desperation for my future, but do not think I am unaffected by you, my lord." The largest smile she had ever seen overtook his face. Charlotte could not help but smile herself as she said, "I never expected such a reaction."

"How could I not smile when my lady has said she is *not unaffected by me*," he replied. "I believe that is the highest compliment I have ever received, my soon-to-be-wife."

She smiled in return, "If this truly is what you wish, you need to go and speak with my father."

He stood and put his hand out to help her up, "Well then, let us get on with the task at hand."

He untied his horse and they began walking, her arm wrapped around his. "Do you really own a castle?"

Laughing, he pulled her arm closer, "Yes I do."

"What of your family—will they accept your choice?"

Smirking, he said, "I believe I was your choice actually." Both laughed and he continued, "I was an only child and my father passed away when I was five. My mother then took me back to her native Italy where we lived until she died just three years later. I have no other family and was returned to England to be raised by my godfather. That is how I became such good friends with the Fitzwilliam brothers as we share the same godfather—the Duke of Hawley. His sons were raised nearly as my brothers. I know they will all be happy for me."

After a few minutes of companionable silence, Ash asked, "What made you so desperate as to seek a husband on your own today? Have you been planning such for a while?"

"No, I would never have done so if it were not for the complete despondency I felt over my own situation. I am a constant topic of conversation among the local matrons, and I recently overheard a conversation between my brothers about my fate and it broke my heart. Last night when my sister and Miss Lydia were joking about today being Leap Day, and what that meant, I decided it was the only way I would ever have the chance to marry."

Tensing, he said sternly, "I may need to have a discussion with your brothers."

"Jonathan was trying to defend me." Looking up at him, she said, "I would not have you angry at him for what was said. James is young and he does not know how hurtful his actions and words can be to others."

"Then it is time he learned, is it not?"

"I would not have you frighten my brother," Charlotte insisted.

"I will promise nothing of the sort, only that I will act in accordance with the deference given to the man who holds the position of soon to become your husband."

Smiling, Charlotte replied, "I could get used to this."

"One of my jobs is to protect you," he replied.

They walked silently for a few minutes more before he asked, "So tell me of your family?"

Charlotte told of her five aunts and four uncles and her numerous cousins, some of whom her sister Maria, along with Lydia Bennet, visited in Brighton. She also told of her father's knighthood two and twenty years before and how drastically their lives changed with that event. They then moved to Meryton and became good friends with the families in the neighborhood, especially the Bennets.

Before the two knew it they were nearing Lucas Lodge. "Lord Ashbourne, my father is gone on business today. Maybe it would be best if you return later when he is home," Charlotte said nervously.

"Nicholas," he said simply.

"What?" she asked in confusion.

"My name is Nicholas, or my friends call me Ash. If you wish it of me, I will leave you for now and will return later to speak with your father," he said.

Nodding her head, she said, "Yes, I do wish it… Nicholas."

He lifted her hand to his lips and gently brushed them over her knuckles, "Then I take my leave of you for now, my lady."

Charlotte blushed and turned to walk away, noticing he did not mount his horse and leave until she was inside. Quickly rushing to her room she closed the door and fell onto her bed, the feelings inside making her nearly burst with excitement. *How could I possibly think I could partner myself for life to a man who does not affect me this way?* Closing her eyes, she could picture the blue eyes and fair features of Nicholas so vividly and she found herself wondering if he looked most like his mother or his father?

CHAPTER

XXIX

Mr Bennet saw his cousin walking quickly through the garden from his study window, so he stepped outside. "Mr Collins, may I have a moment of your time?"

"Oh, yes Mr Bennet. I will be glad to speak with you, but it must not take long as I must leave today. My patroness would not have me tax my dear cousins in extending my stay beyond what is an acceptable amount of time, and it has already passed three weeks since my arrival," he blabbered on, following Mr Bennet into his study.

"Please have a seat, sir," Mr Bennet said, interrupting the speech that would take longer to listen to than the potential answer he hoped to hear from this man. "I will not waste your time or mine, so I will get right to it, sir. Have you considered the terms of the contract presented to you?"

"Well, you see, I am unable to make such a judgment at this time as I have been unable to speak with my patroness. I could not in good conscience even consider such an offer until I know her opinions on whether I should accept it and give up, forever, the land that is naturally meant to come to me."

"Do you have any idea when you will be able to speak with your patroness?" Mr Bennet asked.

"Oh, no sir, I am not privy to the goings and comings of such a great lady of distinction as Lady Catherine de Bourgh."

Knowing he would continue if he were not stopped, Mr Bennet stood and went to the door, holding it open. "Thank you, Mr Collins. I will not hold up your travel any longer. Please let me know as soon as you decide."

Mr Collins sneezed and wiped his nose as he walked out the door. "Yes, I will do just that. I make it a habit to always carry out what I must in a timely manner," he said, cringing inwardly at the idiocy with which he must present himself to this man and hoping the ruse was not found out.

His trunks were soon packed onto the curricle and he was on his way back to London to meet with his cohorts about everything he learned of the intricacies of the Bennet family over the last few weeks. With all this new knowledge they would surely be able to do as they were bid with much more ease.

***

Sir William Lucas was passing the front door when he heard someone knock. Waving away the footman and opening the door himself, he recognized the visitor immediately, "Lord Ashbourne, it is a pleasure to see you. What can I do for you?"

"If you have a minute, sir, I would like to speak with you in private," Ash said nervously.

"Right this way," Sir William led the younger man to his study. "Have a seat, my lord," he offered, sitting after his visitor chose a chair. "I cannot imagine what you would want with me, so I am all anticipation."

"Sir, I will get right to the point." Rubbing his hands together nervously, he cleared his throat and said quickly, "I wish to ask for your daughter's hand."

"My daughter's hand?" Sir William looked confusedly at his guest. "For what purpose, my lord?"

"Why, to marry her, of course," Ash replied.

"Marry her!" He stood, shaking his head in earnest, "No, absolutely not! I forbid it! She is not even out yet, and I will not let that kind of scandal touch my family!"

"She is not out yet? Sir, she is seven and twenty, and from what she has told me, she has been out the better part of ten years."

"You wish to marry *Charlotte*? Not... not Maria?"

"Sir, as your youngest daughter is not yet out, I have never even been formally introduced to her." He stood and went to stand beside the older man, "I wish to marry your eldest, Charlotte."

A smile formed on his lips as Sir William realized the request of this man in front of him. "My lord, I cannot determine why a gentleman of your position would wish to marry Charlotte, but you are such a man to whom I could deny nothing. Of course you have my blessing!"

Ash smiled and bowed to the older man, "I thank you. I cannot imagine my life without her in it."

With a quirk of his eyebrow, Sir William asked, "A love match?"

"She is the best woman I know," Ash said quietly.

"Capital, capital my boy! When shall we announce it? My sons are not home at the moment, so maybe you could join us after church tomorrow?"

Ash smiled, "I look forward to it, sir. There is something else I wish to speak with you about, sir." A solemn look settled upon his face as he said, "It seems your youngest son spoke to another of Charlotte at the Bingley's wedding breakfast. She overheard them and was quite shaken by some things he said. When I found her this morning she was seated by the river, so distressed she was crying."

"My Charlotte was crying?" Pain could be seen in his eyes. "She is not a temperamental person driven to flights of fancy or tears easily, my lord. It disturbs me that James could speak so of her, and within her hearing."

"It disturbs me also, sir."

"Ever since my son went away to Oxford he has come home with fanciful ideas and a haughtiness I cannot condone. He forgets too easily just where my roots are. I may have been knighted, but I was in trade before that, as was my father and his father before him. I want my sons to have better than I, but as a younger son of a simple country gentleman, I cannot promise his life will not be difficult."

"It may just be time he learn this lesson, sir, and I have a few ideas that may leave quite the impression on him," Ash said. At the older gentleman's nod of approval, they discussed the plan to have the earl join them for a family dinner after church tomorrow, at which time the family would be told of the engagement. Ash received permission from Sir William to address any remarks made by James in a manner in which a future husband might be given a little more freedom in speaking than normal, though he promised to not offend the young man in his reproof.

After their plan was well laid out, Sir William stood, "I would guess you wish to see my daughter to tell her of my approval?"

With a small bow he smiled, "Yes; I thank you, sir."

"I will only give you a few minutes alone, then I expect you to be done," he stated with a firm look to the younger man.

"I understand, sir."

"Capital, capital. I will return in just a moment, my lord."

A maid in the hall told Sir William where he could find his eldest daughter. He walked into the kitchen and saw her speaking to the cook. "Charlotte, if you have a minute, I wish to speak with you," he said, trying not to give away the nature of his business.

"Yes, Father." She was unsure if Nicholas had come to ask for her hand yet, so she nervously followed him through the halls.

When he got to his study door, he embraced her and kissed her cheek, "I have had a *certain visitor*, my dear. Can you guess who it could be?"

"He came?" she asked excitedly.

"Yes, he did. Please go to him in my study; you have a few minutes." Sir William saw her close her eyes and take a deep breath before she reached for the door handle. When she disappeared inside, he could not help the swell of his heart at the knowledge that his daughter would be happy and so well cared for.

Charlotte closed the door, her heart feeling as if it would beat through her chest. "You came?" she asked quietly.

He turned when he heard her voice, and quickly crossed the room to her. "Yes, I came. Did you doubt me so much again?"

"I tried not to, but I could not bring myself to admit someone like you would want to marry me."

Drawing his arms around her waist, he eased her head to his chest, "I know you have been ignored and set aside for far too long, and for the pain it has caused I am truly sorry, but I cannot say I am too disheartened as you were saved for me."

She closed her eyes as his soft voice washed over her; she felt herself melt into his embrace. Breathing in deep, her heart started to calm at the smell of his spicy cologne, and for the first time in her adult life, Charlotte felt treasured.

Finally he pulled back, "Charlotte, your father has only given us a few minutes, so I must acquaint you of some things."

"Yes, what is it?"

"Do not worry, it is nothing so disturbing." He gently cradled her cheek in his hand as he continued, "You and I shall be married, do not doubt that. Your father wishes to wait until tomorrow after church services to announce it to your family. He has invited me to join you for a meal here at Lucas Lodge. Does this meet with your approval?"

Smiling, she put her own hand on top of his, and answered, "Even tomorrow I may not believe it to be true."

"But it is," he said as he gently lowered his mouth to hers, kissing her slowly.

The two were barely separated from the kiss when Sir William knocked on the door. Stepping back from her, Nicholas said, "Until tomorrow, my lady," then he quickly left the room.

Sir William entered and closed the door, then he pulled his eldest into a loving embrace, "I do not know what you have done to that boy, but he is positively besotted with you."

"I know not why," she said quietly.

"Because he sees what no one else has taken the time to see in you, my dear. That is the nature of love; it sees what others overlook and puts value in what others dare not notice."

Tears filled her eyes and the two embraced for some moments until Sir William was assured his daughter was composed.

He kissed her cheek and told Charlotte to inform her mother of his specific request for Sunday's meal to be their finest, as they were to have a visitor after church. Charlotte went to relay the message then retired to her room to think in private of all that had changed in just a few hours.

Caroline was annoyed. She had been unable to find her intended target all day. After finally asking the right footman, she was informed Lord Primrose left early this morning. Angered that the *one day* she could further her own suit to him, he was not around, she stomped about the house.

Entering the drawing room and hearing the fussy baby, Caroline loudly grumbled, "WHY does that... that... *baby*... have to be in here? Can she not be taken to the nursery?"

"She just started crying," Louisa said, "and has not been a bother to anyone all day."

Elizabeth spoke up, "Mrs Hurst and I have been enjoying this last hour with your niece." Reaching out her hands to take the tiny one from her mother, Elizabeth offered, "I feel the need to rest, so I will take her to Lucy for you."

Louisa nodded and handed Amelia over. "Thank you, Mrs Darcy." When the door was shut and the two sisters were alone, she stood and walked over to Caroline. Standing nose to nose, looking into her sister's nearly identical face, Louisa said, "If you feel too confined in this house, I shall inform Aunt Hamilton immediately of your need to depart first thing

Monday morning instead of waiting until you are to leave at the end of next week."

"You wouldn't dare!" Caroline said menacingly.

"You underestimate me, Caroline. My husband and I have been left as hosts to those who remain, and David will stand behind me in whatever I decide as far as you are concerned. So which will it be? Will you be more accepting of my daughter having the right to be in any room in which I deem appropriate, or will you be leaving Monday morning?"

Caroline glared at Louisa, her anger seething. "I see the position to which I have been relegated in this family."

"You forget your place too often, and I hope one day soon you realize this before it is too late."

"That baby is nothing more than a farmer's daughter who has been taken in by you; a foundling who was dropped on your doorstep," Caroline replied hotly.

Turning red, Louisa exclaimed firmly, "*She is my daughter.* I would caution you to remember that as you pack your trunks." She immediately left the room to find her husband and Aunt Hamilton determined to avoid Caroline until she could be sent to Town on Monday.

Caroline huffed in exasperation and sat down on the sofa. *What am I to do? To wait another four years is more than I can bear,* she thought. She sat thinking for a few minutes until she heard Mr Darcy and Lord Ashbourne in the hall. *Hmmm,* she thought, Lord Ashbourne is already an earl, and he can have no objections to having me for a wife. She stood and went to the mirror that hung on the wall and checked her hair, tucking a stray strand back and pinching her cheeks. She listened at the door until she heard Mr Darcy excuse himself from the earl and walk away.

Quickly making her way down the hall, she saw Lord Ashbourne as he started to ascend the stairs. "My lord, may I speak with you?" she asked sweetly.

Seeing the look in her eye, he replied, "I do not have time right now, Miss Bingley; please excuse me," then he quickly went up to his room, ignoring the sound of something breaking below stairs.

After a quiet meal and stilted entertainments, with Caroline glaring at everyone equally, everyone determined to retire early. The ladies went above stairs first, allowing the gentlemen a few minutes to talk of the coming travel plans, which explained why Caroline was in such a snit this evening.

When Darcy finally got to his room, he called out through the dressing room door, "Elizabeth, are you in there?"

"I will be right out, William," she replied.

He began readying himself for bed while he waited, humming quietly the song his wife and sister played on the pianoforte this evening.

Elizabeth walked out and smiled. Her husband sat facing away from her on the edge of the bed without his jacket or cravat, hair disheveled and looking out of sorts. This was a side of himself he allowed very few to see. She slowly climbed up onto the bed behind him and wrapped her arms around his chest, leaning down to kiss his scruffy cheek before resting her own cheek on his shoulder.

He turned to her and smiled, "What is the occasion for such an embrace?"

"Because you just looked too charming sitting here in your shirtsleeves with your rumpled hair," she said as she reached up to run her fingers through his dark curls. "I hope our son has your curls."

He reached up to stop her hand, pulling it down to his lips to place a soft kiss on her palm, "*Our daughter* will definitely have your eyes and adventurous spirit." To silence her he turned around and captured her mouth in a kiss.

This debate had gone on since the day William told Elizabeth he knew she was expecting. He firmly believed she carried his daughter, while she was determined to have a son first.

When Elizabeth finally pulled away, she said, "You might be able to distract me, but you will never change my opinion. I know this is a boy."

"Either way, I will be happy," he answered.

"You do seem to have a soft spot for girls," she teased.

"Speaking of my girls, was my sister so very tired? When I knocked on her door Mrs Annesley answered and said she was already asleep."

"She was nearly asleep before I left the room. I think she is enjoying being here and loves to spend time with Mary, but it is quite taxing on her to visit Longbourn so many days in a row. Perhaps it would be best to ask Mary if she wishes to come back to Netherfield Park?"

"Mmmm, yes, I will ask your father tomorrow," he said as he nuzzled her neck, "My family was always even with boys and girls, but in yours the girls are plentiful." He looked into her eyes, "Elizabeth, I know your father's estate is entailed away and that is why you desire to have a boy first, but Pemberley is under no such restrictions. If we have ten girls I would still be happy for our lot."

She smiled, "Thank you, William."

"Bingley can now be counted among the gentlemen of this family, but we are still not as plentiful as the ladies. I must introduce your sisters to some of my friends this Season in hopes of balancing things out a little more evenly."

Elizabeth laughed, *only you would want to introduce my sisters to some of your friends so everything is neat and even,* she thought. "My mother would be ever grateful if you did. Imagine her nerves if she had to plan three or four weddings within a year!" They both laughed at this description of Mrs Bennet. Darcy continued to dress for bed.

"What has cheered you up so quickly?"

"What do you mean?"

"Well, when we were downstairs this evening you were not so cheery, and yet now here you are humming and laughing. What has changed?"

He tapped her nose, "You shall have to wait until tomorrow."

"Why? What is to happen tomorrow?"

William stood to discard his clothes and once again captured his wife in an embrace.

"I will not be distracted this time. What is it? Tell me!"

"I cannot. It is not my news to share," he said, nuzzling her neck.

"Tomorrow I will know?" she asked.

He pulled back to look into her eyes, "Yes, tomorrow you will know all."

"I will let you get away with this only once. If by tomorrow night I do not know, then you will owe me something," she stated.

William held out his arms wide, "Whatever I have is yours already, my dear wife; what more could I give you?"

"Oh, no, if I am not satisfied by the time we retire tomorrow night, you will owe me... hmmm...," she thought, tapping her lip with her finger. "I know—you will owe me a kitten!"

"I am not a cat person, Elizabeth—you know that," a small smile formed in the corner of his mouth as he continued, "but because I am confident you will know tomorrow, I will take on your challenge."

"We shall see!" she said as she fluffed her pillow and settled down in bed.

"Yes, we shall see indeed," he replied as he lay down and pulled her into his arms, his hand caressing the bump that was getting harder to hide beneath her clothes. He sighed when he felt their baby's small yet strong thumping on his palm. "I am certain this little one will not let us keep our secret much longer. I saw your father looking oddly at you as you stood the other day, and I am certain he suspects you are with child."

She smiled and laid her hand on top of his as he continued to caress her stomach, "I know they will understand that I wish Jane to be here when we tell of our news. It is still a long wait until Easter though."

"I have a feeling they will be returning earlier."

She sat up and looked at him, "What? What is it you know that you refuse to tell me?"

He reached for her, urging her back down to her pillow. "Tomorrow," he stated before his lips descended upon hers.

CHAPTER

XXX

Sunday, March 1, 1812

J onathan watched as Lord Ashbourne made his way through the group of parishioners who gathered around talking in the churchyard. He was told the man would be joining them for a meal following the service, but he could not determine why. Sunday was always set aside as a time for God and family, not for social engagements and dinner guests.

He watched as his father merrily greeted the earl, then they turned and followed the ladies on their walk to Lucas Lodge. Jonathan found James and the two speculated about their unexpected guest on the way home.

When the brothers entered the house, they heard their father's booming voice coming from the sitting room where the family gathered. "Well, I guess there is no better time than the present to find out why he has joined us today," Jonathan said as they removed their great coats, gloves, and hats.

Sir William saw his sons enter the sitting room. "Now that we are all here, let us make our way to the dining room." Turning to the earl, he replied, "I am certain you will be impressed, my lord, as my wife is quite pleased with what she was able to find at the butcher's yesterday."

James leaned over and quietly said to Jonathan, "I doubt someone of his rank would be impressed by anything our father could offer him."

Ash, having heard what he said, turned around and replied, "You are quite mistaken. There are many inducements of your father's that impress me greatly." Turning back around he winked at Charlotte, making her blush.

Jonathan saw the wink and his sister's subtle reaction. *Hmmmm,* he thought, *maybe my sister has caught the eye of a worthy gentleman.*

James however did not see, and his next statement enraged Ash when he said, "Maybe he wishes to purchase our prize pig which won top placement at the county fair last year."

Ash felt anger rising in his chest. He flexed his hand instinctively, "I have found something of much greater value, I can assure you."

"Do not tell me Father has sold you his stallion?" James said.

Jonathan saw the looks Lord Ashbourne was giving his brother and he tried to get James to stop goading the earl, "I am sure whatever he has found, it is worth the price."

"Yes, absolutely worth the price," Ash said to Jonathan, a knowing smile forming on his lips.

"I can think of nothing else my father has which would ever induce a gentleman of your stature to sup with us on a Sunday," James replied.

"Can you not," Ash said, looking at Charlotte as they entered the dining room.

Smirking, James said, "It is not as if my sister has brought you to our doorstep."

Ash pulled out the chair for Charlotte, lifted her hand, and placed a kiss on the back of her fingers before he released it. Then he turned and said to James, "That is exactly why I am here."

Sounds of effusions all around the room were drowned out by James comments. "Charlotte? You are here because of *Charlotte*? Somehow, I doubt you are here of your own free will, after all, she is already firmly on the shelf. No one wants her."

Standing to his full height, Ash glared at James, "I most certainly am here because of your sister. Her charms and allurements have proven to me that she is the best woman I know, and I wish to marry her as soon as may be. As for her age, I am glad she has been saved from another all these years for me to now find. She will fill the role of *Lady Ashbourne* quite well, would you not agree?"

James' face turned white and Jonathan helped him to a chair before he collapsed in shock.

"Congratulations, my lord," Jonathan said sincerely.

"I thank you; we thank you," Ash said, squeezing her hand as he sat beside Charlotte.

The rest of the meal was spent discussing the details of the nuptials, and it was decided they would wed before the start of the Season, when the earl would be required to return to London due to his duties in Parliament. Easter was in four weeks, and the date determined to be best for all involved was Tuesday of the week following—the first day of April.

James sat quietly through the entirety of the meal and excused himself from the others as soon as he politely could. He knew he must apologize to his sister, but he was not yet ready to do so, especially with the earl still at her side. He was an intimidating figure and one James was not apt to go up against again anytime soon.

Charlotte wished to tell her best friend in person, so she asked if she and her mother could walk to Longbourn, where they Darcy's were to spend the day with her family, to pass on the grand news.

"Would you like me to go with you? Ash asked.

Charlotte smiled, "Would you not wish to stay and speak with my brother and father, my lord?"

"I will always wish to escort my lady, and any business I have with your father can easily wait until another day. After all, it is the Lord's day," Ash said.

"Then I would appreciate your escort on our walk," Charlotte said with a smile.

The three ladies, along with the earl, set out for Longbourn. When they were gone, Jonathan turned to his father, "Do you care to tell me how this match has come about so suddenly?"

Sir William replied, "It seems it is not as suddenly as it may appear; the man is positively besotted. Come with me to my study and I will tell you all I know."

Everyone was enjoying the Darcy's visit to Longbourn when Lady Lucas, with Maria, Charlotte and Lord Ashbourne in tow, arrived to announce the engagement of her eldest daughter to none other than the Earl of Ashbourne.

Elizabeth was shocked, but one look at her husband and she knew this was why he was confident she would not win their little wager. She hugged her best friend, quietly saying, "I believe we have some things to discuss." The two soon disappeared from the room, not to be seen again for an hour.

Elizabeth closed the door to the morning room and rounded on her friend, "Charlotte Lucas, you sly thing! You never told me a thing!"

"I promise Lizzy, there was not much to tell," Charlotte said. "Sit and I will explain." When the two were comfortable seated she went on to explain everything to her best friend.

"You proposed—to *two* gentlemen?" Elizabeth was stunned. "I never thought you to be so shameless!"

"Shameless! Really, Lizzy, it is not as if I am a wanton lady. I can tell you it was simply out of desperation," Charlotte replied.

"We have discussed this many times over the past few months, but I simply do not understand why you would feel such desperation?"

"I am seven years older than you. I have been out for nearly ten years with no prospects. Even Jane had a beau who liked to write her poetry the year she had her coming out, though I am certain she is glad it did not go beyond that. I have had no prospects though, and am the talk of every matron in Meryton. I could not stand back any longer and do nothing for my own future. I do not want to be the lady who is always staying with her friends in order to be thrown into the paths of their husband's single friends, or the sister who is forever known as the town's old spinster."

"You are right, I will never understand your position." Hugging her, Elizabeth felt tears begin to fall. "I am very glad you have found such a wonderful gentleman. His face lights up when he looks at you, and I can see that you are just as affected by his presence."

Shyly pulling back and looking down at her lap, Charlotte said, "My feelings were never nonexistent, but since yesterday I cannot even begin to describe how much they have grown."

"Do you love him?" Elizabeth asked.

Quietly, she replied, "Yes."

"Then tell him," Elizabeth implored. "You would be amazed how much saying those three words can change your whole life."

Mr Bennet, Darcy, and Ash remained in the sitting room and listened to the ladies discussing the details of the coming nuptials, but when talk of lace entered the conversation Mr Bennet stood, saying, "Gentlemen, I believe we owe ourselves a cigar on such on occasion as this. Might you join me in my study?"

The two stood and removed from the room, gladly leaving the ladies to their talk of lace and trousseaus.

When they were ensconced in the study, each with a cigar in hand and a battle laid out on the chess board that sat in front of them, Darcy spoke, "Elizabeth and I feel it is too tiring on my sister to travel here to Longbourn so often to visit, but she and Miss Mary have such a wonderful friendship. Would you mind if she came to stay at Netherfield again? I know she is to go to Town with us when the Season begins, and that is why you wished her to spend some weeks at home…"

Bennet waved his hand, stopping Darcy mid-sentence, "Yes, of course. If anyone is to understand the trying times your sister has had, it is me. I would not wish to tax her with even more burdens. Feel free to speak with Mary." He sighed heavily, "My girls are growing up too quickly, and you are correct in that I wished to keep her here for at least a few weeks, but it is selfish of me to do so without just cause."

Feeling he was intruding upon a moment between the father and son-in-law, the earl stood and excused himself, saying he wished to peruse the shelves on the other side of the room.

Bennet nodded and had to smile at the far-away look on the earl's face. It was obvious where he wished to be right now, and here with the two gentlemen was not it. He turned back to the chess board and studied the pieces, quietly asking Darcy, "So when are you going to tell everyone your news?"

"Our news? To what are you referring?" Darcy tried to sound convincing.

Mr Bennet looked up from the chess board and quirked his eyebrow, very much reminding Darcy of his wife. "Son, I have seen my wife in that condition six times—you cannot fool me." Moving his piece, he said, "Check mate. It seems for once I have the upper hand on you… in more ways than one."

Darcy smiled and shook his head in amusement, "We never had a chance in keeping it a secret, did we?" He began resetting the pieces on the board as he continued, "We were waiting for the quickening to tell everyone. Then when we arrived, Elizabeth did not want to take attention away from her sister's wedding, so we waited. She then decided she could not possibly tell her whole family without Jane being present, so it was decided we would put it off until everyone is here again in three weeks time for Easter. I just said to her last night that I do not think we are fooling you."

Mr Bennet nodded his head in understanding, "If her mother's flights of fancy are any indication of what you will go through with your wife and her ever changing mind, I have compassion for you."

"So this is normal?"

"Son, when it comes to a woman with child, you will soon learn her mind is the easiest thing for her to change, but the hardest thing with which you must contend. Have patience—I know my daughter well, and she will prove to be quite the challenge for you during the coming months."

"But it will be worth it," Darcy said.

"Absolutely," Mr Bennet answered back.

Darcy heard his wife and her friend walking down the hall and thought it a good enough excuse to take their leave. "I believe it is about time for us to go," he said.

The three went into the hallway just in time to join the two ladies. Darcy reached for his wife's hand and, as they followed the others into the sitting room, he told her of Mr Bennet's approval to have Mary join them at Netherfield as she wished.

Elizabeth said she would extend the invitation, then with a quirk of her eyebrow, she quickly kissed his cheek, "I will find a way to get my kitten one day, William." With that she turned to follow after her friend.

Darcy chuckled, and watched as his wife spoke with Mary, who readily accepted. Then as he walked over to gather Georgiana into his arms, Elizabeth stepped up to his side and drew the blanket over her legs, giving a simple and loving squeeze to Georgiana's fingers. Darcy was touched by the way she accepted Georgiana as her own sister, even with the difficulties she faced, and he felt a swell of pride rise in his chest.

Plans were made for Mary to join them the following day, and the Darcy family excused themselves from the joyous household to return to Netherfield. Darcy insisted they all rest for a few hours, as he did not wish to have his ladies overly taxed when Mary arrived on the morrow especially with the new wedding plans that were to get underway immediately.

Tuesday, March 3, 1812

"Mrs Bingley?" Charles said with a smile as he came into her room.

"Yes, Mr Bingley?" Jane answered sweetly, walking across to meet him.

He drew a missive from behind his back and brought her outstretched hand to his lips. "You, my dear, sweet, beautiful, angelic wife," he emphasized each descriptive word with a kiss to her hand, "have received your first letter with the moniker of Mrs Charles Bingley written on it. I will leave you to read it in private." With a flourishing bow, he left to finish dressing for the day while his wife read her letter.

Jane's heart fluttered at the sight of her husband in just his breeches and shirtsleeves as he walked through the door. When he was gone, she looked down to the letter in her hand. From Elizabeth! She eagerly opened it and read.

> March 2, 1812
> Netherfield Park, Hertfordshire
>
> Dearest Janie,
>
> I apologize for the abrupt start to this letter, but I
> have such wonderful news to relate, and I cannot
> put it off any longer. Are you sitting down? If not,
> you must have a seat before you continue, as I know
> how you will take such news.

Jane looked up and walked over to a chair, sat, then looked back down to
the letter.

> Now are you sitting? Brace yourself for some
> shocking news. Our dear friend Charlotte is to be
> married!

Jane jumped up, "MARRIED!"

Bingley came rushing back into the room, "Did you call me, dearest?"

"She is to be married!" Jane exclaimed.

"Who is to be married?" Bingley asked.

"Charlotte!"

"Miss Lucas?" Bingley was a bit confused. "I must admit, I was so
distracted by my own circumstances I was unaware she was being courted."

"She wasn't!" Jane exclaimed.

"Well then who is she to marry?"

"Oh, I do not know... hold on; I will read Lizzy's letter to you.

"Dearest Janie,

I apologize for the abrupt start to this letter, but I have such wonderful news to relate, and I cannot put it off any longer. Are you sitting down? If not, you must have a seat before you continue, as I know how you will take such news.

Now are you sitting? Brace yourself for some shocking news. Our dear friend Charlotte is to be married! That is not the most shocking news of all though, for you will never guess to whom—it is none other than the Earl of Ashbourne!"

"She is to marry Ashbourne? Well, it seems we were right about those two all along!" Bingley excitedly interrupted his wife. When she looked at him, he replied, "I am sorry dear, please continue."

Jane found where she had stopped reading.

"It seems she has finally been swept away into romantic sensibilities she never knew existed and by an earl no less! They are to be married directly after Easter, as the groom does not wish to wait too long, what with the Season starting in earnest next month. You can imagine the fluttering about Mama and Lady Lucas are doing today. Tomorrow I am to accompany Charlotte to the modiste in Meryton. Lord Ashbourne has said he will be obtaining a special license this week, and the wedding is to take place on the first of April. Charlotte is quite overwhelmed, as you can imagine. She said she would have written to you herself, but your husband once commented that after he married you he intended to steal you away from anything but him for six whole weeks, and nothing, not even letters, could infringe upon your solitude. I believe he made such a statement when Mama had you very busy and he did not get to see you for a few days."

Jane looked up at Bingley, who sheepishly said, "I was a bit put out one day and may have said something of that nature at the Lucas' that evening."

She chuckled, "Well, for the sake of my sister, who I am sure would have come herself if I did not respond to this letter, I am ever grateful you saw fit to deliver this to me today."

Bingley bent down in front of her seat and took her hand in his, "I love you, my Janie." He kissed her on the cheek and replied, "I will leave you to finish your letter in peace. It seems I have some plans to get underway for our travel if we are to return to Hertfordshire in time for the wedding."

Jane again watched as her husband retreated from the room, giggling as he turned and smiled at her from the doorway. She again read her letter from the beginning, happiness for her friend swelling in her heart. Charlotte had finally found someone worthy of her hand and her heart.

Jane folded her letter and wiped the tear from her cheek. She finished readying herself for the day and found her husband sitting at the desk in his chambers. "Would you like some company?"

Looking up, frustration obvious on his face, Bingley stood. "I always take pleasure in your company," he said as he smiled and pulled her into his arms, his lips consuming her own in a hungry exchange.

After a long kiss, Jane asked, "Would you like some help?"

"How did you know?"

"Your face says it all, and I know you do not like to write, especially when something must be written clearly," Jane said.

"You know me so well after only a few short weeks of marriage Mrs Bingley?" Charles teased.

"That particular fault I believe you divulged to me early in our engagement. You said I should not expect to be wooed by fancy words written in a fine hand, and as I told you then, I love you, faults and all," Jane stated as she sat at the desk. She pulled out a clean piece of paper and, dipping a new quill into the ink, she asked, "To whom are we writing?"

"First I must congratulate my friend, then we must write to Darcy and let him know of our change in plans, then there is the posting stations and inn…" his words trailed off when he saw her smiling at his enthusiasm. He walked over and took the quill from her hand, lifting it so she stood. Then he drew his arms around her waist and leaned down close to her lips, and asked, "I just assumed, but never did ask you. Do you wish to end our trip early and return to help your friend with her wedding preparations?"

She smiled broadly, "Oh yes! I have long wished to be there for her just as she has been there for me."

"Then we shall. I must say though, I have enjoyed these few weeks we have shared in solitude and will cherish them all our days, just as I cherish the love you bestow upon me daily."

"Oh, Charles, if anyone is cherished, it is indeed me. You are everything I could ever want or need."

His lips finally moved the small space left between the two, capturing her own in a hot exchange and leaving both breathless.

When they eventually separated once again, Jane sat to write the words her husband dictated, taking great pleasure in signing his name at the bottom and placing *their seal* into the wax of each before laying them on the tray to be posted, her mind a whirl with all the changes that had already come, and more yet to unfold in the coming months.

Bingley saw the smile on her lips and reached for her hand. When she stood he once again drew his arms around her. "Are you truly so happy Mrs Bingley?"

"Absolutely, Mr Bingley."

"I much prefer it when you call me *Charles*."

"I cannot imagine being any happier than I am in this moment, Charles," she said softly just before their lips met once again.

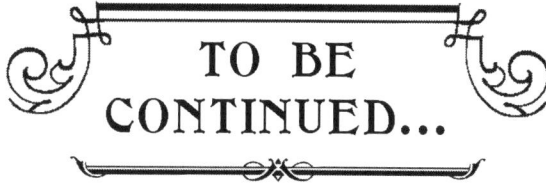

TO BE CONTINUED...

ABOUT THE AUTHOR

Sarah Johnson is a professional juggler in the circus of life! Married to her own Mr Darcy for sixteen years, they traveled the world thanks to the US Army. Now back in the civilian life and settled in Texas, where she grew up, they focus on homeschooling their six children and participating in church and community activities. She can often be found writing a manuscript between spills, science labs, and pencil wars, or late into the night when the house is finally still enough for her imagination to run wild! When she has a few spare moments, she enjoys just about anything crafty — scrapbooking, painting, sewing, quilting, crocheting — basically anything except knitting, a craft she swears few left—handers truly ever pick up well.

A devotee of all things Jane Austen, she enjoys exploring the story lines Jane never lived long enough to give the world. She is often found discussing with her online friends the intricacies of the novels we do have from our dearest author. It is these discussions that often lead to the plot bunnies that have now become many stories over the last few years, and hopefully further into the future as well.

CONNECT WITH SARAH JOHNSON

E-Mail:
sarah.johnson.jaff@gmail.com

Twitter:
@SarahJohnsonPL

Facebook:
https://www.facebook.com/SarahJohnsonAuthor
https://www.facebook.com/sarah.johnson.jaff

Website & Blog:
http://sarahjohnsonbooks.com

Goodreads:
https://www.goodreads.com/author/show/8118710.Sarah_Johnson

17934452R00167

Printed in Great Britain
by Amazon